FIRST POSITION

Praise for Melissa Brayden

"Melissa Brayden has become one of the most popular novelists of the genre, writing hit after hit of funny, relatable, and very sexy stories for women who love women."—*Afterellen.com*

Waiting in the Wings

"This was an engaging book with believable characters and story development. It's always a pleasure to read a book set in a world like theater/film that gets it right...a thoroughly enjoyable read." —*Lez Books*

"This is Brayden's first novel, but we wouldn't notice if she hadn't told us. The book is well put together and more complex than most authors' second or third books. The characters have chemistry; you want them to get together in the end. The book is light, frothy, and fun to read. And the sex is hot without being too explicit—not an easy trick to pull off."—*Liberty Press*

"Sexy, funny and all around enjoyable."—*Afterellen.com*

Heart Block

"The story is enchanting with conflicts and issues to be overcome that will keep the reader turning the pages. The relationship between Sarah and Emory is achingly beautiful and skillfully portrayed. This second offering by Melissa Brayden is a perfect package of love—and life to be lived to the fullest. So grab a beverage and snuggle up with a comfy throw to read this classic story of overcoming obstacles and finding enduring love."—*Lambda Literary Review*

"Although this book doesn't beat you over the head with wit, the interactions are almost always humorous, making both characters really quite loveable. Overall a very enjoyable read." —*C-Spot Reviews*

How Sweet It Is

"'Sweet' is definitely the keyword for this well-written, character-driven lesbian romance novel. It is ultimately a love letter to small town America, and the lesson to remain open to whatever opportunities and happiness comes into your life."
—Bob Lind, *Echo Magazine*

"Oh boy! The events were perfectly plausible, but the collection and the threading of all the stories, main and sub plots, were just fantastic. I completely and wholeheartedly recommend this book. So touching, so heartwarming and all-out beautiful."
—*Rainbow Book Reviews*

Kiss the Girl

"There are romances and there are romances...Melissa Brayden can be relied on to write consistently very sweet, pure romances and delivers again with her newest book *Kiss the Girl*...There are scenes suffused with the sweetest love, some with great sadness or even anger—a whole gamut of emotions that take readers on a gentle roller coaster with a consistent upbeat tone. And at the heart of this book is a hymn to true friendship and human decency."
—*C-Spot Reviews*

Just Three Words

"A beautiful and downright hilarious tale about two very relatable women looking for love."—*Sharing Is Caring Book Reviews*

The Soho Loft Series

"The trilogy was enjoyable and definitely worth a read if you're looking for solid romance or interconnected stories about a group of friends."—*The Lesbrary*

By the Author

Waiting in the Wings

Heart Block

How Sweet It Is

First Position

Soho Loft Romances:

Kiss the Girl

Just Three Words

Ready or Not

Visit us at www.boldstrokesbooks.com

FIRST POSITION

by
Melissa Brayden

2016

ISBN 13: 978-1-62639-602-9

This Trade Paperback Original Is Published By
Bold Strokes Books, Inc.
P.O. Box 249
Valley Falls, NY 12185

First Edition: August 2016

CREDITS
Editors: Lynda Sandoval and Stacia Seaman
Production Design: Stacia Seaman
Cover Design by Jeaning Henning

Acknowledgments

What a journey this has been! Every book holds a place in my heart for different reasons. *First Position* will forever be a labor of love that happened in the midst of some trying circumstances including two hospital stays (don't worry, I'm fully recovered) and my thesis year of grad school (don't worry, I graduated) and the loss of a beloved pet. As a result, I think I bonded with these particular characters in a very unique way, and saying good-bye is hard.

Thank you, Lynda Sandoval, for remaining on board for the wild ride that this book was and as always steering me in the right direction when I second-guess myself or veer off course. You've gone above and beyond for me, and I recognize how lucky I am to have such a fantastic editor.

Len Barot and Sandy Lowe continue to make me happy that I'm published by Bold Strokes Books. I feel supported and encouraged and am happy you're my home. The countless people who work with them to make Bold Strokes run never cease to amaze me. Thank you!

My friends are amazing! Thank you to Nikki, Georgia, and Rachel for existing. You make my world brighter.

Alan should receive some sort of medal for the work he did keeping the world at bay for me in the course of this year, which allowed me to rebound, regroup, and feel like me again. My rock, as always!

My mother, father, sisters, nieces, nephew, and brother-in-law are all worthy of a big acknowledgement for their presence, kind words, and rock-star level of support. You proved yourselves big-time this year!

To my readers, I'd like to take a moment and tell you how much our friendship on the page means to me. Thank you for reading and for your kindness. I received messages, cards, snacks, and even a few "get well" stuffed animals, which made me fight that much harder to get back to this book. I hope you enjoy it.

For Bailey Jeremiah,
who did lots of dancing of his own on those four paws.

Chapter One

A nastasia Mikhelson had come to hate orange plastic chairs.
Yet here she sat in one. Again.

Alone in the hallway, studying the texture of the beveled wall, her heart thudded faster than was probably good for her, but that made sense given the nature of the afternoon. That fast and repetitive beat served as the only sound in the empty hallway, adding an ominous quality to the already nerve-wracking event.

Ana had been counting the days, and more recently, the hours until this meeting with Bill, and in less than twenty minutes, the whole thing would be over, and the fate of her career no longer a mystery. She took a slow breath in an attempt to settle her nerves, because the outcome of this conversation meant everything. She glanced down the lonely hallway in one direction and then the other before finally returning her gaze to the big brown door that marked the entry point to Bill Bradshaw's office. She blinked twice, gave her head a firm shake, and smiled brightly as the door opened. *Nope, no nervous dancer out here. Just a very grateful employee. That's me.*

"Ana? Come in," Bill said. He'd been the Ballet Master in Chief of the New York City Ballet for going on twenty-six years now, and Ana's boss for all of nine. He was tall, lean, and handsome for a man of sixty-one. A shock of white hair topping chiseled features made for a number of notable paintings of him around Manhattan and beyond. Bill Bradshaw was a legend in the dance world and most everyone respected him.

"Thanks, Bill. I hope your afternoon has been an easy one." He pulled her into a one-arm embrace as she passed, and planted a kiss on her temple—his standard greeting—and followed her into his office.

"Not too bad. Not too bad at all. Busy, though." His afternoon would have consisted of one-on-one meetings with each dancer in the company, of which there were close to ninety, for their annual evaluations. In meetings like these, dancers were promoted, counseled on progress, or worse, told their contracts would not be renewed for the following season. For Ana, this meeting was her chance for a promotion from soloist to principal dancer, the highest rank in the company. She'd been a soloist for five years now, killing herself and pushing her body past its limits to make the leap to principal, and then sitting in that orange chair at the end of each season hoping against hope.

She'd been passed over each time.

Maybe Bill believed she hadn't been ready in the past. Or that she hadn't put in enough time. Whatever it was, she was prepared to leave the heartbreak behind her. This upcoming season was hers, and Ana was prepared to tell Bill so herself if it came to it. She was determined not to let anything get in her way. She'd sacrificed too much.

"How's your father?" Bill asked. "I haven't heard from Klaus in a good six months."

"He's doing great," she told him. "Still Papa. He's the guest choreographer at Miami this season. It's going so well, they might want him back for next season, too. Though I doubt he'll accept. He's had a lot of offers."

"Oh yes. I remember hearing that. Lucky bastards to have snagged him."

"Agreed," Ana said, settling into her seat in anticipation for what the meeting would bring. She was, however, familiar with the obligatory small talk about her father before any major conversation about her own career. Klaus Mikhelson had achieved fame as a world-renowned Russian ballet dancer before immigrating to the United States in the late seventies and doing the same thing here. As one would imagine, he received tons of attention. Thereby, Ana had been compared to her father her entire life. The fact that she'd not seen the same success had been…hard. On both of them.

"Well, tell that old fellow I said hello and that I owe him a drink," Bill said, sitting.

"Will do." Ana smiled good-naturedly and wondered about that moment. Would she also be informing her father of her promotion? Or rather, trying to explain to him that she was once again passed over for principal?

Ana glanced around Bill's neatly organized workspace and waited as he settled in for the meeting. She caught sight of a folder open on his desk, her own headshot visible on top of the stack of papers inside. "So, you've been with the company for nine years now," he said, and glanced up at her.

"That's right." She kept her voice even, professional. "And I want to thank you for the opportunities that have been afforded me, Bill. I feel I've grown immensely as a dancer since coming here as an apprentice."

"Six injuries in that time," he said, looking up from his notes. "How's your ankle doing? Any pain?"

"Stronger than ever." And it was. Two surgeries and months of physical therapy had her back at work and pushing past the pain of what had been a crushing injury two years prior—not that injuries were anything new.

He nodded and bowed his head again. "Glad to hear that. I have to tell you, Ana, that Roger and the other choreographers all feel that you really came into your own last fall in *Orpheus*. That was a good part for you. A step forward in your dancing."

"I'm thrilled you thought so. I loved the work we did on that ballet but, Bill, I'm ready for more. I put two years in as a member of the *corps*, and six as a soloist. That's not even counting my apprenticeship."

"And you feel this is the year you want to emerge as a principal dancer in the company? Is that it?"

He looked skeptical, but she couldn't let that deter her.

This was the moment she'd waited for. She sat forward in her seat and met his gaze head-on. "I do. No one can match my technique, and my commitment is unwavering."

"I don't know that technique is enough, Ana. You have to want it from here," he said, a hand to his gut. "Dancing can't just be precision. It has to come with an element of fire. Do you understand? Passion."

"I have it. Dancing is my oxygen, Bill, and I will leave every part of me on that stage. You know that. I'm the first soloist in the door each morning and the last one out after a performance. I've worked my whole life for this opportunity, and if you give it to me, you won't be sorry. I'll work day and night for you."

He reclined in his chair and regarded her as she organized her second-tier argument. "Okay," he said simply.

Wait.

What did that mean?

"Okay?" Her hands went instantly numb, and a warm shiver moved up her spine. Was this the moment she'd been waiting for since she was six years old and watching *The Nutcracker* from the third gallery at Lincoln Center? Was she actually a principal dancer with the New York City Ballet?

"That's what I said. It's your year, Ana. I have a feeling." He leaned across the desk as if he had very important words to impart. "But you can't let up. Do you hear me?"

"I won't."

"The second you do, it's over. The competition these days is like none other I've seen. The ability and technique is unrivaled, thereby your commitment has to be that much more to stay ahead." She nodded, knowing how true his words were. The competition among company members was, in fact, ferocious. And while most of the dancers were friends just as much as they were rivals, Ana kept to herself, never taking her eye off the goal: to be the best. "You're one of the most gifted dancers I've ever worked with, but you know what your dancing lacks, Ana?"

"Tell me."

"A heartbeat. I need you to breathe life into your performance. You're all technique. Gorgeous technique, I'll give you that, but it's sterile. Clinical. If dancing is your oxygen, I need to see that on onstage. Put that passion into your movement. It doesn't matter how beautiful your extensions are if you don't move your audience. Do you understand?"

"I can do that. Thank you, Bill." It was the automatic answer, as it was the same note she'd received throughout most of her career. The words stung acutely, but she'd find a way to improve, because it was too important not to.

When she arrived back at her apartment two hours later after a barre workout, she wanted nothing more than to celebrate—maybe indulge in a rare glass of bubbly for the momentous occasion. She'd purchased a bottle just in case. It had been undoubtedly the most important day of her life thus far, and she should take a moment to commemorate it. As she moved to the refrigerator, she stopped cold at the handwritten note she'd placed there as a daily reminder.

Better is always possible. Good is not enough.

She took her hand off the door handle and discarded the idea of a celebration, running her fingers across the words. She needed to stay in tip-top shape for the opening of the season, and champagne was not on her approved foods list.

Still smiling to herself over the events of the afternoon, she took the time instead to roll out her muscles from her morning dance class before sitting with her phone in her hand, ready to place the call she'd waited years to place.

"Hello, my darling," her father said upon answering. His Russian accent had grown thinner but was still recognizable. "How did it go? What happened?"

Ana felt as if her heart would burst from her chest. At just the question, she had tears in her eyes. "Well, Bill had many complimentary things to say." She swallowed the emotion in an attempt to give nothing away. Buildup was always better, wasn't it? "He said to tell you that you owe him a drink, by the way."

"If he comes to Miami, we do the drink. Now, did he give you promotion or are you stuck for another year?"

She paused, drawing out the moment. Before saying the words, she closed her eyes, vowing to let them wash over her. "I'm now a principal dancer with City Ballet, Papa." She took a breath and waited.

"Anastasia!" he said. "At last. This is fantastic."

"Thank you." The tears rolled freely down her cheeks now, but they were happy tears, so she let them fall.

"Did you ask him why he waits so long?"

She opened her mouth to answer and then closed it again, not sure how to handle his deviation from the main idea. This was the best news of her life and she wanted to celebrate, not dwell on why it hadn't happened sooner. "Of course not. I was too happy with the news. I've waited for this for a long time, plugging away."

"Better late than never! I am proud of you, Kotik." The term of endearment, meaning "kitten," dated back to when Ana was five years old and lost her mother in a car accident. Her father had become her custodial parent from that point on. He wasn't an overly affectionate father, but he'd been there for her. "Casting for the fall season is happening soon, yes?"

"This week. There's a new work of Roger's that I'm dying to dance. It's the season opener. Contemporary and edgy. This would be something different for me."

"For your career, what is best? What's going to advance you the most amount?" The ever-present question seemed to surface whenever they spoke. How could she get ahead and how fast could she do it? Little else mattered to him, which placed a lot on her shoulders.

"I think it *would* be beneficial, yes."

"Then you must earn the lead, my darling. No less than lead."

"I will, Papa. I'll speak to you soon."

They said their good-byes and Ana clicked off, her emotions twisted the way they often were when she spoke to her father. Just once, she wanted to luxuriate in a victory rather than focusing on her next battle. He'd been happy for her news, but only briefly, because he already had his sights set on her next goal.

But then again, so did she.

Suddenly, a cluster of voices echoed in the hallway, made up of singing and cheering and words of congratulations. As the building was comprised of many of the dancers from the company, it was common for them to congregate in the hallways, even more so on a day that would bring about big changes in the company. They'd discuss who'd been promoted, who'd been let go, and which students from the School of American Ballet would be coming on as apprentices in the new season. She smiled, happy for their success, and moved closer to her door to listen to the chatter. Part of her wanted to join the group in their happiness, share her own news, and celebrate with her colleagues. Maybe they'd go out that night to the bar across the street, or stay in and gather in someone's apartment. She smiled at the thought and what that must be like. Actual friends. And while it would be seemingly easy to walk into that hallway and join them, something held her back. She stared at the Post-it across the room and remembered.

Better is always possible. Good is not enough.

The best thing she could do for herself right now was stay focused. As much as she might want to push it all aside for a good time, the season would be cast soon, and she couldn't let anything distract from her objective.

Chapter Two

W"hat's the house look like?" Natalie Frederico asked as she raced through the stage door, shrugging from her size-too-big green cargo jacket and glancing at the wall clock as she passed. She had never been good at call times, which meant she now had exactly twenty-two minutes to get herself in costume and makeup for the ten p.m. curtain. Not a big deal. She'd make it.

"We're at capacity," said her stage manager, Eddie, following her down the narrow, dimly lit hallway to her makeshift dressing room, formerly a storage closet. Her life was anything but glamorous.

"Sold out for the fourth straight week, then. Why the hell are we being tossed out of here again?" she asked, still pissed that they were forced to close the show so unexpectedly. "We play to standing room only six nights a week and Terrance is evicting us? This space has been our home for the past two years, and then we're just tossed?"

"Maybe because you only charge ten dollars a ticket in a garage space that only seats a hundred and fifty? He's a businessman, Nat," Eddie explained as he followed her. His glasses leaned off-kilter on his nose again, and Natalie took a minute to straighten them, ruffling his curly hair for good measure.

"He's a fucking capitalist," she said. "Money doesn't make the world go 'round, Ed. Assholes like Terrance need to figure that out." She took a seat in the fold-up chair she'd set in front of a mirror. Voilà, instant dressing room.

Eddie held up a finger as she applied eyeliner just under her lower lid. "Right. Except that it does. I mean, objectively."

"Yeah, well." She couldn't exactly argue further, as money *was* the reason the owner was giving her and her cast the boot. *Wheels*, the show she'd conceived of, choreographed, nurtured, and now danced in alongside eight of her closest friends, was playing its final performance that night. The devised dance piece had not only received fabulous write-ups in all the Los Angeles trades and dailies, but had a nightly waiting list of die-hards intent on getting tickets to the generally sold-out show. For some of them, it was their tenth or fifteenth time seeing the piece. And why wouldn't it be? *Wheels* was easily the most kick-ass production Natalie had ever been a part of, incorporating video projections, modern dance, classical ballet, and even a couple of skateboards (not ridden by her). They were a hit with the downtown crowd and lauded by the uptown. A win-win and she couldn't have been more proud of the work.

Yet it had all come crashing down due to lack of cash.

She shook her head in frustration. Sure, she could have upped ticket prices, but it went against what she believed in. Art for art's sake mattered more than a big box office take. She danced for herself and not some guy with a checkbook bigger than his face.

"For what it's worth, I'm gonna miss working on the show with you," Ed said to her in the mirror, his cheeks pink with emotion. Before she could stop herself, she turned and pulled her friend into a tight embrace because she'd miss him, too, the little nerd. The project had been a labor of love, and that was exactly what she felt for the show and everyone involved. A tight ball of emotion rose in her throat, because tonight was the end of something very special.

She turned back to the mirror, reining in the sentimentality. "We'll do another show. We'll get started next week. Find a new space."

Eddie hesitated. "This one is going to have to be my last, Natalie. The rest of the guys are out, too."

She stared at him, nonplussed. "Wait. What do you mean?"

"We had a talk last night."

"Without me?" She straightened and faced him, aware of the now seventeen minutes she had until curtain. "Why would you make that kind of decision? This is what we do and we're good at it. Everyone?"

He nodded. "We all feel it's time to move on. We made the decision as a group."

"Minus one," Natalie supplied. She reached for her pointe shoes. She wouldn't need them until the second half of the show when she shifted from modern to ballet, but they needed to make it to the stage with her.

"I'm sorry we didn't tell you. But we knew you'd talk us into staying on. Your passion for the work is contagious, but I can't make my rent," Ed told her in defeat. "You can't either."

"So?" The bravado helped her push past the reality of that statement. "We'll figure it out."

"Sadly, I don't want to figure it out," Ed told her. "Everything is crumbling around us and all you care about is the next show, the next gig, the art of it all. As romantic as that sounds, I'm not twenty years old anymore, Nat. I need to figure out my life."

She closed her eyes against the statement. She'd heard it before. From her mother. Her father. Her friends. And now here it was from members of her own dance company.

"What does Morgan say?" Eddie asked, pulling her back from her thoughts.

At the mention of her girlfriend, Natalie smiled. "She thinks what we do is awesome and supports me one hundred percent."

"Yeah, well, she'd say that if you'd announced you were taking a gaggle of prairie dogs on a field trip to Mars. She's not just your girlfriend, she's your number one groupie."

Natalie lifted a defensive shoulder. "So she's supportive. Big deal."

"Exponentially so. To a fault, and you know it."

"Is this a tough-love talk? Because it's starting to feel like one." She'd known Eddie for years. He'd come to her first solo show and had become an instant fan, attending every performance she'd given for weeks. In the end, he'd asked to contribute in any way he could and had turned into the best stage manager she'd ever worked with. They'd become friends along the way.

He met her eyes, seeming to give up on the argument. "I love you. You know that, but maybe it's time for a little stability in all of our lives."

She nodded, though sadness tugged. "I better get ready. Twelve minutes till go time. See ya out there."

Once she was alone, Natalie studied herself in the mirror. Her medium-length brown hair, now streaked every other strand with blond highlights, was pulled up on the sides and fell freely in the back. Her makeup was appropriately dramatic for the show, and the overdrawn green eye shadow matched the shade of her own eyes nicely. She blinked back at herself, willing her head to get in the game in the midst of the bomb Eddie had just dropped. "Focus, Frederico. You have a last show to dance."

But the weight of Eddie's words hung over her like an all-knowing rain cloud, and she blew out a melancholy breath. She was twenty-seven years old, and in her ten years as a dancer, she'd learned one key lesson: art trumped commerce. It was the reason she'd stepped away from a promising career that had her on the fast track to becoming a world-class ballerina. She cringed at the word even now. She'd had the agent, scholarships from all the top schools, and the scouts at her feet after winning a national ballet competition at thirteen. The newspapers had named her the most promising young ballet dancer in the western half of the country. After that, she'd given professional ballet a whirl, but the structure and the extreme focus on technique had her unable to express herself in the way she wanted to. Correction, *needed* to. To Natalie, dancing was her fix, but dancing *her own way* was a far more potent drug.

Things had been rough lately. She could admit that.

Putting together quarters to come up with her next meal had grown tiresome. As good as the write-ups had been on *Wheels*, it was getting harder and harder to stay one step ahead financially. She loved dancing, but the scramble to keep her head above water was taking an intense toll. With Terrance evicting them, and the company scattering, Natalie would be starting from the ground up with a new show and a new crop of dancers. That would take time.

And time didn't come with a paycheck.

Hell, couldn't anything ever be easy?

"Places, everyone," she heard Eddie call from down the hall. She gave her head a little shake and moved to the small stage, taking her place and waiting there in the dark as the music rose and pulsed around her, the techno beat vivid and all encompassing. Once the light hit, Natalie was off. The choreography was slow at first, by design, but the tempo picked up and the projected images behind her were timed to the beat. Robotic lighting followed her every move. As the show played on, she danced with a fire behind her fueled by desperation at her present set of circumstances. Feeling like her back was against the wall, she put it all on that stage. The music moved through her, ushering her steps, wild and carefree, but angular and accurate at the same time. Fifty-two minutes later, she took her final bow alongside her friends, absorbing the thunderous applause for the last time. By the end of the performance, she'd made a decision.

This was the end of the road.

It had to be.

And that just about killed her.

❖

The afterparty at Mustang Mike's was in full swing when Natalie arrived. The bar had turned into the go-to spot for cast and audience members alike to gather after each show and kick back until the wee hours of the morning. Prior to arriving, she'd taken an extra few minutes in her dressing room to pack up her things and say a mental good-bye to a show she'd grown to love. With a lump in her throat and a box under her arm, she'd taken a last long look at the place before switching off the lights for good.

The end of an era, she thought to herself. Sharp. Razor edged. Painful.

But she shook off the blistering sting because it was time to celebrate what they'd accomplished, and it just so happened Natalie was very good at celebrating—as in A-plus caliber.

When she appeared in the doorway of the bar, the patrons broke into applause and whistles, which progressed to hoots and hollers that lasted well past when they should have. God, it felt good. She took a minute to let it settle over her before making her way around the jam-packed room, hugging her friends and thanking them for a job well done. She also graciously accepted the compliments from audience members who'd enjoyed the show and stopped her to say so.

"Ms. Frederico, would you sign my program?"

"Natalie—can I call you Natalie? That was a kick-ass show. I loved the skateboards. Was that your idea?"

"You were awesome tonight, Ms. Frederico. I've never seen anyone dance like that. My friends were right when they told me to get tickets."

She smiled, nodded, signed, and answered any and all questions.

Interacting with people who saw value in her vision was one of the perks of the job that never got old.

And then at the end of the bar, she was met with the apologetic faces of her fellow dancers, their eyes downcast and their expressions guilt-ridden. When she came to Misty, who'd been with her in the early days before there even was a full-fledged company, she paused.

"Good show tonight," Natalie told her.

"Thanks. So we heard Eddie talked to you," Misty said, taking her hand.

Natalie nodded and gave Misty's hand a squeeze. "It sucks, but I get it. All good things have to come to end eventually, right?"

Misty nodded, and Angelo, another dancer, joined the conversation. "So you don't hate us?"

Natalie shook her head. "You know that's not my style."

"You're an inspiring leader, Natalie. Maybe one day we can all come back together again," Misty offered. "Restored and better than ever."

"I hope so," Natalie said, though she knew the chances were slim to none. In a way it felt like graduation day, where they all headed off into the boring world and got suit-and-tie jobs that would put food on the table and kill the adventure forever. "What will you do in the meantime?"

"Work for my dad's insurance firm," Misty said with a grimace. "Maybe find a way to teach a dance class at night. What about you?"

It was the million-dollar question. What exactly *would* she do? The thought was interrupted when two arms snaked their way around her middle. She turned to see Morgan's dark eyes dancing back at her. She wore a black dress that hugged her curves and left little to the imagination.

"You were amazing tonight. And hot. Beyond hot." Natalie moved into her girlfriend's embrace but was intercepted with an open-mouthed kiss that woke her libido in a big way. Perhaps there'd be a little one-on-one time with Morgan later. For now, however, there was a larger goal. Drink a lot, party a lot, and forget the future that loomed in front of her, large and imposing.

She pulled back from the kiss. "Let me talk to these people, then we can kick back with everyone."

"I'm not going anywhere."

In one quick move, Natalie was up on top of the bar and facing the room. She held up her hands, which brought the rumble of voices to a gentle hush just as someone killed the volume on the music. She looked down at all the expectant faces, friends, supporters, and colleagues. The sight tightened her throat with emotion. "So this is the end of something important, I guess. *Wheels* was one of those shows that you'll always remember, and dancing with you guys," she said, directing her focus to her fellow dancers, "was an honor I won't likely match. I think tonight has to be a celebration of the work, and I for one, am ready to honor it with large amounts of alcohol. Who's with me?"

The bar erupted in cheers and the music blared as she jumped down in time to have her first cocktail of the night placed in her hands. She downed the Crown and Diet and joined her friends on a makeshift dance floor in the middle of the bar. The night turned into one Natalie wouldn't soon forget. They danced, they talked, they hugged, they drank. Just after four a.m. she stumbled into her studio apartment with Morgan's mouth on her neck.

If it all had to end, at least she went out with a bang.

Tomorrow was the start of something new. She just wasn't sure what.

❖

Someone was knocking on the door. The rat-tat-tat had yanked Natalie unceremoniously from her slumber, and she wasn't thrilled. *Damn it.* She glanced around the room with one eye scrunched. The sunbeams from the skylight ripped across her face and prompted her to glance at the readout on her clock. Just past one in the afternoon.

Rat-tat-tat-tat.

"Hold on a sec," she mumbled, getting up in search of her robe. Pulling it tightly across her naked body, she made her way to the door, acutely aware of the screaming muscles she'd earned from last night's performance.

Rat-tat-tat.

"Oh my God, I'm going to have to kill you," she said loudly and flung open the door. Standing there on her doormat was a suit. One with a man inside. Which was the best way she could think to describe the visual. There was definite tweed. And the suit had a hat in his hand. "What's up?" she asked him. "What can I do for you?"

He stared at her, as if trying to determine her species. "Natalie Frederico?" He glanced up at the number above the door. "Do I have the right…"

"I'm Natalie. And you are?"

"Roger Eklund. Pleased to meet you."

She turned her head to the side and took a moment to roll the familiar name around in her foggy-from-sleep brain. "As in the dancer?"

"I'm a choreographer now, and was hoping we could talk. I saw your show last night. Can I come in?"

"Um…" Natalie glanced behind her at the disheveled apartment that probably mirrored her own appearance. No wonder he hadn't recognized her. Behind her, a variety of dance shoes and costume pieces littered the floor, and her bed stood unmade from the night before. Morgan must have headed into work at the coffee shop without Natalie hearing her leave. But this was an interesting turn of events, and her curiosity was piqued. Roger Eklund was the real deal, a well-known ballet dancer from the eighties and now a resident choreographer at New York City Ballet, if she remembered correctly. She'd seen recordings of his work and had always been impressed. She eyed him now, curious as to what he'd want with her. "Can we maybe meet somewhere? There's a café at the end of the block. I could get changed first."

He didn't hesitate. "Half an hour?"

"I can do half an hour. See you there."

Pulling her hair into a ponytail, Natalie selected a pair of boyfriend jeans and a black T-shirt advertising the Ramones. Some mascara and lip gloss later and she was off to meet Roger and figure out what the deal was. She found him in the corner booth of the sleepy little café that smelled scrumptiously of waffles and bacon.

"I ordered you some coffee," he said as she slid into her side of the booth. "I hope that's okay."

"Thanks. It's perfect."

"I didn't know what you take in it, but I'm sure they can bring whatever you like."

"I take it black," she said, and eyed him. "So what's this all about?"

"I saw your show last night."

"Right. You mentioned that." She grinned until the knowledge that the show was now closed hit and pulled the smile from her face. "You're a guy who knows his stuff. I've always admired your work. What did you think?"

"I thought it was indulgent and had too much going on."

Natalie took a moment and sipped her coffee, the criticism rolling off her back. "Well, everyone's entitled to their opinion. Yet despite those issues, you're still here this morning, meeting with me. So, what gives?" In the back of her mind, Natalie couldn't resist hoping he'd come to her because he was interested in investing in the show. Maybe there was a chance to transfer to another venue, and if this guy had the funds to do it, well, she was all ears.

"We've met before," Roger said. "Do you remember?"

Natalie nodded. "I do, but I'm surprised to hear you remember. It was back when I was enrolled at the School of American Ballet, right? You taught a couple of master classes. Everyone was in awe."

He ignored the compliment. "You were good back then. You stood out as a prodigy, a word I don't often use."

"You mean before I up and quit?" SAB had been a suffocating institution, and after just eight months in New York, she'd dropped out and headed home to California, where she could relax and be a human again. Dance the way she wanted to, sans all the rules.

"Before you quit, yes. I was in town earlier this week, doing some scouting when I saw your name on a flyer and memory struck. I thought I'd drop in on the show."

"Just so you could look me up later and criticize it?" But she said it with a smile, hoping he knew she was only ribbing him.

"The show was creative, but you were the standout yet again."

"Thanks. That's nice of you to say, but we're an ensemble."

"The ensemble was shit. You were the only draw."

"Okay." She drew the word out, not knowing exactly where to go with the backhanded compliment. The waitress delivered a basket of toast, which gave her a moment to gather her thoughts. "So you're not here to talk about the show, then."

"I'm not, no. I want you to come to New York." He poured milk into his coffee as if what he said were the most casual thing in the world.

"I've already seen the sights, but thank you."

"I'm talking about the New York City Ballet. I think you'd make an interesting addition to the company."

Whoa. Okay, she took a moment with that one. "I gave up ballet years ago."

"No, you didn't," he said matter-of-factly. "It was all over your show last night, just mixed in with a lot of other unnecessary style and media. But quite frankly, that's what has me interested. That style. The risk taking."

"Let me get this straight. You want to offer me a contract with City Ballet? What would Bill Bradshaw have to say about that?"

"Bill has given me license to bring in a choice few new dancers via unconventional means." What he meant was that it was rare for City Ballet to hire from outside the School of American Ballet, and she definitely didn't graduate from SAB.

She stared at him, still dumbfounded at the whole series of events. "I'm honored, truly. But it's not going to happen. Classical ballet, again? Tried it. Wasn't my scene."

"And you have so many other amazing opportunities that *are* your scene?"

She opened her mouth to argue, but what could she say? That she planned to pore over the want ads that very morning? See if craigslist might have anything interesting? The truth was she'd be waiting tables by next Tuesday, or worse, schlepping it in retail. She imagined herself in khaki pants and a red Target polo and cringed.

"Tell me why you want me, because I don't see what I can offer you."

"We're looking to revamp. Bring in some new blood, instill an edgier vibe at City Ballet with our fall opener, and that's you."

"So, City Ballet with a side of rebellion?"

He sipped his coffee and smiled. "Something like that."

She sighed, still not believing that she was even considering this. "If I did take you up on your offer, when would I have to be there?"

"Yesterday. The company reconvenes in September. That gives us enough time to work together for some long and hard weeks. Get you back in shape for what's ahead."

She shook her head. "I'd have to find a place to live, figure out the logistics."

"The company can help with that."

"Am I seriously entertaining this idea?" she said to the table.

Roger grinned and sat back against the booth. "It seems that you are."

❖

"The New York City Ballet!" Morgan yelled. Her blond hair was streaked pink this week, and she clutched two bags of Chinese take-out she'd yet to set on the table.

"I know, right?" Natalie said, shaking her head in mystification. "It's kinda out of nowhere, but when I think about it, I don't know what else to do. It's either ballet in New York or I'm the next counter girl at Hank's Dry Cleaning."

"Yeah, Hank's an asshole," Morgan supplied.

"And more than a little handsy."

Morgan nodded, taking it all in. "It's an awesome opportunity for you, babe."

"It is. And, at least this way, I'll be dancing. Plus, the guy, Roger, gave me zero time to think it over." She reached for the stack of shirts on her dresser and tossed them into her suitcase. She studied her pointe shoes and wondered if it was best to just leave them. City Ballet provided shoes for all of its dancers probably on a daily basis, and hers wouldn't fit the bill anyway.

"New York City Ballet. That's a big deal."

Natalie straightened. "It is. I guess."

"You're downplaying. You always do that. You're gonna be famous and on billboards and dancing in front of the prim and proper. I have a sudden urge to make out with you."

Natalie moved to her, smiling. "I doubt there'll be fame involved. I mean, how many ballet dancers can you name? But it is pretty cool. Thousands of dancers shoot for City Ballet each year. Most never make it into SAB, and of those that do attend and graduate, only a handful are offered apprenticeships with the company."

"And that's you now? A fancy apprentice?" Morgan's hands were under her shirt, caressing the bare skin at her back in a way that always made her relax.

Natalie shook her head. "That's the really crazy part. The company is divided into ranks. Apprentices on bottom, then the *corps de ballet*, who are the background dancers, followed by soloists, and then on top, the crème de la crème, are the principal dancers. Morgan, they're bringing me in as a soloist."

"You're serious right now?" Morgan stole a kiss. And then another.

Natalie nodded. "That's why it has to be so quick. Roger Eklund is the resident choreographer and he wants me in New York a few weeks before rehearsals start to get my technique in shape for his new ballet."

"You don't seem happy," Morgan pointed out.

"It's just that I don't know whether to laugh or cry." She walked back to her bed and sat down. "It's nice to know they want me, but this is not exactly what I would have picked out for myself. It's ballet. And not the cool kind."

"Well, you're going to make it cool. It's what you do and probably why they want you." Morgan paused and took a seat on the bed next to Natalie. "So you're off to fancy New York and I'll be here, waiting tables."

"You could come with me," Natalie offered. It would be a big step for them, but why the hell not? Natalie met her eyes and touched her cheek. Morgan was a sweet girl and had always been her number one fan and biggest supporter. They had a lot of fun together, and she hated to see that end. But from the apologetic look on Morgan's face, her moving to New York didn't seem to be an option.

"I don't know that I can just uproot my life right now, Nat. I love LA. All my friends are here."

"I understand," Natalie said through the pang in her chest.

"So what does this mean for us?" Morgan asked. "Because we're good together, you and me."

Just apparently not good enough for you to move. "Nothing has to change. I'll come home when I can. You'll visit me in New York. We'll take in the city together. It will be a time." Morgan's lips were on hers before she could take her next breath, and the momentum of the kiss drove her backward until they fell onto the bed in jumble of laughter and limbs.

"We're gonna be fine," Morgan told her, slipping her hands back under the hem of Natalie's top. "And I'm now dating a full-fledged ballerina. How hot is that?"

Natalie smiled. "Why don't you show me?"

Chapter Three

A na sat in the corner of the dance studio sewing her pointe shoes the first day back from the summer break, which always felt a bit like the first day of school. Extra energy. New faces. Hopeful smiles for what was to come. Deciding not to concentrate on any of that, she instead focused on sewing her shoes onto her feet, taking pride in the fact that the task, which had once taken her forty-five minutes, now took her five. Each dancer had a unique preference when it came to their pointe shoes, and Ana was no different. She preferred an elastic drawstring to a canvas one, and a strong shank with a little extra glue in the box for stability. Putting away her needle, she stood, stepping up on the box to break the shank in a little each way. Not too stiff, but still sturdy. Excellent.

"Congratulations, Ana," Audrey Wilder said as she passed behind Ana in the mirror. Audrey had just been promoted to soloist herself, snatching up Ana's vacated spot. Audrey's had been one of the celebratory voices she'd heard in the hall that day.

"And to you," Ana said, and smiled briefly. She watched as Audrey, always bubbly, joined her group of friends. They sewed their own shoes in a small circle, chatting as they worked, catching up on anything juicy that might have transpired since the close of last season. Ana looked on, as always. She wasn't a part of that group, but then again, that was by design. She could idealize having a social life all she wanted, but there was only so much time in a day.

"Well, if it isn't the newest principal," Jason Morales said, and pulled her into a bear hug. Jason was one person she was especially happy to lay eyes on. They were often paired together for any given *pas de deux*. He was easily her closest friend in the company, and she was lucky to partner with him. With Jason, she could always trust she was in good hands. They danced seamlessly together, and perhaps that trust was the reason she let her guard down a bit with him. Jason understood her in a way most people didn't.

"You might have to put up with me a little more now," she told him, making reference to the fact that they were likely to be paired even more frequently as a result of her promotion.

"More so if you're cast as Mira to my Titus." He slid her a knowing look, and she felt a twist of nervous energy in her stomach at the prospect of winning the role she'd been fantasizing about for months now.

"I'm afraid to even think about it," she confessed to him. "Maybe it won't happen."

He leaned in close to her ear and lowered his voice. "It's our season, Mik. Trust me."

"Don't jinx it." Of the roles in the upcoming fall season, she wanted Mira most, the lead in *Aftermath*, a never-before-performed ballet choreographed by their own Roger Eklund. Mira was a greedy, contemptuous woman, but by the end of the ballet, she'd been changed and reformed by her love for Titus, who fought both heaven and hell to be with her. The piece was modern in its telling, and thereby different from the ballets she was normally cast in.

"Please. It's as good as done. The part was practically written for you." He winked at her, and she smiled, bolstered by his confidence in her ability.

"Thanks, Jase."

"Just make sure I look good up there. Rippling muscles should be your focus. Let them draw you into me. People will love it." He bounced his eyebrows and biceps, pulling a laugh from Ana. After years working alongside each other, she understood his humor, as testosterone driven as it could sometimes be.

Around them dancers chatted amiably as they prepared for the day of dance ahead. New apprentices would spend most of the day with the *corps de ballet* learning the ropes. But for her, today was a new beginning. As principal now, she'd spend time with the choreographers preparing for the season ahead. This was her chance to wow Roger with the work she'd done over the break. Her extensions had never been longer, her form never more precise, and her endurance was at an all-time high. God, she hoped he'd notice.

Marjorie, one of the instructors, led class that day and walked the company through a series of barre exercises. "Lift your chest," she said to a new apprentice as she moved through the group. "Toe out," she said in correction to a member of the *corps*. For Ana, the exercises were simple, a way to prepare her muscles for what was ahead. Just as they moved into the second repetition, the door opened and a girl with a dance bag rushed in. On cue, every head in the room swiveled in the direction of the new arrival.

"I overslept," the girl whispered loudly to Roger, who sat along the sidewall. He nodded curtly and refocused on the class, as did the rest of the dancers. But Ana found her attention captured. The girl went about putting herself into a pair of shoes, taking nearly ten minutes to do so. Ana was embarrassed for her, if anything. The first day as an apprentice, a coveted position, and she showed up late? Not the best first impression, and in front of the whole company no less.

The girl hurried into position at a barre along the wall and joined the warm-up. But something about her snagged Ana's attention. She was familiar in a way, though Ana couldn't pinpoint just how. As they worked, she continued to steal glances at the new dancer, who had her brown hair with noticeable blond highlights pulled back into a ponytail. She was maybe five foot five, not especially tall for a dancer, but from what Ana could tell, her technique was strong for an apprentice. Her turnout was impeccable, and her control quite measured and precise. Plus, she was beautiful. The type of girl people noticed in a crowd. Whoever she was, she'd probably do well here, if she could just work on discipline.

When they broke for lunch, she saw the new girl talking to Roger, which was unfortunate, as she was hoping to have a discussion with him herself. In fact, she'd been gearing up for it all morning. He'd be integral in casting the season along with Bill. She waited patiently for her turn, but when the conversation concluded, Roger headed off in the opposite direction just as Ana raised her hand and opened her mouth in an attempt to snag a moment. "Damn it," she said under her breath.

"Oh, hey," the girl said, turning to her and then pointing after Roger. "Were you waiting to talk to him? Totally sorry."

"Not a big deal." A pause. She had green eyes, the new girl. Bright green eyes, and she didn't seem as young as Natalie had first concluded.

"So, I'm Natalie. My first day."

Natalie. Suddenly a vague memory sparked. "Wait. Were we by chance in class together at SAB?"

"Maybe for a few months. I wasn't there long. What's your name?" She had a very laid-back vibe, different than most of the dancers here. And those big green eyes were incredibly expressive.

"Anastasia Mikhelson. Ana."

Recognition flared and Natalie pointed at her. "Yep. That's right. Klaus Mikhelson's daughter."

"The one and only," Ana said flatly, once again feeling pigeonholed.

"We *were* in class together. You were the star pupil who used to shoot me *behave* looks whenever I got bored and made cracks about tutus, which we can all admit are entirely worthy of ridicule based on name alone."

It all came back to Ana in a sharp tumble. "Right. You're *that* Natalie." Natalie, who used to organize loud sleepovers in the dorm room across the hall, keeping Ana awake. Natalie, who rarely rehearsed, but seemed to know the combinations anyway, who whispered during class and got on Ana's last nerve. She hadn't been sorry to see her leave school, quite the opposite. But the series of events didn't add up. "So how are you here now?"

Natalie shrugged. "I wish I could tell you, Ana Mikhelson. I identify with that confused look that's creasing your brow right now, as I don't really understand it myself. That Roger guy showed up in LA and offered me the gig. It wasn't like I could say no when I'm flat broke. So here I am. Destined for ballerina life after all, it seems."

Ana narrowed her gaze. "Wait. He offered you a *contract*? No."

"Yes."

"That doesn't happen."

Natalie raised a knowing eyebrow. "Apparently it does."

"Except it doesn't. You're saying Roger Eklund just handed you an apprenticeship when there's a line of graduating seniors at SAB waiting for this very opportunity?"

"Not exactly." Okay, that was better. Maybe Natalie was here on a trial basis before any apprenticeship was officially decided upon.

Apparently they were working differently at City Ballet this season. "Not an apprenticeship. They made me a soloist," Natalie said.

Stop the world.

Had she just said that?

Was reality as Ana knew it imploding?

"I'm sorry. A soloist? As in you just skipped over two ranks at the most prestigious company in the nation?"

"Right. Something about needing to fill a gap in the company."

Ana took a moment, turning her head to the side as she regarded Natalie. "That's impossible."

A small smile crept onto Natalie's lips. "You seem to have a lot of reasons why things can't happen in life. Yet here I am." She offered a little wave. "Hey."

"Yet here you are," Ana repeated mildly.

"Why do I get the feeling that you're not thrilled to see me?"

"It's not that. I just—I mean, in the past—It took me *years*... Do you know how many people..." For the first time in her memory, Ana couldn't string together a series of intelligible words because the injustice at play had her thrown. *Thrown.*

"While you figure out the direction of that sentence, I'm going to introduce myself around, see if I can make a few friends. Good to see you again, Ana. Let's hang out soon. Drinks are on me." Natalie backed away looking every bit pleased with herself, and Ana cringed internally. No, no, no. This wasn't happening. It couldn't be. This Natalie girl had just waltzed in and claimed a spot that thousands would have killed for, after not even putting in the proper time? Make that zero time.

"Ana, were you looking for me?"

She turned. Roger. Right, she needed to get her game plan in order. What had she lined up to say again? "Is it true that the new dancer, Natalie, has been made a soloist?" Yeah, that hadn't been it at all. Damn it.

He studied her with a less than interested gaze. "It's true. We thought it was time to get some new blood in here. Shake things up with a dancer who falls slightly outside the City Ballet box." With a twinkle in his eye, he walked away.

"Wait, Roger!" She shook her head and forced herself to focus on the goal.

"Yes?" he asked casually over his shoulder.

"I wanted to tell you how excited I am about your new ballet. I'm beyond interested in auditioning for Mira."

He raised an eyebrow. "I always pegged you for more of a classics lover. A Balanchine enthusiast."

"I love Balanchine. I love Robbins. I do. But I'm just as passionate about dancing new works."

"Your style fits the older ballets. There's a formality to the way you dance, Ana. I'm not sure you could lose it to tackle something so modern."

She'd heard it a million times before. "Right. But *Aftermath* could be my chance to do just that." She decided to put it all on the line. "I'm just asking for a chance, Roger. Please. Let me dance for you and you can make the call."

He looked thoughtful a moment and nodded. "Meet me in studio four after lunch. There'll be a couple of other dancers there as well. I'll walk you through some of the variations and we'll see. That's all I can promise. A chance. I've always admired your work, Ana, I'm just not sure you're the best fit."

She didn't let that last comment faze her because she knew what she was capable of. The smile hit her face before she had time to control it. "Thank you, Roger. I'll be there."

Ana walked away with a sense of excited purpose. She had a shot now and wasn't about to blow it. Jason was right. This was her season, and she was ready to reach out and grab it.

❖

"So what kind of work did you do in LA?" Audrey asked, her blond curls bouncing. Natalie had only known Audrey for about an hour now, but those curls had bounced throughout most of it. Natalie leaned back in her chair and surveyed the two girls across the table from her. After she'd introduced herself to a group of dancers, Audrey and her friend Helen, who also happened to be soloists in the company, had invited her to lunch at their favorite deli across the street from Lincoln Center. Of course she'd accepted. With no friends in the city, she was eager to get to know some of the company members, gauge whether or not there was any kind of nightlife to get in on. Her time in New York couldn't be all work. Plus, maybe they could offer some insight into the inner workings of City Ballet. She already felt like she'd screwed up once with that late entrance this morning. She should maybe work on not ruffling feathers again.

"Let's see...in LA, I stuck with devised dance, mostly," Natalie told Audrey, focusing on the question at hand. "A mash-up of styles in which ballet, modern, and experimental are thrown against some mixed media."

Helen, of the perfect skin and gorgeous figure, sat next to Audrey absently twisting her straw. She was African American, and if she hadn't been a dancer, she surely could have made a go of it as a model. "Mixed media as in..."

"Video projections up against still slides, grunge music up against baroque. You name it. I'm into opposites and how they relate to each other because I think in the end everything is connected. It's just a matter of how."

Helen shook her head and leaned forward, captivated. "That's so outside of anything I've ever done that I'm ridiculously envious of you. I'd love to work on a show like that. Explore outside-the-norm themes. Chart my own course."

"Nothing's stopping you." Natalie pointed at Helen with her own straw. "Well, except the whole world-class ballet career you have going."

"So you believe opposites attract?" Audrey asked, digging into her turkey melt and leaving a dot of mustard on her cheek in the process.

Natalie didn't hesitate. "I think they can. Don't you?"

Audrey shrugged. "I'm all for it. Speaking of opposites, I wish that stockbroker guy in 2D would throw me up against the wall in the elevator and make me scream his sexy stockbroker name. How's that for opposites? It's probably something like Chip or Blake, and I can make excellent work of a name like Chip or Blake. But in my experience, the buttoned-up types don't do well with the less-than-normal schedule I have to keep."

Natalie smiled at the unexpected confession. "Stockbroker guy, huh?"

Audrey nodded. "He's like Clark Kent as if played by Jake Gyllenhaal. I want him to be my Superman love slave on the daily. Does that make me shallow?"

"That makes you Audrey," Helen countered. "One foot gingerly in your own damn world. It's why I keep you close by. You make me look put together." That earned Helen a tempered glare.

Okay, so Audrey was man-crazy. That could be fun on a slow weekend. "Let me ask you something," Natalie said quite seriously. "How does he feel about mustard?"

Helen chuckled, understanding the reference. Audrey, however, stared at her blankly. "I'm not sure. Why do you ask?"

Natalie halfway pointed at Audrey's cheek. "Because you have some. Right there."

"Maybe Superman could lick it off," Helen said.

"You're not funny," Audrey told her, but the smile on her face said otherwise. With her napkin, she dabbed the mustard. "Listen, I would lure that man in any which way I could. I'd paint my body in mustard if that did it for him."

"Sigh," Helen stated. "We have to have that talk about limits again. Do you want to end up an old mustard maid? You have to play harder to get."

Audrey sulked into her Diet Coke.

"What about you?" Helen asked Natalie, shifting the focus. "Boyfriend?"

"Girlfriend."

"Shut up," Audrey said, eyes wide. She raised a fist in victory. "Finally, a lesbian in the company. Well, at least the first we know of. The boys in City Ballet have had the market cornered on homosexuality for too long."

Helen met Natalie's gaze. "Audrey's a fan of diversity."

The curls bounced again. "I am. And now I have a new lesbian best friend."

"We're best friends?" Natalie asked.

"Obviously. Just look at us."

Natalie picked up on the fact that Audrey was simply being playful, but she had to hand it to them. These girls were fun, and she honestly *could* see herself becoming friends with them.

"So where do you guys live?" Helen asked. "You and your girlfriend."

"Morgan's back in LA. We'll be doing the long-distance thing. But I'm downtown on Fourteenth Street. The company helped me snag a place at a price that won't break me, which helps." Helen and Audrey exchanged a triumphant look. Natalie pointed at Helen and then Audrey. "What does that mean? The knowing glance thing happening right now."

"We're neighbors," Audrey explained, clearly pleased with this new turn of events.

Helen nodded. "You're living among a ton of dancers from the company. City Ballet gets killer deals on those units on Fourteenth, as one of its biggest benefactors also owns half that building."

"You're kidding. We live in the same building? What floor are you guys on?"

"We share a two-bedroom on eight."

Natalie smiled, liking the way this was going. "I'm in a one-bedroom on seven. How did I not know this was a company building?"

"You just had to ask the right folks," Helen said. "You gonna eat that pickle?" And without waiting for a reply, she stole the spear from Natalie's plate.

Yeah, they were going to get along great.

CHAPTER FOUR

Natalie was still amazed that she was not only back at Lincoln Center, but employed this time. She stared up at it now as they ascended the steps after lunch, captivated by the series of buildings surrounding the iconic fountain she remembered from her youth. The David H. Koch Theater was world famous, and if all went according to plan, she'd be dancing on that stage. While it wasn't exactly the kind of work she would have dreamed up for herself, there was a history to the New York City Ballet that had her respect.

Audrey and Helen took the extra few minutes before Natalie's scheduled afternoon session with Roger to show her the warm-up rooms just prior to the stage, as well as the costume and shoe shops, and the greenroom set aside for them to congregate. All the key spots that would help her get through the day as a member of the company.

"And you'll need to speak to Henry about customizing your shoes. He can set you up after a brief consultation. Or you can try on a bunch of company members' shoes and see if any of them work for you, style wise."

"I have to have a sturdy shank," Natalie told them, already dreading the idea of her shoes dying on her in the middle of a performance. "Or I'm done for."

"Henry's your man. Make him your best friend and you'll never long for the right kind of shoe."

"Good to know."

Once they looped back around to rehearsal studio four, Natalie turned to them. "Hey, thanks for looking out for me today. I owe you each a drink."

"And we plan to collect. There's a bar across the street from our building. McKenna's. An Irish pub. You should find a bunch of us there tonight to commemorate the first day back. Stop by and tell us how the session went."

"I might do that," she told them and then gestured to the door behind her. "How come you guys aren't called to this work session?"

Audrey didn't hesitate. "Because this session is exclusively for *Aftermath*, the first show of the season. Only girls in consideration for Mira were invited."

"Who did you pay off?" Helen asked her. "Soloists aren't often considered for leads."

"Still trying to figure that one out for myself."

"You must be hella good, little Miss Natalie," Audrey said.

"I guess I'm about to find out." Natalie pointed at them. "McKenna's?"

Helen nodded. "That's the place."

Her new friends took off and Natalie headed into the studio. Inside she found Ana and her less-than-friendly vibes stretching on the barre on the far side of the room. She passed Natalie a sidewise glance before continuing her warm-up. Closest to Natalie was a tall, dark, and handsome guy on the floor wrapping his knee and across the room another couple of female dancers Natalie had yet to meet. Everyone seemed to be in their own space, keeping to themselves.

"Hey, is this the session for Roger?" she asked the male dancer quietly, feeling the library-like concentration happening across the room and not wanting to break any sort of code. Well, at least not on the first day. There'd be time for that later.

"Yeah, he should be here in just a sec. You Natalie?"

She nodded.

"He mentioned you. Welcome to City Ballet."

"Thanks. Still a little surreal."

He extended a hand from his spot on the floor. "Jason. I'll be dancing Titus, at least for today."

She knelt next to him. "I don't see any other guys here. Does that mean the role is yours?"

He smiled, hope noticeable in his eyes. "Generally. I imagine I'll know for sure before today is through. As should you."

"Right." She tossed a glance across the room at her competition. "They any good?"

Jason nodded. "The best we have. Especially that one." He inclined his head in Ana's direction. Her dark hair was pulled into a knot on top of her head and she wore a blue leotard with black tights underneath. The perfect body for a dancer, Natalie thought, taking in her long arms and legs. Ana was graceful, elegant, even in the midst of warm-up. "We've been partnered together for years, so I have to root for her. No offense. Best wishes on a killer audition, though."

"Thanks. Sounds like I'll need it."

Roger had talked to Natalie a little bit about the ballet he'd be working on, and she understood that part of her reason for being there was for this particular role. He needed someone who could bring a more visceral quality to the dance, and she was ready to give it her best shot. Her only fear was letting him down.

She removed her light hoodie and rolled her now-bare shoulders, ready to get this thing going. After a few barre stretches of her own in the excruciatingly silent room, she turned as Roger joined them.

"Come, come," he said to the group, beckoning them closer. "Let's have a chat before we begin." She moved to Roger along with Jason and Ana and the others, ready to hear whatever it was he had to say. "We're going to spend the next hour learning the choreography to two different sequences from *Aftermath* and see where we're at when we finish. Yeah?"

"Sure," she said, and the others nodded and exchanged a knowing glance. Translation: we'll see who's still standing. Natalie decided it should be her. She didn't come all the way to New York to dance in the *corps*.

The trouble was that the combinations were anything but easy. In fact, this was some of the most complex choreography she'd yet to encounter, and half an hour in, Natalie felt like she was three steps behind and primed to fall farther as they continued. Ana, however, had yet to miss a beat, and the reserved smile she passed Natalie's way as they headed into a five-minute break could be described as taunting at best.

"Doing okay?" Ana asked and took a drink from her water bottle.

"I'm fine. You?"

She raised a shoulder. "I'm great. I love what Roger is doing with this piece."

Natalie wiped the sweat from her forehead with her towel and felt her calves pull from the challenges thrown her way. She'd been training with Roger diligently, but keeping up with Ana added a whole new element to the process. Ana was quicker to pick up the choreography and had this undeniable grace about her that Natalie could never duplicate. She simply didn't come with that kind of elegance.

Roger reentered the room, scribbling something on his notepad, probably all of the things that she'd screwed up in the first half of the session. Perfect. He whispered quietly to the two girls nearest the door, and they began to pack their dance bags. Had they been cut? Was it down to her and Ana, and if so, how had that happened? Roger stalked farther into the room and glanced up at the remaining trio from his clipboard. "Can I see the realization and reversal moment between Titus and Mira? Jason, why don't you dance this one with Ana?" The two nodded and headed to the center of the studio as Natalie took a seat along the wall.

They began to dance, slowly at first, light steps that mimicked the music. Jason reached out his hand for Ana but she stayed just out of his grasp, moving in short jumps around him. He beckoned a second time and she spun into his arms just in time for the lift. It was beautiful. Stunning even, when it came to the mechanics of the dance, but the fire hadn't been there. The reason for Mira to give in to Titus wasn't clear. The performance lacked the one thing she knew she could bring to the exchange: depth.

Jason placed Ana onto the floor gently and the two of them turned to Roger, awaiting further instruction or feedback. Roger simply stared and tapped his pen against his teeth, the only sound in the room. Finally, he turned to her in some sort of quiet frustration. "Natalie, would you mind?"

"Of course not." She moved to the floor, passing Ana on the way. As their eyes met, the challenge in Ana's cool stare was evident. *Top that.*

But Natalie didn't have time to dwell, as moments after she took her position next to Jason, the music trickled toward her. She had to get out of her own head, that much she knew. Thinking through the precision of the steps would trip her up, and the only way she knew to survive this was to feel the music. To let it move through her and pull her along. Technique be damned.

So that was what she did, living within each beat, following every crescendo, and if that meant that she missed one of Roger's steps, then she'd make up for it with passion, grit, and fire. In that moment, she became Mira, moving into Titus's arms as he lifted her in triumph.

As Roger's assistant killed the music, the room fell into silence. "Whoa," Jason said quietly to her as he placed her back on sturdy ground. "That was complex. You about ripped my heart out."

She turned to him. "That's the goal, right?"

He nodded and passed a concerned glance to Ana, who looked on, the air of superiority now stripped from her in a way Natalie couldn't help but enjoy. She passed a look back. *How was that?*

"Again," said Roger, a pensive look on his face. "Ana first and then Natalie." It went on that way for the better part of two hours, as one girl danced, then the other. The session included notes from Roger, corrections, and discussion about character and craft. Natalie gave what had turned into the most grueling audition of her life everything she had and then looked on as Ana did the same.

At the end of her last combination when she was breathless, spent, and in pain from the demands of the choreography, Roger's voice interrupted her recovery.

"Jason, you'll dance Titus in *Aftermath*," he said resolutely.

"I'm honored, Roger. Thank you," Jason told him.

They made decisions that fast around here? Natalie took a deep breath and waited for the verdict.

Roger turned to Ana and Natalie's heart dropped. "Ana, I want you to dance Mira in the production." Quite contrarily, Ana gasped and smiled, her hand immediately on her heart. "Three nights a week," he finished. "But as the part is a demanding one, as you've seen today, Natalie will dance Mira the other three nights." Just as quickly as the smile had been on Ana's face, it dimmed. But Natalie didn't care. She'd just been handed an opportunity on a platter, and for her first day on the job, things were going pretty damn well. While ballet wasn't what got her blood going, there was something about Roger's choreography that had her hooked, her interest held.

"Just like that?" Natalie asked.

Roger smiled at what might have been her naïveté. "Not exactly, darling. You have a great big mountain of work ahead, and I don't envy you. Your form is still inconsistent and at other times quite choppy, and I can't have that in my show."

Natalie lifted a shoulder. "Well, say what you really think, Roger."

"You'll get there, but not without working day and night." Roger glanced to Ana, who seemed to enjoy this exchange. "And you. Your dancing is flawless, pristine even, but it's missing the magic. There's no soul there, only finesse. And you can't tell a story with finesse alone. At least, I'm not willing to let you."

She nodded resolutely. "I'm up for it."

"So that brings me to a plan of action," Roger said, addressing them both. "You will rehearse together as you prepare for the part, and that is quite intentionally by design. Natalie, you embody everything that is Mira, but your technique is lacking. You can learn from Ana. Likewise, it's my hope that you'll help Ana in return." He nodded curtly. "I'll see you back here at ten a.m. ready to start what will be a strenuous rehearsal period prior to opening. I hope you're both ready for what's ahead."

Once Roger left the room, Natalie let out a whoop in celebration and turned to the others, fully expecting them to join her. She was met with a reserve she didn't quite understand. Why the hell weren't these ballet people celebrating? Was muted emotion part of the job requirement? Ana's response to the news was to go about packing her dance bag, and Jason smiled conservatively.

"Hey, you guys. This is huge," she said to them. "Exciting! So why is no one excited? Isn't this the kind of thing that you work really hard for around here?"

Jason nodded and passed a glance Ana's way as if to seek permission. "You're right," he said finally, breaking into a full-on grin and pulling her into a hug. "Hey, congratulations. I look forward to us working together."

"I think this requires more than congratulations," she said as he released her. "This is fucking awesome. We should celebrate. Get a drink somewhere immediately, paint New York some festive colors. Ana, you're coming with us. Don't argue."

"No, I'm not." Ana turned to her. "I don't drink when I'm in rehearsal."

God, could this girl be any less fun? And this was who she was supposed to be working with day in and day out for the next few weeks? "Surely you can make an exception for today," Natalie said. "The day you were cast as the lead in a new work at City Ballet? I have all the faith in you."

"Actually, I can't."

"Ana doesn't go out much," Jason supplied.

"No?" Natalie asked, shaking off the annoyance at Ana's continued refusal to have a pulse. She focused on Jason instead. "Well, what about you? You up for some extracurricular?"

He exchanged another check-in glance with Ana. Were these two in some kind of relationship she should know about or simply codependent for the sake of it? "Um, yeah, I'd love to celebrate, actually," he said, seeming genuinely excited at the concept. Poor Jason, the guy probably needed an outlet if Ana was his go-to.

Natalie clapped her hands. "Great. Let's do it."

"You sure, Mik?" Jason asked one last time.

"I'm sure. You guys knock yourselves out."

"I don't know that we'll get that far," Natalie offered playfully. "But the night is young and I hold hope." The comment earned exactly zero response from Ana, which was not a shocker. Natalie returned her focus to Jason. "Audrey, the one with the fun curls, said there's a place across from the company apartments on Fourteenth?"

"McKenna's," Jason supplied. "I know it well."

"I'll grab a shower and meet you in front of the bar."

He passed her a smile. "You're on."

Ana watched as Jason and Natalie left the dance studio, and a pang of something unnamed struck. Was that jealousy? Maybe she should have just gone with them. Shoved it all aside. Hell, she'd just been cast in the role of her lifetime, the one she'd been waiting for since she'd first joined the company all those years ago. But discipline told her that her time was better spent resting her muscles and eating a healthy dinner so she could be back here the next morning in tip-top shape and show Roger that he hadn't made a mistake casting her. Could that Natalie girl do the same? Doubtful.

As she pushed open the door to the outside, her phone buzzed in her dance bag. She fished it out just in time to take the call.

"So how did it go?"

She hadn't checked the readout before answering, but her father's deep voice tipped her off. "I got it, Papa. I *got* it."

"You are the lead? He cast you?"

She laughed, loving the excitement she heard in his voice. At long last. "He did. I'll be dancing Mira three nights a week. Another girl will do the other three performances."

"You are sharing the role?" he asked. "Why? Why must you do the share?"

"It's a physically demanding part, so it's split between two dancers."

"When I was a dancer, there was no sharing. We danced the parts given, demanding or no."

"And I could have, too, but it wasn't my call."

"A ridiculous call it is, because you could dance alone." A pause. "She is good?"

Ana considered this. "Her technique is scattered, rough at best, but she has this presence, Papa. She infuses her performance with a lot of emotion, and it works. I see why she was cast."

"You are better. Remember this always." Ana closed her eyes at the proclamation, wanting to live up to his expectations, though they had always been so very high. "You have what she doesn't. Precision. Show Roger. You can do this, Ana."

She nodded as a crisp wind blew across her body, prompting her to pull her light jacket tighter around her midsection. "That's the plan. Will you come to a performance?"

"I will try to come to New York before the show, it closes. We can have a dinner after. Sardi's. My treat."

"I'd like that."

"I love you, little Ana. Work hard. Make me proud."

"Love you, too, Papa. I will."

Night had fallen by the time Ana began her walk to the train, wincing each step of the way. Her left foot, which had given her trouble here and there throughout her off-season training, was making itself known today in startling color. She'd pop some Advil when she got home. In the meantime, she pushed through the pain with each step. Nothing new.

When Ana arrived back at her apartment, she did what she always did. Struggled with the key in the lock. The building was an older one and the lock had given her trouble since she'd first moved in. As she jiggled the key in the door, first to the right, and then to the left, she tossed her head back in frustration when neither trick worked. Three calls to the super and still no new lock.

"That door steal your boyfriend or something? I'm sensing a lot of hostility over there."

Ana turned at the voice behind her, only to stare into green eyes she'd recently come to know. Natalie exited the apartment across from hers, then closed and locked the door. With a *key*. Rewind.

"Do you live here?" Ana asked. "In that apartment?"

Natalie patted the outside of the wooden door as if it were her friend. "I do. Seems we're neighbors as well as colleagues."

"Great," Ana said, purely out of civil requirement. That was when she noticed Natalie's changed appearance. Gone were the leotard and leggings. Instead, she had her hair down, a look that quite prominently showcased the blond highlights in her otherwise brown hair. She wore slim-fitting jeans with a hole in the thigh (the kind you buy that way), and a tight black T-shirt with the words "Do Over" in pink letters.

"Why are you looking at me like I'm dressed as an astronaut?" Natalie asked and brushed casually at her cheek, as if to wipe away an errant smudge.

Ana realized she'd been staring. "Sorry. No, just…long day. Zoned out for a sec." She'd be lying if she didn't admit that Natalie looked great. With those big green eyes and full lips, she was gorgeous. Onstage, she mentally corrected. She was simply evaluating Natalie's appearance for stage. Nothing more. She was, after all, Ana's competition and the most *annoying* person on the planet to boot. Couldn't forget annoying.

"It *was* a long day, which is why you should join us across the street rather than fight with your door any longer. It's sad, and that door deserves a break."

"I told you, I'm not really in the mood. And it is not sad. Why would you say it's sad? It's a door. It's just fine."

"Are you *ever* in the mood?" The question felt provocative, but Natalie was smiling and that somehow softened the effect. "If my memory serves from years ago, you keep to yourself a lot, which can't be much fun."

"I do and it's just fine."

"Come out with us, Ana Mikhelson. Live a little. Aren't Russians known for having a good time?"

"They're not, actually. Quite the opposite. But then, I've never lived in Russia. Another time," Ana said, and turned to her door, intent on getting in her apartment if it killed her. She wrestled with the key, jiggling it from side to side aggressively, shoving her body weight against it.

"You really hate that door, don't you? Want some help?"

Ana made an after-you gesture and stepped aside in frustration. Natalie removed the key from the lock, and with very little force slid it easily back into the keyhole and turned it gingerly to the left until they heard a quiet click. "See? Just needed a softer touch. This door doesn't hate you. You should try being its friend. There might be a larger metaphor there." And with that, Natalie headed off down the hallway, hips swaying slightly.

"Wait. How did you do that?" Ana called after her.

"I've been told I have really good hands," Natalie called without looking back.

Ana felt the blush almost immediately and pushed it to the side in favor of exasperation. So Natalie had not only swooped in and conquered City Ballet, making friends with half the company and then landing a lead role without any preamble, but she also came with the magic touch. Fantastic. Ana pushed her way into her apartment and stared at the darkness, which, after Natalie's blatant assessment, felt a little…unfun.

❖

When Natalie and Jason had arrived at McKenna's, a group of familiar faces called out to them, eager to hear the news from the casting session. It seemed she didn't have to look much farther than across the street for any kind of nightlife.

"So it's cast?" Audrey asked in shock. "You're saying the *Aftermath* leads are a done deal?"

Natalie nodded at the faces along the long table of fellow dancers and pointed to Jason. "You're looking at Titus." Right on cue, Jason smiled triumphantly and fist-bumped one of the guy dancers two seats down. As music pulsed from the speakers along the walls, the table broke into a combination of cheers and applause.

"And who's dancing Mira?" Helen asked.

"Ana," Jason supplied. The girls seemed to sink a little at the proclamation. Whether it was on her own behalf, Natalie wasn't sure.

"Well, good for Frozen," Audrey said somewhat reluctantly. "She probably needs something like this to cheer her up, given she seems kind of unhappy with, you know, Earth."

"And Natalie," he countered, pointing at her. "Did I forget to mention that? They're splitting the role due to the physical demand."

Her new friends turned to her in silent shock, their eyes wide. Helen's hands made their way to her mouth in beauty-pageant-win-slow-motion.

"Shut up," Audrey finally said. "You were cast?"

"As the lead?" Helen finished.

Natalie nodded. "Shocked the hell out of me, too."

Helen stared at her, shaking her head. "Who are you? And where did you come from? Things like this don't happen at City Ballet." But Natalie could tell that Audrey, Helen, and the rest of the dancers, who now passed the news down the table, seemed to be genuinely happy for her, if not a little mystified.

She smiled at them. "I don't presume to know why any of this is happening. I show up and I dance."

"Well, you danced the hell out of that audition," Jason said, signaling the waitress for a couple of beers for them. "New girl or not, you make people want to watch you when you perform. It's all kinds of awesome." The comment landed and resonated with Natalie.

"Thanks, Jason. I hope you'll be watching me carefully during our second *pas*. That lift scares the hell out of me. I'm not sure how I'm gonna pull it off."

"Trust that I have you," Jason told her. "That's all you have to do."

"It's been a while since you danced a *pas* in a show with someone other than Ana," Audrey pointed out.

Jason considered this. "Ana and I have always worked well together, and Bill sees that." There was something about the way he said it that let Natalie know that Jason was a little gone on Ana. Interesting…

"Well, at least she'll give you the time of day," Helen said. "The chill I feel when she walks past isn't just from the air-conditioning. She definitely hates me."

Jason tapped his finger on the table. "She does not. You guys just need to get to know her better. If anything, she's shy. That's what we're talking about here."

"You think we haven't tried to get to know her?" Audrey countered. "We call her Frozen for a reason. You're the only one she's friends with. It actually makes me a little sad for her."

Natalie leaned back in her seat and reflected on what she knew of Anastasia Mikhelson. "She was that way in school, too. Kept to herself. Didn't say a whole lot and then danced us all under the table."

"We were a couple of years behind," Helen said, motioning to Audrey, "but we heard the stories."

"You guys went to school together?" Jason asked Natalie, now intrigued.

"We were the same year at SAB until I dropped. She used to roll her eyes at me on the daily. I have a feeling she still does. I'll say one thing for her, though." Natalie ruminated on what she'd witnessed that afternoon. "She's a beautiful dancer, you guys. Measured. Precise. I could never do what she does."

The others nodded in agreement and Helen shook her head. "When it comes to technique, no one touches her."

Natalie accepted the beer the waitress placed in front of her and raised it to the group. "I think little Miss Ana just needs some loosening up. And now that we'll be working so closely together, I will make it my personal mission to see that it happens."

Audrey clinked glasses with her. "Best of luck, grasshopper. Take a coat. You'll need it."

Two hours passed in a blur of war stories, drinks, and getting-to-know-you conversation. Natalie learned that Jason had dated several female members of the *corps* but had yet to fall in love, and that the dancers at either end of the table, Boomer and Marcus, had just gone through a nasty breakup and weren't quite ready to coexist just yet. The company, in fact, seemed loaded with inner drama that Natalie planned to stay on the periphery of. Hurt feelings, rivalries, and good old-fashioned jealousy were all alive and well in City Ballet. Yet in the midst of it all, these dancers worked together to create the most sought after and critically lauded ballets in the western world.

And Natalie was now a part of it all.

As she made her way across the street with Audrey and Helen en route to their building, Natalie found herself high on life and encouraged by the choice she'd made to follow Roger to New York. She was doing it—holding her own with these ballet folks and having some fun in the process. Maybe this place wasn't so bad after all.

"Hey," she said, stopping their progress in front of the elevator. Audrey and Helen turned to her mid-laugh, sobering once they caught the sincerity in her demeanor. "I survived my first day, and part of that is because of you guys. So thank you."

Audrey, who was extra warm and fuzzy due to the beverages she'd consumed, pulled Natalie into a tight hug. "You're gonna do just fine here, Natalie whatever-your-last-name-is. You're a cool girl." And then because Audrey forgot to release her, Helen politely pulled Audrey's arms off Natalie, who regarded her new friend in amusement.

"You guys don't drink too often, do you?" Natalie asked.

"Not in the course of the season," Helen said. "But we had to celebrate the first day back and your victory! Now I have to go home and crash so I can find a way to learn the new choreo in class tomorrow."

"Night, you party animals," Natalie said as the elevator let her off on the seventh floor.

"Don't wake up Frozen," Audrey said from the elevator in an overinflated whisper. Natalie shot them the thumbs-up sign and headed down her hallway in an exaggerated creep for the benefit of her new friends. Once the elevator door closed, she straightened and passed Ana's door. She paused a moment, wondering if inside Ana was already asleep or perhaps working meticulously to organize her pointe shoes in age order. She suppressed an eye roll and headed into her apartment, intent on not letting thoughts of Ana Mikhelson and her pristine technique ruin her buzz.

Chapter Five

O ne, two, three, four, five, six." Roger stood in the corner of the room and clapped out the beat as Ana moved through the new combination that would serve as the ballet's opening sequence. Music from the piano echoed across the studio's expanse. The choreography was intricate, and the timing everything. Ana had arrived early that morning to warm up properly, to prep her body, but found the regime interrupted when Natalie joined her.

"Hey, Ana M.," she'd said upon entering the space.

"Good morning." Ana had passed her a glance as Natalie slung her dance bag onto the chair and went about pulling her hair into a ponytail. She took a spot at the barre and began to stretch just a few feet down from Ana.

"We had a great time at McKenna's last night. That's a pretty cool place. Have you been?"

"I have, yes," Ana said, and pressed her torso to her shin, willing herself to concentrate on her warm-up. However, Natalie apparently had other ideas.

"One of the things I really like about New York—everything's so packed together. I had forgotten."

"That it is." If she kept her answers short, maybe Natalie would get the picture and let her focus on what she was there to do, work. She wasn't interested in being best buddies with the other dancers, and certainly not Natalie, of all people.

"So have you lived here your whole life?" Natalie asked brightly. "In Manhattan?"

"We lived in Brooklyn and commuted to the city."

"I imagine it must have been quite a head trip, growing up with a famous father."

Ana moved her stretches to the floor. "I wouldn't know the difference."

Natalie laughed wryly, and the robustness of the sound had Ana's attention. It wasn't put on or obligatory. She had a feeling Natalie wasn't into pretense. "Trust me. When your parents are nobody from nowhere, it makes things a little more complicated."

"In what way?"

"You know, standing in line with hundreds of other kids in the rain in front of a theatre. Dancing with a number on your chest hoping to get noticed and offered some kind of chance."

Ana bristled at the implication and straightened from her spot on the floor, now fully involved in the conversation, her defenses engaged. "Are you saying I've gotten to where I am because of who my father is?"

Natalie's eyes went wide. "Absolutely not. I'm just saying it couldn't have hurt, as far as the number wearing went."

"And how would you know that?" Ana felt the anger hit and the surge of energy that moved through her at the challenge. Natalie had touched on a sensitive topic, as Ana had spent much of her life working overtime to prove herself as a worthy dancer in her own right.

"Listen, I'm not professing to know anything. I would just imagine if Klaus Mikhelson were my father, I might have had a few more contacts in the dance world starting out."

Ana lifted her hand in the air. "Yet here you are anyway. Skipping the hard stuff. I don't remember the entire story, but what was it that brought you to SAB all those years ago?"

"I won a national competition and it came with a scholarship. I couldn't have afforded it otherwise. My dad works in insurance, and my mom stayed at home with us. Two brothers totally obsessed with football, and me."

"So you were handed a fantastic opportunity and you walked away." Ana couldn't fathom it.

"It wasn't where I was supposed to be."

"And this is?"

Natalie seemed to make a decision and knelt next to her. "Can we back up? Because I feel like I've upset you, and that was so not the goal of this little powwow. Quite the opposite actually, so how about some sort of peace offering?"

"I'm fine. Just ready to get started. Can I have a little space?"

Natalie held up her hands and stood, exasperation in her eyes. "Your wish is granted. God, do you ever lighten up? I'll give you one thing, Ana. You're certainly consistent."

Shortly after the exchange, Roger had joined them and they'd embarked upon one of the more grueling rehearsals Ana could remember participating in. All the while, the interplay with Natalie from earlier loomed over her like a thick, dark raincloud, pulling at her for reasons she couldn't quite assemble. Consistent? What did that mean? And then there was the feel of Natalie's eyes on her as she danced, which made Ana feel self-conscious in the most irritating sense. Because of course Natalie would watch her work. That's what this joint rehearsal was for, to prep both of them for the same part. Still, she found Natalie's presence distracting, and its effect grated on her.

In fact, everything about Natalie Frederico annoyed Ana.

As Ana spun across the floor, she felt that aggravation move through her in one wave after another. Natalie's unprecedented hiring into the company. *A leap.* The cavalier manner in which she'd arrived late for the first class of the season. *A pirouette.* The coveted role she'd snagged without even trying. *Frappé.* The fact that Ana couldn't shake thoughts of her. *Land and pose.*

She heard the final notes reverberate and fade and relaxed from her ending position to find Roger, and secondarily, Natalie staring at her with interest.

"What was *that*?" Roger asked.

She took a moment with the question, knowing that she'd been less than present on the run-through. "Sorry. I think I was distracted. I can try again."

Roger moved to her quickly, a new intensity crossing his features. "Distracted in the best way possible, apparently. You came alive in that variation. I don't know who that was out there, but I want her back."

She inclined her head, struggling to understand. "That's what you *want*?"

He motioned to her dance space. "That was the first time you've shown me any kind of character. Visceral. Aware. Raw. I don't know what you tapped into just now, but I need more of it. And fast. Natalie, you're up. Same variation."

Ana took a seat along the wall, still mystified by the feedback and grappling to piece together exactly what she had done so she could find some way to replicate it in the future. The problem was that she simply had no clue. She ran through her technique and realized that nothing had changed. Instead of beating her head against the wall in confusion, she blew out a breath and watched Natalie dance.

At first she smiled as she watched, taking enjoyment in the extensions that she knew fell slightly short of her own and the posture that wasn't quite there, mentally patting herself on the back as the stronger dancer in the room. But then something unexpected happened. Ana's critical eye, that ever-present need to critique each and every movement of a fellow dancer, drifted away and she lost herself in the performance. Something she hadn't done since she was a child, watching her first few ballets from the fourth ring of Lincoln Center with her nanny. The thing was, Natalie didn't just move with the music, she melded herself to it in a heart-wrenching playout. The longer Ana watched, the more it affected her. Whether she wanted to admit it or not, Natalie knew how to communicate each nuanced emotion through dance. She wasn't a precise dancer, but she delivered a moving performance, which counted for a lot.

The rest of the afternoon had them learning more of the choreography, side by side in front of the mirror with Roger's assistant. As much as Ana concentrated on her own understanding of the work, she stole glances at Natalie here and there, her interest piqued at Natalie's process, how she transformed each beat into an expression of character. Because maybe there was something she could learn from this process after all. Who would have thought?

"Where you headed?" Natalie called after her as she pushed through the glass double doors into the chilly air outside. Dusk had fallen in full effect around Lincoln Center, and the sidewalks bustled with people headed to shows, dinner, or home from work.

"My apartment," Ana answered.

"I'm headed home, too. I'll walk with you."

"Fabulous," Ana said half to Natalie, half to herself. Her natural inclination to avoid people kicked into gear but she did her best to override it.

They walked in silence to the train, dodging pedestrians along the way. "I thought it was a productive rehearsal," Natalie offered as they descended the stairs to the Sixty-Sixth Street station. "Can we talk about your amazing breakthrough?"

Ana took a beat with that. "Are you being sarcastic?"

"Not at all."

"Oh," Ana said, as guilt struck. She turned to Natalie and leveled with her. "I'm bad sometimes. With people. And their styles of communication."

Natalie passed her an amused grin. "You just need more people practice. Good thing I'm here."

"Right," Ana said nervously, wondering what that meant exactly. Was Natalie expecting they'd spend much time together?

"Roger was right, you know. Something came over you and you took off during that third run-through. You were virtually on fire. In a good way."

"I wish I could tell you what it was," Ana said. They arrived on the platform and she met Natalie's eyes. Something about them seemed kind, devoid of judgment, and that allowed Ana to say what she did next. "Honestly, I have no idea what it was, and now my head is a mess trying to figure it out. I didn't change a single execution. If anything, I was distracted."

"Thinking about what?"

She opened her mouth to answer and then closed it again. She couldn't tell Natalie that she'd been thinking about her and how wildly frustrating she found her. "My grocery list."

Natalie laughed. "Riveting."

"See what I mean?"

"I do. Sounds like you're screwed."

"Exactly what I'm saying." They were laughing now, which was new…and kind of refreshing. They stood in silence on the train until Natalie turned to her.

"Okay. So I'm thinking that it had to be something beyond technique. Maybe your grocery list distraction freed up a part of your brain, and your self-awareness fell away. Either that or your grocery list inspired some major emotional responses. My advice? Don't overthink it. Let it float back to you on its own."

Ana raised an eyebrow. "Let it *float* back to me? I'm not sure that's the best course of action. I'm looking for something a bit more, I don't know, results oriented. I'm going to be up all night dissecting it all as it is."

"Here's the thing. You can't control everything. Sometimes you just have to let life happen." The F train made its first stop, which freed up two seats they immediately snagged.

"Easier said than done," Ana said.

"I don't know about that. Have you tried it? Letting go for a bit?"

Ana thought on this. "Seems counterproductive."

Natalie leveled her with a long look. "That's a cop-out, and you know it. Now answer the question for real. Like a human. This can be part of your people practice."

Ana took a moment because no one had really called her out, pressed her this way. "Fine. I have had moments of letting go in my life. Just not a lot of them."

"And how did those go?"

Ana glanced around, looking for an escape hatch. "Do we really have to talk about this on the subway?"

"No one is listening to us." Natalie hooked a thumb at the guy next to her. "Ear buds, see?" She pointed at the men standing in the aisle. "Thinking about work." She pointed at the old woman across the way staring at them intently. "Okay, so she's into it, but no one else. Hello, ma'am." The woman raised a hand in greeting and seemed to appreciate being included.

"Fine," Ana huffed, and then nodded politely to the woman. "Hi. Okay, so when I let go...it can best be described as slightly terrifying."

"And what else?"

"Um...a little bit exhilarating, if I'm being honest."

"It would be kind of a time waster if you weren't. And? What was the end result?" Natalie smiled, waiting on her answer, and Ana couldn't help but smile back despite her best efforts. Natalie, she was finding, was a little bit contagious.

"It can be a release."

"Of course it can," Natalie said emphatically. "And if you don't release the tension that's building up inside you, sooner or later, you're gonna blow."

"I'm not gonna blow."

"Are too."

"Are you seriously arguing with me about this? You barely know me."

"I know you. I also know that the release can be amazing amounts of fun. You should try it."

"I'm fine. Thank you, though."

Natalie looked at her like she'd just said the most pitiful thing on planet Earth. "Listen, I don't want to offend you, because we have this whole working together thing that we're trying to embrace, but you kind of have one note."

"One note. Did you just call me shallow?" Ana asked, incredulous. Had that actually just happened? As in, to her face?

"I might have, yeah, but it's not as bad as it sounds."

"In what universe is shallow considered a good thing?"

Natalie nodded. "I see your point."

They rode in silence the rest of the way to their downtown stop, and not the comfortable kind. Who did this girl think she was exactly, to waltz into Ana's life and start making unflattering declarations when they were just getting to know each other? The awkward part was that they now had to walk the remaining distance to their across-the-hall apartments. Oh, she had to say "kudos" to the universe for that little stunt. Nice work. Across-the-hall apartments? Seriously?

Natalie, however, was apparently not finished and raised one finger as they walked. "About the shallow thing, I don't think that's the word for it. I'd rather go with uptight, resistant to change."

"Which is so much better," Ana said, staring straight ahead. "You're batting a thousand here, champ."

"C'mon. Would you disagree?"

Ana sighed. "No, I *am* uptight. I realize this. Embrace it, even."

"Do you? I can't help but wonder if you loosened up a bit, maybe your dancing would, too."

She ruminated on the concept, the point valid. "And how do you propose I do that?"

Natalie bumped Ana's shoulder with her own in a move that caught her off guard. "Stick with me."

Ana regarded Natalie out of the corner of her eye. "Yeah, I don't know about that. You're a wild child and beyond irresponsible."

"Thank you. And you don't have to know. Leave that part to me." Natalie's phone buzzed in her pocket. She pulled it out and stared at the readout before smiling at the screen and typing back. "My girlfriend," she said casually. "There's a spider in the corner of the kitchen and she has this whole thing about them."

"Oh," Ana said, processing the new information. "Do you need to go help her or...?"

"Would be a long trip. Morgan's in LA. We're doing the long-distance thing, which sounds easier than it is."

"Oh, I see," Ana said. The thought of Natalie with a *girlfriend* prompted an annoying tightening in her stomach. She pushed the sensation aside, along with the tingles that danced across her skin. That had been a stupid reaction, as she was so *not* into Natalie. "I imagine that's difficult. The long distance."

"Yeah, but we're doing okay," Natalie told her. "Well, at least I am."

"She's having a harder time?" Ana wanted to know more, as this new side of Natalie intrigued her beyond what she wanted it to. But at the same time, she realized the question was intrusive. "I'm sorry. You don't have to tell me. That was rude. I shouldn't have asked."

Natalie paused in front of their building. "Hang on, because you're doing that uptight thing again. You asked me a simple question, and it's perfectly okay to ask those, so now I'm going to answer. Morgan's always been a little more needy than I am when it comes to having people around her. I've just always had a more independent streak. I love being with her, and prefer it, but I do okay on my own, too."

"I get that about you. Morgan's a pretty name."

Natalie smiled. "It is. Speaking of hearts and stars and everything Cupid related, what about you? Who gets your blood going these days?"

Ana took a moment, instantly uncomfortable with this new line of questioning. "What do you mean?"

"I'm trying to get to know my new colleague. That was code for 'are you seeing anyone?'"

"No," Ana said, willing the elevator to arrive a little quicker. "No one. No real time for that kind of thing."

"Well, that can't be true. We have tonight free, for example. You could be on your way to a hot date."

"Yeah, but once the season starts, I'm booked most nights, and holidays are all but nonexistent, as we have sold-out shows. People outside of the world of ballet don't understand that kind of schedule. They want you home on Christmas."

Natalie nodded as they approached their respective apartments. "Maybe you should look *inside* the world, then. Jason's pretty great, and you guys look hot together." The notion was a ludicrous one, and Natalie must have seen it on Ana's face. "Is that a no to Jason then?"

"A definite no. I adore Jason, but outside of working together, he and I are strictly friends."

"So no making out on the side?" Natalie said, teasing her. "Even just a little in the darkened corners of the theater. Darkened-theater kissing can be a total turn-on."

"Nope. Never."

"Okay. I can accept that. However, I'd like to point out that just because you haven't considered it, doesn't mean he hasn't. I have a feeling that Mr. Jason wants to get hot and heavy with you." Natalie raised an eyebrow and tossed her a knowing look. "And I've picked up on this after only a handful of days, so..."

The idea was insane.

Plus, in Ana's very limited experience with romance, guys had never really worked out for her. A date here or there, but nothing ever took. In fact, the only time her interest had been piqued had been with Roxanne, one of their stage managers. They'd had a little bit of fun together when she was twenty-two, before Roxanne headed out on the road with a touring company. Nothing really since. But Jason? How had she missed this?

"Really?" she said to Natalie, lowering her voice even though there was no one around. "You think he's attracted to me?"

"Um, I *know* he is."

"Do you mind telling me what makes you say that?" It was an honest question, as she wasn't especially skilled at these kinds of things—as in the kinds of things that involved *people*. And reading them. And interacting with them. Natalie definitely seemed to be better at it.

"Well, for one," Natalie said as she leaned against her apartment door, "he stares at you a lot. That's a pretty big tip-off. He checks in with you constantly to see if you're okay, or what your reaction is to a given circumstance. He looks out for you, roots for you. But quite honestly?"

"Yeah?"

"There's a heat there."

"A heat?"

"Yeah, a heat. If we were to take the temperature of those once-overs he's passing you, his eyes moving up and over your body, it'd be off the charts."

As Ana listened to Natalie talk about heat, her gaze settled on Natalie's mouth, taking in the way her lips moved as she formed words. For whatever reason, Natalie's mouth, and all things related to it, fascinated her.

"Huh," Ana said, shaking herself free of the focus. "Well, I'll have to pay more attention, then. To Jason, I mean."

Natalie pushed off the door and grinned. "And maybe keep an open mind. He's a nice guy, Ana. You two could have baby ballerinas."

"He is nice. But probably no to the future family."

"Understood."

Ana sighed and turned to her own door, wrestling with the key in the lock once again.

"Ease up a bit," Natalie told her. "That's it. Now turn your wrist ever so slightly to the left."

The lock clicked beneath Ana's fingers and she turned to Natalie. "Thanks. For the door help and the…uh…extracurricular insight."

"No problem. See you tomorrow, Frozen."

Ana recognized the nickname and spun around. "Freeze. What did you just call me?"

Natalie faced her and clapped. "Kudos on such an appropriately thematic response. Wouldn't have predicted it."

"Don't deflect. I can't believe you just called me that to my face."

Natalie thought on this. "I mean, someone's got to. Don't you think? Now get some rest so I can dance circles around you tomorrow."

Ana opened her mouth to speak, but the audacity of Natalie's words and the in-your-face challenge left her grappling. Ana wasn't used to people addressing her so unabashedly, and she found herself stripped of a comeback. "Yeah, tomorrow," she said lamely, and escaped into her apartment. But as she ruminated on the evening, she realized she had actually enjoyed the talk with Natalie, which was a surprising turn of events. Maybe they'd find a way not to kill each other after all. Maybe they were even on their way to becoming actual friends.

Crazier things had happened…

On her own now, Ana flipped on a light, stared at her apartment, and surveyed her options. She considered going over her notes from rehearsal or rolling out her muscles. Somehow her typical evening rituals just didn't really grab her. Three and half minutes later, she was curled up on the couch rereading Suzanne Farrell's biography and eating a couple Double Stuf Oreos, for God's sake. See? She could let loose when she wanted to. Deviate from the plan. Natalie Frederico didn't know what she was talking about.

❖

"Oh fuck," Natalie managed as she stared through one eye at the clock on her bedside table. "Fuck, fuck, fuck. Tell me I didn't do this." She scrambled out of bed and did her best to ignore the god-awful screaming pain that shot through her head as she moved. The sunlight streaming through the window into her bedroom was like some sort of message from Satan that not only had she royally screwed up, but this hangover would spend the day reminding her of that, one painful second at a time.

She struggled to remember the events of the evening prior as she hopped in and out of the shower, shrugged into her dance clothes, popped some aspirin that would probably do no good, and raced to the train. She'd gone to McKenna's with Audrey around ten. That part she remembered. Audrey had jumped ship around eleven thirty, because apparently she was fifty times smarter.

"If I don't sleep, I'll crash and burn at work tomorrow," she flashed on Audrey saying. But damn it, Natalie'd stayed back with a couple of the guys and—*oh my God, that's right*—they'd done shots. More than two, which would have knocked her on her ass. She'd been trying to prove she could keep up with them, which was ridiculous of her, because at her height and weight, there was little chance.

By the time she made it to Lincoln Center she was over half an hour late for *Aftermath* rehearsals and she'd missed the morning class altogether. As she entered the studio, music played and Ana was already in the midst of a run-through of the third movement. Natalie hurriedly put herself into pointe shoes and warmed up on the side, all the while trying to clear her head and find a way not to throw up then and there.

"Glad you decided to grace us with your presence," Roger said snidely once Ana finished up.

"I apologize. Overslept. Won't happen again."

"See that it doesn't. Same section as Ana, then?"

"Of course." As they passed each other on Natalie's way to the center of the room, Ana sent her a questioning glance, to which Natalie simply shrugged and shook her head.

As the pianist began to play, Natalie danced, wincing against the bolt of pain that shot through her head and neck with each slight movement she made. She was behind the music, that much she knew, but her stomach churned and she wasn't sure how much longer she could dance without it turning on her fully. Finally, knowing she couldn't go on, she held up a hand. Out of breath and feeling a little dizzy, she leaned over, her hands on her knees. Jason was by her side instantly.

"Hey, Nat. You okay? You need some water?"

She grabbed the water bottle he handed her and downed a few swallows. "Everything all right over there?" Roger asked.

"I'm not well today, I'm afraid."

He walked to her, and gave her a frustrated once-over. "Take the day. I'll work with Ana. Let's take ten, everyone, and attempt to recover from this train wreck of a rehearsal."

The room scattered in different directions and Jason walked her over to the bench where Ana sat. "I'm sorry you're feeling bad. Is there anything I can do?" Ana asked.

Natalie dropped her voice. "Just a really dumb and stupid late night. I'll be all right. Just need a few hours."

Ana sat back, nonplussed. "You're telling me you're hungover, right now? *Hungover?*"

"Can you keep your voice down, please?"

"Perfect. That's just…perfect." Ana dropped her towel onto the bench next to Natalie and walked away without another word.

Natalie didn't feel exactly great about what had happened at rehearsal and spent the rest of the day on the couch with a large bottle of water. A little after seven, there was a knock at her door. To say she was surprised to see Ana, Artic princess, standing there was an understatement.

"Hey," she said.

"Hi." Ana ran her fingers through her hair. "Do you need any aspirin or anything?"

"No, I'm good. But thank you."

"What about dinner? Have you eaten?" While she still seemed annoyed, the fact that Ana had gone out of her way to stop by and check on Natalie floored her. Apparently Ana did care about other humans, and it was kind of a gratifying revelation.

"No, I'm good," Natalie said, gesturing into her apartment. "Gonna hit up some Top Ramen soon, dinner of champions. I told you I'd feel better in a few hours."

"Great." Ana turned to go, but then doubled back. Her eyes now carried conviction, anger even. "What you pulled today wasn't okay. I just want you to know that."

"Listen, I get it. I guess I'm used to later in the day rehearsals, so this early-morning stuff—"

"Is your job," Ana finished authoritatively. "And I'm not sure you do get it. As in, at all. But we're dancing in the same ballet, and what you do affects the rest of your cast. Don't come to rehearsal hungover ever again." Ana didn't wait for a reply. She turned abruptly and headed to her own apartment.

"Ana."

At the use of her name, Ana paused and faced Natalie. From the look on her face, it was clear that this was a topic she had some strong feelings about, and Natalie couldn't blame her. The ballet mattered to her a lot, and Natalie hadn't treated it with the same care. To Natalie, what had happened today hadn't felt like a huge deal, but maybe it should have.

"I behaved unprofessionally today. I hope you'll accept my apology."

Ana ruminated on this for a moment. "While I appreciate the sentiment, I'd much rather you just never do it again. It's that simple."

"Understood. You have my word."

When Natalie returned to her apartment, the conversation with Ana hovered and picked at her no matter how many times she tried to shake it. It wasn't her goal to make a bad impression, but she'd apparently done so anyway, and it bothered her.

Damn it all.

❖

"And rehearsals are going well?" Morgan asked.

Natalie used her shoulder to hold the phone to her ear as she purchased a MetroCard to see her through the week. "Well, we're a couple weeks in, and it's going as well as can be expected."

A total lie.

She flashed back to Roger pulling her from that day's rehearsal in frustration, losing his temper and storming from the room when she and Jason couldn't manage the lifts that he and Ana did so effortlessly. She was falling short of his expectations in a major way, and the days were beginning to take their toll.

That wasn't to say he seemed happy with Ana's progress, either. She'd been sidelined just as often. If anything, it seemed like he worked with one of them until he couldn't quite stand it anymore and then swapped them out for sheer variety. It sucked to feel like she was doing a poor job, but she genuinely didn't know what to do to correct the situation, afraid that her body, which already felt broken and sore beyond anything she'd ever known, couldn't handle much more.

Things with Ana had been strained following her hangover happenstance, but as the days went on, Ana seemed to relax a little and offer Natalie a smile here or there, sometimes an actual conversation.

"I knew you'd be a superstar in New York," Morgan purred into the phone. Except Natalie wasn't one. She was anything but. Though she didn't feel like sharing that information with Morgan, which felt strange, as they'd always talked easily about everything back in LA.

"What about you?" Natalie asked. "Tell me what's going on in your life before I lose my signal."

"Oh, not much. Waitressing, partying, waitressing, and repeat."

"Did you look into that temp agency we talked about? That could lead to something more permanent down the road. You've always talked about working in an attorney's office."

"Nah," Morgan said. "I'm good with where I'm at."

"Since when? You hate the diner."

"It's been okay recently. Plus, it gives me free time to have fun, do what I want."

"Okay," Natalie told her. "As long as you're happy."

Morgan had never been terribly ambitious, instead choosing to put most of her focus on Natalie and her career. And while it was great to have Morgan in her corner, now that they were so far apart, she had expected Morgan to put more into her own situation. "So I thought we could talk about Christmas." But there was no answer. "Morgan? You there?" She glanced at her phone. Damn it. She'd lost her signal as she moved farther into the subway station, and now she clicked off the call with regret. One of those days where it felt like nothing was going her way. A hot bath and some dinner called to her, and she couldn't get home fast enough.

What she found when she arrived left her reeling for a whole separate reason. "What the hell?" she asked the empty apartment with two inches of standing water on the floor. She moved quickly around the small space, picking up anything important that rested on the floor and moving it to higher ground and simultaneously dialing the number for the super on her fridge. She so did not need this right now. God.

"Leak from upstairs," the super told her casually half an hour later when he finally showed up, chewing gum at the same pace a hummingbird flapped its wings. He stared at the large wet spots on the ceiling as they continued to drip and stream water. "Pipes are old. I'll need to shut off the water to the unit upstairs, but that'll take out your water, too. Sorry 'bout that."

She stared at him. "So what am I supposed to do? My place is flooded, there's still water coming in, and now I'm left without running water of my own?"

He nodded, chewing away. "Uh, yep. Should probably stay with a friend so we can figure it all out. I'll see if they'll adjust your rent."

"I don't have anyone to—"

"I'll call when we're up and running again. Might want to grab some towels to put under your door. Isolate the problem." He gestured to the room at large. "We'll get some fans in here tomorrow and dry it all up. Should just take a couple days, though. Sorry for the inconvenience."

He headed to the door and she followed, hot on his heels. "Wait, wait, wait. That's it? Sorry for the inconvenience?"

"Listen, lady. I didn't sneak in here and cause the leak. I didn't time travel to 1920 and construct the building. Nor do I foot the bill for new plumbing, like some kind of John Rockefeller. It's New York.

Lotta history here. Including those pipes. Gum?" he asked, holding out the pack as some sort of consolation prize.

She blinked at him in measured patience. "No, I'm good."

"Suit yourself. I'm Sal, by the way. Salvador. But folks in the building call me Sal. So you could, too."

"Nice to meet you, Sal."

"Welcome to the building." And after six to ten more passes at his gum, the door shut and Natalie was left there. Alone. In standing water. With no ability to take that hot bath or cope with life. To top off the sundae of suckage, her muscles screamed in agony from the paces she'd put them through.

Taking a deep breath, she did what she had to and marched into the hall, prepared to start knocking on the doors of everyone she knew in the building. Starting with right across the hall. Ana answered after a few short moments and eyed Natalie cautiously.

"Hi."

"Hey," Natalie said back, and ran her hand through her hair, frustrated at the whole situation. "So here's the thing. My place is flooded. A pipe is leaking upstairs or in the ceiling or somewhere mysterious as ordained by God, and I need a place to crash. I know that you live on your own, so I thought maybe there was a couch I could take up residence on until this whole wet and gross apartment thing is resolved."

To Natalie, such a request wouldn't have seemed like a big deal coming from a friend or a coworker, but the look on Ana's face told an entirely different story. "You're asking to stay *here*?"

"Yeah, I mean, if it's all right. I don't want to put you out. I can ask upstairs."

Ana glanced tentatively behind her, and that's when Natalie noticed her attire. Jeans and a soft-looking white T-shirt. No dance clothes. No shoes. Ana looked like a person. A very pretty person, in fact. Her hair was down, and it fell just past her shoulders in subtle waves, thick and dark. She stood there, barefoot and relaxed, and for a moment, all Natalie could do was stare, take her in, forgetting the trajectory of the conversation altogether. She'd always thought Ana was attractive, but this was different-level attractive.

"I guess that would be all right."

"You guess what would be all right?" Natalie asked blankly, trying to get her mind back on track. And her mouth was dry all of sudden? Why was her traitorous mouth dry all of a sudden? Not cool.

Ana stared at her in mystification. "You staying on my couch. Isn't that what you asked? I'm sorry. I'm confused."

"Yes!" Natalie said and pointed at her, finding her footing again. "That is exactly what I asked. Awesome of you to say yes. I'll, uh, grab some stuff from the flood of the century over there and be right back."

"Okay, just, um…I'll leave the door unlocked, I guess. Or you could—"

"Perfect. And I will open it when I return." Seriously? Had she just said that? Her conversation skills had taken a ten, apparently, and hit up the break room.

After packing a bag, Natalie left her soggy apartment and headed across the hall to Ana's drier, more comfortable place. The apartment was the mirror image of her own. However, the place came with touches that indicated Ana had lived there a great deal longer than Natalie had. In other words, Ana's place was fully decorated. A comfortable beige couch with green accent pillows sat across from a matching beige and green chair. The curtains over the window at the back of the room, also beige, blended nicely. On the walls hung artistic photographs of dancers like Jacques d'Amboise, George Balanchine, and Margot Fonteyn. Inspiration, Natalie imagined. The living area was open to the small kitchen that offered enough room for approximately one and a half humans to stand in its nook. She found Ana sitting on a stool at the kitchen counter that divided it from the living room. She seemed to be going over something in her notebook.

"Knock, knock," Natalie said symbolically when Ana didn't immediately notice her.

Ana glanced up. "Hey. Come in. I was just recapping today's rehearsal."

Natalie set her bag near the sofa and picked up one of the green pillows to examine absently. "Recapping?"

"Oh, you know, going over all of my notes, making sure I've internalized the day's work." Ana must have noticed Natalie's piqued interest. "You don't do that?"

"What? Go over work after leaving work? I guess I did back when I was working on a show of my own, when I was at the helm and everything fell to me."

"You don't consider a lead role in a prestigious ballet just as important?"

Natalie dropped the pillow, not liking the sound of that sentence, and took a seat on the sofa. "No, I guess you're right. It just feels different somehow. Working for someone else."

Ana swiveled in her chair and faced Natalie, something clearly pulling at her. "Can I ask you a question?"

"Go for it."

"You're really talented."

"Thank you, but that's not a question."

"But it doesn't seem like you care."

Natalie took a moment with the statement that was still not a question. "Of course I care." She paused. "Care about what exactly?"

"Your job. Do you even like ballet?" The look on Ana's face held judgment, and Natalie felt her defenses rise to meet it.

"I like ballet."

"But you have no passion for it."

Natalie drew in a deep breath. She decided to level with Ana about her love/hate with the art form. "I walked away from the ballet world because it didn't seem the best fit for me. You must have seen that at the time. The structure, the rules made me feel like I couldn't breathe. I wanted to dance for me, and that's what I've spent the past few years doing. But maybe that was the young and rebellious version of myself, because since I've joined the company, I've found a new appreciation for the work. Ballet is pretty awesome. I'm sorry if I haven't made that clear."

Ana stared at her and nodded, seeming to let the information settle. "Roger wanted us to help each other, so I want to uphold my part of the bargain. And do that. For you."

Natalie readied herself for whatever Ana had for her. She could be big about a little criticism. "Okay, in what way? Do you have some sage veteran advice or something? Lay it on me."

"You have to work harder."

"Okay," Natalie said, drawing the word out. Except she did work hard. She was known for her work ethic…just not in the realm of commercialism.

Ana sat a little taller in her chair, energized now. "No, not okay.

You have to put in more time. Discipline yourself. Never show up late to a class or rehearsal, and when you get home, it doesn't stop there. You have to keep working. Because that's what it takes to succeed in this business."

"Wow. You've been thinking a lot about my shortcomings, haven't you?"

"Well…yeah. Because it's important."

"And because I drive you a little crazy. Admit it."

Then and there, Ana looked caught and tried to backpedal. "What? I never said that."

"You didn't, but you're thinking it and it's often written all over your face. It's okay to say so. In fact, it's part of what I have to teach you in return. To loosen the hell up."

A pause. Ana forced a smile and gave her head a little shake. "Fine. Okay. You drive me a little crazy. There. Out in the open."

"More than a little. I drive you up the wall. I always have." Now Natalie was smiling. "Admit it."

"I admit it," Ana said. "It's true. You have a way of…"

"Getting under your skin?" Natalie asked and moved until she stood next to Ana at the counter.

"Yes," Ana said, and met her eyes unabashedly. "I don't know what it is about you that just gets me…worked up." Natalie raised an eyebrow and held her gaze, enjoying the panicked expression that appeared on Ana's face at her choice of words. "Not worked up. More like—"

"Too late," Natalie said and headed around the counter into the kitchen. "It's already out there in the universe. I work you up, a declaration I embrace fully." She glanced around.

"What are you looking for?" Ana asked.

"Your booze. It's been a forever long and difficult day. I think we need to have a drink together to unwind and celebrate this new advancement in our friendship."

"I don't drink—"

"When you're in rehearsal. Right, I've heard it before. I'm a little bored of it."

"And you shouldn't either. Discipline, remember?"

Natalie sighed. "Tell you what. I'll back off my vices for the remaining rehearsal period for *Aftermath* if you'll indulge a little right here and now. A happy compromise."

"To what end?" Ana asked, clearly skeptical.

"To relax, unwind, hang out. It's what people do. It's time for you to be a person, Frozen."

"Really?" Ana stared at her, nonplussed. "Again with the nickname?"

"I feel like you should embrace it. Claim your title."

Ana seemed to contemplate this before making a decision. "No."

"Great. Then we're in agreement. Booze. As in, where is it? Am I going to have to build an ark and head back across the hall to find my own stash? I can do it, but will need to maybe put on some waders."

"Don't you have a bad track record when it comes to drinking the night before a rehearsal?"

"In fact, I do," Natalie said. "I'm glad you brought that up. The difference is that we're not going to get drunk. We're going to be responsible. In fact, I'm putting you in charge of responsible drinking because I find you just that trustworthy."

"Fine." Ana sighed and pointed to an upper cabinet. "There's some sort of whiskey my uncle gave me for Christmas up there." In order to reach the shelf, Natalie had to push herself onto the counter and rise up on her knees. "Please don't fall. I don't want to have to explain to Roger that you broke a leg on my watch. It would look like I did it on purpose, which on consideration is not such a horrible idea."

"Fantastic. We've now reached the portion of the evening where you threaten bodily harm. We definitely need this drink." Natalie climbed down, whiskey in hand. She stared at the ornate bottle with a series of consonants she couldn't begin to assemble into a word. "This looks like it's in Russian."

"That's because my uncle is Russian. My whole family is."

"No accent on you, though, which I find highly suspicious."

"Because I've lived in the United States my whole life."

Natalie located two glasses and poured the drinks. "Your mother's Russian, too?"

"Yes. She died in a car accident when I was two. She was also a dancer. Not as well known as my father, but she was well on her way."

The thought of a young Ana losing her mother caused the smile to dim from Natalie's face. Her own mother, flighty as she was, had been a big part of her childhood, and she couldn't have imagined growing up without her there. "Hey, I'm sorry. I didn't mean to bring up—"

"Don't worry," Ana said with a dismissive gesture. "I'm fine. I don't really remember her except for some fragments, so...Hey, how about that drink?"

"Right," Natalie said, rallying from the dip in spirit. "Straight, or with a mixer?"

"Please. I'm Russian." Ana held out her hand for the drink. "I can handle it." Natalie raised the glass and surveyed the dark amber liquid before handing it tentatively to Ana.

"Straight-up Russian whiskey for the Russian. Not gonna lie and say it doesn't scare the hell outta me. Cheers." The two clinked glasses and Natalie headed to the couch. She stood before it and held her arms out. "So this is where I live now. This couch is what it's come to."

"I'll have you know," Ana said, joining her there and leaving a space between them, "that this couch is really comfortable."

Natalie pushed down against the cushion with her hand. "I can agree to the softness."

"And you can't exactly come in here judgments flaring, especially after I gave you Russian whiskey. Last I checked, you were homeless." Ana had that emphatic look on her face again. The one that said there was no room for disagreement. Natalie found it kind of...sexy in a way. How worked up Ana got over little things.

"You can relax that angry furrow between your eyebrows. I happen to agree on the merits of the couch."

"I'm glad." Ana sipped from her glass and grimaced. "Wow. Okay. This is strong."

"Doesn't matter. You're Russian." Natalie enjoyed teasing Ana. She tossed back a swallow of the whiskey herself but had to take a moment with the kick. Definitely strong, beyond her usual fare. "I, however, am not Russian and can admit this stuff is deadly."

"Because it is. And the Frozen moniker," Ana said, taking another swallow and gesturing with her glass, "is not who I am. Let me just say that. Is it warm in here?" She glanced around and took another pull from her glass.

Natalie laughed at how quickly the drink seemed to be taking effect on Ana. "It's the alcohol and probably the fact that you rarely drink any. Does the nickname bother you?"

Ana shrugged. "I don't love it. But it's always kind of been my reputation, ya know? I'm focused and I'm shy, both of which make me keep to myself. Not a great combination for making friends."

"You are focused. I'll give you that."

"More than the average person, and I don't leave a lot of time for much else. There's not a ton I can do about that. It's who I am."

"You're doing something about it right now."

"How so?"

"You're hanging out with me. Being a person. Pushing past the shy. And you're actually not so bad at it. I find it shocking."

Ana studied her. "Thanks, I think," she said, and took another drink. "It's not that I don't want friends. I do. I think I would like having friends. Friends look kinda nice, actually. I just don't really know how to go about being someone's pal exactly."

It was clear to Natalie that Ana was loosening up now, which was nice to see. "Well, I think you have to start by incorporating the word 'yes' into your vocabulary. When someone invites you somewhere, you say yes. It will probably freak you the hell out at first, but you'll get past it."

"So that's the secret to your social prowess? Saying yes?"

Natalie held up a hand. "Within reason, Frozen. I'm not a social whore."

"So noted," Ana said, looking thoughtful. She headed into the bedroom and returned a couple of moments later with a pillow and a couple of blankets. "You'll probably need these."

"Look at you and your impressive generosity."

"I said yes to *you*, didn't I, staying here?"

"You did. And that's kind of huge, so thank you."

They locked eyes again and Natalie felt the warmth hit her cheeks. Had Ana always been this amount of hot? Her brown eyes were captivating tonight...and friendlier, open. Maybe that's what it was. Walls were coming down. They just needed to get to know each other better.

"Have you ever been in love before?" Natalie asked. She didn't know where the question came from, but there it was all the same, falling from her lips without preamble. "Since we're getting to know each other and all."

Ana glanced at the ground and then back up to Natalie's eyes, running her thumb across the rim of the beveled glass in her hand. The *empty* glass. Before answering the question, Ana rose and poured herself a second drink, which given how things were going, Natalie was all in favor of. "I thought I was once."

Wow, okay. Natalie wasn't expecting that answer and was now all kinds of intrigued. She downed the rest of her drink and held her glass out to Ana, who poured a healthy replacement. "Tell me all about him. Don't leave anything out."

Ana blew out a breath and resumed her spot down the couch from Natalie. She looked skyward before speaking, doing that lip-biting thing that, once again, snagged Natalie's attention. Now, that was a visual she could study for hours. "There was this stage manager that worked with the company for a time. I was young, still dancing in the *corps*, and my attention was captured in a big way."

"Okay, and then what happened?" Natalie brought her knees to her chest in excitement.

"We had fun together for a while. The sex was great."

"You little minx!"

Ana held up one finger. "But my dancing suffered and I pulled away. As a result, she left the company and took a job with a touring group." She covered her eyes with her hand. "And I cannot believe I'm telling you this."

Natalie replayed the last sentence of the story in her head to be sure she'd heard Ana correctly. "You just said *she*. You're saying you were involved with a woman?"

"Right. That's what I said."

"I would never have—"

"What? Is that really so crazy?"

Natalie sat up, palms out. "No. No. Not at all. I just…didn't see that coming necessarily. As in, at all. No wonder you're not interested in Jason."

"He's a great guy, just—"

"No, he is—"

"The greatest. Just not really the greatest for *me*."

"No, I would imagine not."

A pause hung in the air between them as the newfound understanding settled. The energy in the room had shifted and things felt noticeably altered. New, if Natalie had to categorize it.

"Not that I have time to date anyway," Ana said, pulling them from the silence.

"You should rethink that," Natalie told her. "I'm serious."

Ana laughed, now completely unguarded from the alcohol. "Please. No one wants to date Frozen. You and I both know that much."

"Um, no, we don't at all. You're an attractive woman, Ana, and a professional ballet dancer, which is sexy all on its own. Trust me, there are people who would line up to date you. I know *women* who would line up to date you."

"Thank you," Ana said quietly. "Maybe someday. I mean, I would like that." A pause. "What about you? You're in love, yes?"

"Yeah," Natalie said automatically, and then marinated on the question. "I mean, I think so."

"You *think* so? C'mon, I told you about my thing." Ana tossed a pillow at her, and Natalie smiled at the new playful behavior. Ana could be fun.

"No, I am," Natalie said, though it *was* a really big question. "Love is hard to categorize. It's a subjective emotion, right? Different for everyone. But Morgan's pretty awesome, and when we're together we have an amazing time. So love? Yeah. At least the closest I've been to it." The words out loud sounded lackluster, even to her own ears. She pushed the thought away for examination later.

Ana nodded. "You smile when you talk about her. You light up. One day I'd like to have that look on my face."

Natalie nodded. "You will. You just have to stay open to the possibility. And as we've found tonight, Russian whiskey is not a bad place to start. Within reason, of course."

"Of course," Ana said and stood. "As the appointed officer of responsible drinking, I should probably let you get some rest. We have class tomorrow morning and rehearsal after. We cannot be late. Got it? Not even a minute."

"You're bossy when you've had a drink," Natalie said, staring up at Ana, all alluring and gorgeous in that white T-shirt, its V-neck dipped to subtle curves. She should really stop objectifying her friend.

"Yeah, well, your fault."

Natalie shot a victorious fist in the air. "I'll take it. Corrupting the innocent everywhere I go."

"Good night, Natalie," Ana said, and rounded the corner into her bedroom.

"Good night, Frozen." The sound of quiet laughter trickled from the bedroom. Natalie shook her head as she went about turning the sofa into a bed for herself, reflecting on the very unexpected evening. There was way more to Anastasia Mikhelson than she once thought. Way more.

She was human and came with hopes and dreams and fears and a sex life of her own.

Who knew?

Chapter Six

A na's earliest memory was of sitting in the corner of a dance studio and watching her parents rehearse a *pas de deux* from Balanchine's *Allegro Brillante*. She wore a purple tutu of her own and did her best to mimic her mother's movements, which earned a laugh from her mother that she could still hear to this day. She treasured that memory, one of the few she had of her mother, and pulled it out whenever she needed cheering up or a reminder about why she pursued the work she did.

There had never been any doubt about what she would be when she grew up.

Dancing had been in her blood. Still was.

Ana glanced at her watch as she crossed Sixty-Second Street and mentally celebrated that she had time to stop at the deli on the corner for a chai latte and a plain bagel, one of her favorite indulgences, before work. As she hurried across the street, the ever-present burst of pain in her left foot said hello, and she winced in reply—her least favorite part of her job. Ana did what she always did and pushed the recognition from her mind entirely. If she paid no attention to the pain, she gave it no credence, it would fade to the background. At least, it usually did.

She gave it a shot and concentrated on the day ahead. When she'd left her apartment that morning, she had been a little surprised to see Natalie still fast asleep on her couch, given that they were attending the same morning class. Ana had paused and stared down at her houseguest, debating whether to wake her or leave her to her own devices. What she found herself doing instead was taking in how unexpectedly peaceful Natalie looked as she slept. Her hair fell delicately down one shoulder, with one hand pulled in beneath her chin. Natalie's go-to vivaciousness had been tucked away for the night, it seemed. The easy smile Ana'd grown so accustomed to on Natalie was also gone, and in its place was the face of angelic girl, curled into herself on the couch, the covers shrugged to her waist, revealing a black camisole and the smooth olive skin of Natalie's bare shoulder, which led Ana's gaze to the curvature of Natalie's neck, and downward to the dip in her cleavage, a visual that sent a warmth through Ana that—okay, no more of that, thank you very much. Work to do! Ana gave her head a little shake in annoyance and grabbed her jacket from the coat rack across the back of the door.

"Class in an hour, Natalie. Don't be late," she said without looking back. The mumbled reply from the couch gave her additional pause. She sighed and faced her houseguest. "Hey, Natalie. You awake?"

"I am now," Natalie said, her voice scratchy from sleep. "You make it hard not to be."

"An hour until class," Ana told her firmly.

"Yeah, I'm aware. Thank you." She took firm hold of the blanket and snuggled herself beneath it in a display that had Ana kind of jealous. Natalie, all relaxed and cozy, looked like she had all morning to luxuriate under that blanket. How was that even possible, given the day ahead of them?

"Okay," Ana said, consulting her watch. "I just say that because the train is crowded this time of morning and you only have—"

"You realize I'm an adult, right?" Natalie raised her head and regarded Ana through one eye, as the other was scrunched up.

"I've had my doubts."

That seemed to have snagged Natalie's attention, as she sat up fully on the couch, exasperated now. "As fantastic a drill sergeant as you would make, you're a much better ballet dancer and should stick with that. I got this waking up part taken care of, okay?"

Ana held out both palms and then let the topic drop, refusing to battle this girl who was determined to do things her own way. "Fine. You're right. See you there."

She'd shaken off the exchange on her way uptown in favor of enjoying her morning, and thus far, she had. Ana took a last swallow of her chai latte before rounding the corner to the shoe room to check with Henry about the custom adjustments she'd asked for. There were a few dancers from the *corps* already there, consulting with Henry's assistants. The two young girls nodded to her politely and made way for her to pass, intently watching her as she did so. She nodded in return, then remembered her new social directive and added a smile. It seemed to have made a difference, as the girls smiled back.

Ana remembered what that was like to be them, looking up to the more established dancers in the company and hoping one day that might be you. Yet here she was, at last a principal dancer, and she didn't feel much different than she had dancing in the *corps* herself. Maybe it hadn't sunk in just yet...

"Ana," Henry said, emerging from the back of the shop with a box in his hands. "Special delivery for you, my dear. They've arrived. Pairs and pairs of them." He flipped open a box to reveal a rather large supply of pointe shoes that had been specially adjusted for her by her shoemaker in London.

"They're here!" Ana exclaimed, cradling a shoe wrapped in plastic in her hand and examining it. Gorgeous. There was nothing more personal to a ballet dancer than her pointe shoes, and achieving the perfect design was everything. In search of it, Ana continued to tweak and tuck each year.

"I know you've been waiting," Henry said, his eyes sparkling as he began stacking the shoes onto the shelf with her name on it. She and Henry had worked together to come up with this most recent adjustment, cutting down some of the fabric on the sides and back of each shoe so she'd be left with less bagging in the satin, making the shoe nice and tight, tailored to her heel. She couldn't wait to sew herself into a pair for class that morning, already excited for the cleaner lines she knew the shoes would provide. "Thank you, Mr. Henry. I owe you."

"All you owe me is a beautiful performance. I already have my seats picked out for *Aftermath*. On one of the nights *you're* dancing the part."

Ana smiled at the show of support, and the friendship she had with Henry. Frozen or not, she'd established several relationships that mattered to her, and Henry was at the top of that list. "I will do my best not to let you down."

"You could never, Ana." He threw a glance to the front of the room and then quietly just to her, "So how's this new girl? It's been three weeks now."

"Oh, um, Natalie? She's...coming along." She thought back to the visual of the innocent-looking girl on her couch, who really was anything but. "She's coming along, a talented dancer."

"Not as talented as you. Impossible."

She placed an appreciative kiss on his cheek. "Thank you for the vote of confidence, Henry. I'm off to sew myself into a pair of kick-ass new shoes."

"Let me know how they feel."

"Will do!"

She moved to the studio and joined her colleagues in warm-up for class. She made an effort to smile more, exchange pleasantries with the other dancers, Natalie's words about loosening up ringing in her ear whether she wanted them there or not.

"Hey, Ana," Helen said as she snatched the spot next to her on the floor. "How are rehearsals going?"

"You know, not as smoothly as I'd hoped, actually."

Helen straightened from mid-stretch and regarded her. The surprised look on her face told Ana that she hadn't been prepared for a substantive answer to her question. *That's because you never offer one*, she reminded herself. Her go-to would have been "fine."

"Oh yeah? What's up?"

Ana decided to make the effort and confide in Helen, who'd always seemed like a nice enough person. So she took a breath and went for it. What was the worst that could happen? "The choreo in the ballet is difficult, but the character stuff has been a whole separate challenge. I'm not much of an actress, I suppose, and finding that out the hard way."

Helen turned to her. "I have a feeling you're better than you think."

Audrey joined them. "Who's better? Me? Am I better?" She dropped her dance bag and went about unlacing her boots.

"I was telling *Ana*," Helen said, adding extra emphasis to her name, "that she's probably doing a much better job in *Aftermath* than she thinks." Audrey's head swiveled in Ana's direction expectantly. Her blue eyes held interest and blinked at Ana, awaiting further explanation.

"Because I think...I might be crashing and burning."

"Not what Natalie says," Audrey offered.

Ana paused at this new angle. "Natalie's talked to you about rehearsal?"

Audrey smiled. "Says you're always a few steps ahead of her."

"Well, that part's true," Ana said. When Audrey's eyebrows shot up, she played back the sentence in her head and tried again. It sounded different than she meant it. "What I mean is in terms of picking up the steps, yes, I'm quicker. But she's got the character worked out in a way I haven't, and when she dances, it's kind of…electric," she said. "You should see it."

"Thank you."

Ana turned to see Natalie standing behind her and felt the blush hit her cheeks instantly.

"I'll take electric," Natalie said and met her eyes and held them.

Ana shook her head. "I just meant…that you show a lot of emotion when you perform."

"Guilty." Natalie sat down with the group and went about sewing herself into her shoes, a task she didn't quite finish before it was time for class. Ana shot her an I-told-you-so look as she left to take her spot at the barre, to which Natalie only shrugged.

For the remainder of class, Ana should have been concentrating on the exercises, on her form, or even how wonderful her newly cut shoes felt on her feet. Instead she tracked Natalie's movements, hyperaware of her place in the room, her form when they moved away from the barre into *arabesque*, and the concentration in her green eyes. Natalie had all the makings of a world-class ballerina. She just didn't want it badly enough. Why wouldn't she put in the work?

"Are we having fun yet?" Natalie whispered to her on a break.

Ana turned to her, anger flaring. "You could be really good. You're beyond talented."

Natalie inclined her head to the side and regarded her. "Okay. That was apropos of nothing. But I appreciate the compliment, even as angrily as you delivered it."

"It's frustrating is all," Ana said and reached aggressively for her water bottle, which she didn't even want.

Natalie grinned. "And you're all fired up about it. Is this because of this morning? I just needed a few extra minutes of sleep, and look." She gestured to herself. "Here I am. I'm sorry if I was grumpy. I blame Russian whiskey."

Ana brushed off the comment. "You need to pull in your hips when you move into *arabesque*."

"I do?"

"Yes, and use your stomach muscles. Keep them tight."

"Okay," Natalie said sincerely, blinking back at her with those big expressive eyes. "I can give that a whirl."

"Don't 'give it a whirl.' Just do it. It'll make you better. And get here on time." With that Ana stalked away, unable to fathom why she seemed intent on helping Natalie.

"Hey, Ana?"

She paused. "Yeah?"

"Maybe we could work on some of that after rehearsal tonight? Stay a little late in the studio and hammer it out?" She tucked a strand of hair that had fallen from her ponytail behind her ear in a move that had Ana struck. Mesmerized. Enraptured. "Ana?"

"What? Right." She ruminated over the proposition, knowing it was a good suggestion. Plus, the look on Natalie's face was so hopeful, and Ana couldn't find it in her to say no. In fact, she wasn't sure she wanted to. "Yeah, okay."

"Great. See you then."

❖

Picture-perfect extensions.

Impeccable turnout.

Unmatched control.

Natalie stood there, awed as she watched. Ana exhibited a weightless existence as she moved quickly on her toes through the expanse of the studio.

Natalie shook her head and drummed her fingers against her upper lip as she took in Ana's performance of the new variation Roger had added. She'd been watching her dance the *Aftermath* solos for a better part of an hour. How it happened, she wasn't quite sure, but somewhere along the way, she'd lost herself in the beauty and the rhythm of the ballet. The more she watched Ana dance, the more in awe she became.

Of Ana herself.

Her ability.

Her body.

Jason looked over at Natalie and smiled. "She gets better every day."

"Understatement," Natalie said and threw her towel at him good-naturedly. "She was born to do this." When Ana danced, ballet was more than just a stuffy niche of what Natalie referred to as real dancing. It was…beautiful. Art on display, right in front of her eyes.

"What?" Ana asked, as she came off the floor, all eyes on her.

"Looking good out there, Mik," Jason told her.

"Well, that's the goal, right?" she tossed back to him.

Roger gave notes to his assistants in the corner, likely about to bring rehearsal to a close for the day. They'd gone hard for five hours and made some decent progress. Ana especially.

"Until tomorrow, everyone!" Roger shouted. "We'll be in the larger studio, incorporating the background dancers as they appear in the underworld sequences. Natalie, you'll be up first. Come prepared, please."

"Got it." Natalie stood and stretched. Somewhere there was a bucket of ice water with her name on it. Icing down her muscles would be the only way she could dance those combinations again the next day. Because God, her body screamed.

"Are we still on?" Ana asked her, toweling off.

After dancing for the last hour, she still had energy for more? She was kind of a ballet machine, this girl.

Natalie stared up at her. "Um…I'm game, if you are."

"Great. Why don't we take fifteen and meet back here? We can go over the opening and I can show you a couple of tricks I think will smooth out your transitions."

"Cool. See you then."

Natalie took the time to roll out her muscles and decompress a little in the green room. When she returned to the studio, the lights were at half and the place was now empty, everyone having packed up and headed home for the night. She stared at her reflection in the mirrors that lined the wall. Her hair was up, but strands had fallen here and there throughout the day. She pulled the rubber band out entirely and gave her head a little shake, prompting her hair to fall to her shoulders. In the corner of her eye, she saw Ana's reflection watching her from the doorway and something decidedly sexual moved through her, making her very aware of her body and the effect Ana's stare had on it. Was she crazy, or was there an abundance of chemistry there?

"Hey," Ana said, still in the doorway. "I'll put on the music and we can go from there." In the empty room, her quiet voice echoed.

"Ready when you are," Natalie said, and took her spot in the middle of the room for the opening sequence. Something about the one-on-one work session had her nervous, that her flaws would be so clearly on display. She shoved the unease aside and took a deep, settling breath. Once she heard the music, she was off, but it was only a matter of moments before the room came to a halting silence, causing her to halt as well. She turned to see that Ana had paused the music and was walking toward her with purpose.

"The thing is that you're too liberal with your movements. Too loose. You bring this whole reckless quality to the character, and it works, but for the sake of form, you have to tighten up."

"Right. I've heard that before from Roger. Okay, cool. I'll try again."

Except when she did, the results were much the same. Ana shook her head. "The choreography is there but you lack precision. You have to finish each extension before moving on or the transitions are muddled."

"I thought that's what I was doing."

"It's not," Ana said matter-of-factly. "You're rushing. But don't get frustrated. It's going to take time. Try again and focus on that one thing. Finish what you start."

Natalie danced until the music stopped and again turned to her tutor. "Better, you did just what I asked. But now you need to pull yourself in. Keep your hips underneath you." Ana moved until she stood behind Natalie and met her gaze in the mirror. "Feel that?" Ana asked and placed her hand against Natalie's abdomen. Natalie nodded, hyperaware of the contact and the warmth that hit her cheeks and spread downward.

"I do."

Ana's voice was quiet in her ear. "You're going to pull in here, and push through the toe."

Natalie nodded at Ana in the mirror, the contact unbroken. She could feel Ana's breath tickle her neck, and with Ana's hands still on her body, her mind wandered to places outside her control. As if sensing the shift, Ana took a step back and released Natalie, moving them on from the charged moment.

"One more time."

Natalie nodded and focused on what she needed to do. As she spun on her toes, she took Ana's advice, pulling in just beneath the touch she could still feel against her skin. She closed her eyes, concentrated, and before she knew it, she'd made it to the end of the variation. When the music came to a stop this time, Ana didn't say a word.

"Well?" Natalie asked. "Any better?"

Ana blinked back at her, as if awaking from a dream. "Yes. That was...beautiful actually." And then, finding herself again, "But there's more to cover."

"Okay. I'm game."

They spent the next ninety minutes going through a proverbial list in Ana's head of the techniques Natalie had apparently been murdering throughout their entire rehearsal process. While it was a humbling experience, the thing was, Ana was dead-on each time, and her fixes were working. They were the same notes Roger had given her from the start, but Ana explained them in a way that made sense to her. It wasn't easy for Natalie to put the notes immediately into her performance of a ballet her body had already memorized, but if she worked at it daily, she was confident she could incorporate the notes more fully and improve. Hopefully before opening night.

"Are you ready to try the whole thing together?" Ana asked.

Natalie raised an eyebrow. "All of it? Might be kind of hard without Jason."

"I can fill in for anything that's not a lift or the flying shoulder sits. We can just mark those. I can support you enough through the rest, though." Ana shrugged her hoodie off her shoulders.

"Wait. You're dancing with me?"

"Don't look at me like that. It's not like I haven't seen the choreography a million times."

Natalie stared at her in mystification, her mind rolling through the sequences she'd come to know and then imagining it all happening in Ana's arms, rather than Jason's. The idea alone made her heart stop and her stomach tighten. She tried to smile it away, but she faltered, the idea of the intimate contact overwhelming her senses. But she didn't have time to linger, as Ana joined her in the middle of the floor. Natalie assumed her opening pose and Ana wrapped an arm around her from behind, just as Jason would have, and extended her arm along Natalie's.

Only it felt nothing like when Jason did it.

Not even close.

Was this even the same ballet?

The music began and they leapt into motion. Dancing side by side. Ana took her by the hand and led her upstage, never breaking eye contact. Natalie moved into her body and then away, just as always, only this time her temperature climbed. She spun. They danced, Ana's hands on her waist, her stomach, her thighs. The flashes of emotion, the give and take of the characters, added a whole other element, and dancing through that dynamic with Ana…had her body thrumming beneath Ana's touch.

Though they skipped the lift, Ana caught her at the end of the *pas de deux* and pulled her close, ending the sequence flush with each other.

"You did great," Ana said in her ear, and held her a moment longer as Natalie's breath came in short little gasps, part exertion, part arousal. Ana released Natalie solemnly, nodded to her, and headed back to the bench. Okay, so she hadn't been the only one who had felt the electricity back there. That much was now clear. She stared at the ceiling, understanding that this was a slippery slope they were on, and she had to find a way to maneuver it gracefully.

"Have you ever thought about teaching?" Natalie asked, focusing on the work. That could be her new plan. Take a page from Ana's book and make it all about the show. Ana considered the question as they gathered their things to head home. It had been a more than productive session, and she owed Ana big-time.

"Not really," Ana said. "Why?"

"You'd be amazing at it. The way you explain yourself to a dancer is refreshing. You're direct and clear. Plus you're knowledgeable and patient. The patient part is kind of surprising, I have to admit."

Ana laughed quietly. "Why do you say that?"

Natalie tried to find the best way to explain. "You're wound kind of tight, no?"

"Okay, I can cop to that."

"So patience with others is not exactly what I would have expected."

Ana shrugged as they departed the studio together. "I'm hard on myself. I have high expectations, but it's not like I want others to fail. Quite the opposite. I want you to be good."

"You just want to be better," Natalie said knowingly.

"Well, who doesn't?"

They walked in silence much of the way to the train. Natalie was tired from the day, sore from dancing, and her mind extra cognizant of this new and overwhelming attraction to the one person who drove her up the wall. Ana had, for the most part, presented herself as uptight, overly ambitious, and quite often, closed off. What about that combination had Natalie lusting after her was a mystery. The problem was, she now knew there was more to Ana than that, and she for damn sure couldn't get Ana out of her head.

But it wasn't like anything could come of it.

Natalie had Morgan, who was so much easier, less complex, and always on her side.

But that understanding didn't stop her from stealing a glance or two at Ana as they walked. The sky was dark and her hair blew back in the chilly autumn wind, highlighting what were surprisingly delicate features.

"Where do you go when you dance?" Ana asked her. The question shattered the silence. The wind picked up and Natalie braced against it, shrugging her jacket tighter around her shoulders.

"Where do I go?"

"In your mind. It's like something takes over. I've seen it."

"I think it's about harnessing emotion. Some of it's my own. Some of it belongs to the character. It's about tapping into yourself and seeing what you have to give. What you feel."

"I don't do that too often."

"You don't do what?"

"Let myself feel."

Natalie stopped walking right there on the street corner, which brought Ana to a halt next to her. "And that's a total shame. You know that, right?"

Ana nodded. "But I did tonight. When we danced."

Tingles traced the outside of Natalie's skin. "Did what?"

"Felt something." A pause. "You don't have to say anything to that. In fact, I'm not even sure why I told you. I shouldn't have."

The comment surprised Natalie and she wasn't quite sure what to say. Instead, they walked on in silence. "Me too," were the words she heard leave her lips after a few long moments.

Ana turned to her, so many questions apparent in her eyes, but she didn't say anything. As they walked, Natalie stared up at the darkened sky. A sliver of moonlight peeked out. The street was fairly quiet for that time of night in the city, and she took a moment to enjoy the serenity. Ana slid her hands into her jacket pockets. "Sometimes I think I must be the most boring person on the planet."

"Trust me. You're not."

"I'm beginning to wonder. All I think about is rehearsal, injuries, hair, makeup, and pointe shoes. Lately, I've been thinking about more, though."

"You have?"

"Strangely, yes. It's really all your fault. Or all your credit, depending on how you look at it."

"Explain it to me, then."

She looked thoughtful for a moment. "Okay. I guess I could try. It's like I've taken the blinders off. The world's bigger than I sometimes realize, and spending time with you has, I suppose, reminded me of that."

"I don't know how much I actually had to do with it, but that's an important realization," Natalie said. "There's so much more to life than what you do for a living. Don't forget the *more*, Ana."

The evening had taken a heavy turn, but when they arrived back at the apartment, Natalie knew she wasn't ready to say good night. In order to hang on a little longer, she needed to do something to bring them out of it, to lighten the mood. She hung her cargo jacket on the back of Ana's door and gestured to the TV that didn't seem to get a lot of use, if she took into account the books that were stacked in front of it. "Want to see what's on?"

Ana looked at her like she'd asked for an elephant ride through downtown and sat on the floor to roll out her muscles. "What's on what?"

Natalie shook her head. "Things are worse than I thought. Did you know that this square box turns on and lights up?"

"I wondered why they were so popular."

"May I?" Natalie asked.

"Be my guest." Ana smiled at the meaning of her statement. "In fact, you are."

"You enjoyed that little playout."

"A tad," Ana said. "What are we watching?"

"It doesn't matter. That's kind of the point."

"It doesn't matter?"

"Nope. We're looking for mindless and entertaining. No redeeming value required for decompression TV, and no deep thinking. None."

"You seem to have thought this through."

"Thought it through? I've perfected the art. I'm a pro at mindless and entertaining. Boom," Natalie said, and pointed at the screen. "*Funniest Home Videos*. This can't be beat in terms of mindless. Are you watching? Because this is important. You need to watch."

Ana stared at the screen a moment. "Ouch. That kid just fell face first in the snow. Where are his parents?"

"Behind the camera, but he's laughing, so all is well."

"I'm not so sure."

"I am. I'm a *Funniest Videos* regular. Take notes."

"In progress."

As the show played on, Ana eventually made her way onto the couch next to Natalie. Every few minutes she chuckled quietly, and as time went on, her body did seem to relax. She'd pulled her feet beneath her and sunk back against the cushion in a display Natalie couldn't describe as anything other than adorable. It was genuinely the most relaxed Natalie had ever seen her, and on Ana, relaxed looked...hot. Though lately, everything on Ana seemed hot. Natalie had developed some sort of complex...or crush.

"What's next?" Ana asked, as the credits rolled. She was clearly enjoying herself and seemed lighter, girlish even. Natalie flipped through the stations until she landed on a home repair show.

"Perfect. This is where we get to watch people other than ourselves take run-down houses and turn them into beautiful homes without either one of us having to lift a finger."

"My kind of work," Ana said and they settled in to watch. Thirty minutes later, Natalie pulled the blanket she'd folded that morning across her lap.

"You cold?" she asked Ana, who nodded and accepted a section of the blanket. They were close now, and Natalie felt Ana's leg brush against hers and swallowed against the rush of something potent that hit her at the contact.

God, she couldn't go down this path with Ana.

She just couldn't.

But at the same time, she was curious as to what was suspended between them, and that curiosity nudged her closer to the girl who'd been her nemesis just weeks ago. What was it about Ana that had captured her attention and would not let it the hell go? Whatever it was, it sucked up all the air in the room and made Natalie crave things best left untouched. She couldn't remember the last time she'd legitimately craved.

"I should say thank you," Ana said, her cheek against the couch as she faced Natalie.

"For what? You're the one who helped me tonight back at the studio."

"I wasn't talking about work. I was talking about this. Life. All of it." Ana seemed shy all of a sudden and sat forward on the couch so she wouldn't have to look at Natalie. The vulnerability was a whole new shade on her. "This was fun. I still need to go over notes before bed, but I feel better somehow. Decompressed."

"Because you're just being a person. Chillin' on the couch."

Ana laughed. "I've never thought of myself as someone who 'chills on a couch,' but I embrace the moniker."

"Well, now you can. A prima ballerina capable of chillin'. An impressive combo, Ana M."

They sat back and watched two more episodes of *Fixer Upper* before Natalie felt the weight of her eyes take over. She fought against the impending sleep, but must have lost the battle. When she awoke, the room was dark and silent...and warm. Warm in the best way. The kind you want to curl into and never leave. She glanced down to find Ana asleep against her shoulder, her hair tousled and covering one eye. Natalie's mind struggled to piece together the circumstances, but came up short. Didn't matter. She enjoyed it—the closeness and the warmth Ana brought. With a satisfied sigh, Natalie pulled Ana in closer and fell back asleep.

Chapter Seven

The poster on the stark white wall in front of Ana showed the image of a transparent foot. Inside the drawing, she could see each bone, tendon, and ligament that made up one of her most precious commodities, and she marveled at the intricacies so small, but capable of ruining her whole life.

With the pain now nearly overwhelming her ability to dance, she'd come to a specialist she'd grown to trust. Dr. Santillan had seen her through a fractured ankle and pulled ligaments and had even performed surgery when she blew out her knee. Ana trusted him implicitly and knew that he would help her get control of her situation.

Because there had to be a fix.

Even if it was temporary.

She could sideline herself after *Aftermath*'s closing, if that was what it took, but this show was too important for her to let anything get in the way.

The door opened and Dr. Santillan smiled at her, but Mayday!— all was not right. Ana's stomach dipped because that smile didn't quite reach his eyes.

"So what's the verdict?" Ana asked nervously before he could say anything. He held the MRI of her left foot, which he'd surely just come from studying. "And how do we fix it?"

"Well, that's the thing," Dr. Santillan said, and took a seat on the black stool across from her. "It's a bit more complicated this time, Ana. The tendinitis in your foot has progressed. Your longus tendon," he said, pointing to the bottom of her foot on the dark paper, "has become so thin from the strain of dancing that we're dealing with full-on tendinopathy."

A chill moved up her spine. She immediately shook it off and focused on the matter at hand. "And what's the fix for that? A steroid injection? Something to bolster its strength again?"

He shook his head in apology.

"I don't know what tendinopathy is." She wasn't sure she wanted to, either. She glanced at the ceiling for some sort of reprieve from what she was about to hear. Her palms were cold and sweaty, and suddenly it felt hard to achieve more than a shallow breath.

"It means the tendon is so overrun with small tears that it's exceptionally vulnerable, thin, and weak. As a ballet dancer, you're forced to maintain a variety of unnatural positions on your toes and ball of your foot. Eventually, in my experience treating dancers, it becomes a test of whose body can withstand the conditions longest. You're close to thirty now, Ana, and it's possible that your body is done."

"It's not done." She refused to entertain that concept. "How do we treat the tendon? That's what we should be talking about."

"Rest and immobilization for seven to ten days will help alleviate the immediate inflammation and thereby the pain, but if you continue to dance on that foot day after day at intense levels, you're going to be right back to square one. There's no escaping it, Ana."

"Taking ten days off right now is not an option. I'm about to open in a new ballet, the most important role I've ever danced. I need you to help me make it through."

"I can't do that." Dr. Santillan gestured to her foot. "You dance on the foot in the condition that it's in now and the tendon could snap at any second. If that happens, then it's all over. There's nothing I can do. No more dancing."

An icy shiver moved up her spine and her limbs felt thick and heavy. She placed her hand over her heart to somehow stop the rapid thudding and take control of this situation. "So your advice is to just quit? That's in no way an option."

"I don't think you understand how serious this is."

She turned her head to hide the tears, now hot and full in her eyes. "So I'm supposed to just walk away from the job that I love more than anything on the planet? The only thing I know how to do?" She knew of dancers who'd been in her position before. They transitioned to choreography or teaching. She'd just never imagined that kind of life for herself. She was a professional ballet dancer, damn it, and at the height of her career. Ana wasn't going to let anyone or anything interfere with that.

"Please tell me this isn't happening," she whispered.

He placed a hand on hers, but the news didn't change. "I wish I could."

As she walked home that night, she allowed herself to feel the pain beneath each step. In a way, it made her feel as if she were facing the enemy head-on. She had to acknowledge the problem before she could fix it. Then and there, she formulated a plan. Instead of pushing the pain aside, ignoring it as she danced, she would instead pay more attention and keep careful tabs on how her foot felt at any given moment. She could take breaks in rehearsal if necessary, let Natalie fill in for her. But there was no way she was pulling herself from *Aftermath* altogether. The idea was insane. She would worry about what came after the show later. Tell Bill she needed some time off, if it came to that. No need to rush to any rash conclusions just yet. One day at a time.

"So how was your appointment?" Natalie asked when she arrived home. She was in the process of retrieving a mug from the microwave and wore yoga pants and a soft sweatshirt that drifted off her shoulder just a tad.

"Just a check-in with my foot guy."

"And all is well?" Natalie handed the mug to Ana and pulled a second from the cabinet. She really was learning her way around the place, and after several days of having her there, the initial unease of a houseguest had waned. Ana had started to look forward to seeing Natalie when she arrived home. Shocking really. And who knew how much longer that could be, given that they were now completely replacing the faulty pipes in Natalie's apartment. There were definitely worst sentences she could be dealt.

"As well as could be expected, given what we do. Can I ask you something?"

"I'm confident you can. What's your question?"

"How many injuries have you had?"

Natalie raised her eyebrows. "How long do you have?"

"See? That's my point. Injury is just a part of the job. Oh, what is this?" she said, inspecting the contents of the mug that smelled delicious and warmed her hands.

"Hot cocoa. An important part of one's daily nutrition. Especially when it's cold out."

"I think I love it." Ana took a sip and closed her eyes in surrender as the thick chocolaty goodness extended its warmth to her throat. "Now I know I do. Yeah, that's nice. I'm gonna hold on to this."

"Just trying to earn my keep," Natalie told her, purposely beaming.

"I'm starting to believe you."

"About that. Sal-of-the-gum-chewing said the guys are wrapping up across the hall. Tonight could be the last night I force you to hang out with me."

"They lie," Ana said. "Ten bucks says you're here tomorrow. I'm familiar with Sal and his miscalculations." In actuality, Ana was in no hurry to have Natalie move home, something she wasn't fully ready to admit to Natalie, or maybe even herself.

"Yeah, well, I'm not sure that's a bet I want to take. But we're off topic. How many injuries have you had in *your* career? I mean, if we're swapping stories."

Ana whistled low. "Okay, so three majors resulting in two surgeries, and so many minors I've lost track. But I'm not complaining. It's what I signed up for. When you're a dancer, you get up in the morning and make a checklist of everything that hurts and then head to work. There's no stopping and reveling in the pain or you've just been beaten out by another dancer who's mentally stronger than you and can rise above it."

Natalie took a seat on the couch next to Ana and turned her body to face her. Ana had come to recognize Natalie's thoughtful face, which she had on now. Knitted brow, downcast eyes, pursed lips. Almost like she'd pulled into herself to think things over. "Yeah, okay," Natalie said, finally raising her gaze, "but there have to be limits."

"No. Limits are for people who don't want it bad enough. Very few people make it to where we are. You do what you can for your body to make it to the next rehearsal. I take vitamin C, vitamin D, magnesium for fatigue, and Advil as an anti-inflammatory. Every day. You do it too. I've seen you."

"Well, yeah, but there's still going to be a day that I can't dance anymore. Regardless of what I tell myself, that day exists on a calendar somewhere in the sky and is headed my way. Injury is always possible, and it's the reason you have to have a plan B. For example, I plan to get by on my sexy lips. Look what happens when they get all pouty. I really think I could be an honorary Kardashian if I work hard enough. Or maybe not work hard at all. That might be the key." She demonstrated her pout, which made Ana smile in spite of her troubling afternoon.

Honestly, she admired Natalie's ability to remain lighthearted about a subject matter that had her panicked, terrified even. That was yet another way they were different. "I don't have a plan B. Dancing at this level is my everything."

"I get that, but—"

"Can we talk about something else?" Ana asked, the discomfort of the dicey topic getting to be too much. The news she'd received today was jarring enough, and she needed a way to divert her attention. "Maybe we could watch TV again."

Natalie stared at her. "You're starting to resemble a regular person over there. It's freaking me the hell out."

"Goal achieved," Ana said and grabbed the blanket off the back of the couch, tossing half to Natalie. She remembered waking up in the early morning on this very couch, lying very much against Natalie. The physical closeness and the way her body had thrummed still played vividly in her memory.

"Perfect," Natalie said. "Let's veg."

After flipping through several other mindless options, they settled on the Home and Garden channel, and enjoyed heckling the overly pretentious couple shopping for a vacation home to purchase in St. Thomas.

Natalie shook her head ominously at the screen. "Oh no. He's not happy. This is not good. This house will require him to walk an extra fifteen feet to the beach."

"The fifteen feet will crush him," Ana said. "How can he possibly be expected to spend time in a place like that?"

"He can't. It's preposterous to imagine he could. I don't know what that realtor was thinking. Fifteen feet is too far to walk. Those people need sand under their toes yesterday, damn it."

Ana laughed and turned her head against the couch to face Natalie.

"Why is it when I spend time with you, I forget everything else?" It was a legitimate question, but not one she meant to voice out loud. She felt the pink hit her cheeks almost instantly. "You don't have to answer that, it was entirely rhetorical and probably not—"

"I don't know," Natalie said anyway, meeting her gaze. "I've never really had a friend like you before."

"Like me how?"

"Someone so different from me and frustrating as hell."

"Hey," Ana said, and bopped her with a pillow. "You're the frustrating one. Trust me."

Natalie caught the pillow and pulled it from Ana's grasp. "I'll amend. Frustrating as hell and dangerous with fluffy weaponry."

"Yeah, well, don't tempt me."

"That sounds like a challenge," Natalie shot back, her eyes flashing amusement. "But you're pretty cute when you're aggressive. So, bonus."

The comment landed, and Ana had to take a moment. Natalie thought she was cute. Unsure what to do, Ana did what she did best. Deflected. "We should get back to the show," she said, gesturing awkwardly at the television. "Fifteen feet hang in the balance. Kind of a big deal."

Natalie nodded and the amusement dimmed on her face. "Fifteen feet it is." But then a few moments later, "Stop hogging the blanket, Frozen." And a laughter-filled tug-o'-war ensued.

❖

Natalie checked her watch and took a long pull from her water bottle. She had time for a two-minute break to catch her breath and hydrate before stealing another thirty minutes of rehearsal before class that morning.

She'd never been an early riser and almost didn't recognize herself as she stumbled into the rehearsal studio at seven that morning. But the motivation had been simple. The work Ana had done with her had been golden, and the adjustments she'd made to Natalie's dancing had made a huge difference, but it would take work for them to have full effect. Maybe listening to Ana, who knew a thing or two about formal ballet, wasn't such a crazy idea.

Because, okay, she *could* work harder.

Get up earlier. And stay later.

She was seeing exciting changes, not just in her dancing, but in her understanding of the whole ballet world, and that had her motivated to make her mark. She would do whatever it took to get better and do the best possible job she could. The more she saw her work pay off in rehearsal, and it was, the more of herself she wanted to give.

"That ballet is going to be gorgeous," Helen said from the floor of her apartment, later that night. Natalie and Audrey lay flat on their backs alongside her, dead to the world from their long day at work.

And it had been a *day*.

"You think?" Natalie asked, with barely enough energy to move. "Once I get so far in, I can't see the show as a whole anymore. It's hard to tell if it's going to be good. Forest for the trees. That kind of thing."

Helen shook her head. "Better than good. It's going to pull a ton of buzz and put you, Ana, and Jason on the map in this city. Trust me, Roger is a visionary and the musicality of the ballet is genius."

"You know what else would be genius?" Audrey said from her spot on the floor. "If someone would bring me a bucket of ice so I could soak my poor, overworked ankle."

"I'd get you some, but that would require *movement*," Natalie said. "I'm against movement in all its forms at present. I'd take movement to court and sue its ass off if I could."

"Who can we call to bring us ice?" Audrey asked in full pitiful mode.

"Ana," Natalie said matter-of-factly. "I was on in the run-through today, so she should be extra fresh. I can get her ice tomorrow when she's me. I'm nice that way."

It had been five days since they'd moved out of the studio and begun rehearsals with the larger cast of *Aftermath*. They were now running the show in its entirety onstage each day and had just two weeks before opening. Natalie had rehearsed with the cast earlier that day and Ana was on tomorrow. She would watch Ana and take notes through rehearsal. Watching Ana, Natalie had found, was not exactly a great thing. Watching Ana tended to lead to thoughts of Ana, which led to the occasional daydream of Ana…which she had to figure out how to stop, because it continued to escalate and there was only so far one could—

"Text her!" Audrey said, pointing at the ceiling in lieu of Helen. "She's been extra cordial lately, saying hello first and everything. She smiles and it's really quite pleasant."

"On it."

"You're rubbing off on Ana, you know," Helen said. "I think you guys are good for each other. A yin and yang kind of thing."

"We're just friends," Natalie said, perhaps more emphatically than necessary.

"What more would you be?" Helen asked, eying her slyly.

Helen, she was finding, didn't miss much, and Natalie might have just shown her cards. Wait—there were cards? What cards? She had no cards. She had Morgan, who was her girlfriend. And Ana, who was her...Ana. She shook off the entire, disturbing line of thought.

"I was in awe of you during the run-through today," Audrey told Natalie. "It's like you're a professional or something."

Natalie laughed. "Aww, you noticed."

"Seriously though," Helen said, pushing up onto her elbow. "Like everyone else, I was a little skeptical when they brought you in. But after the last few days, I get it. You're the real deal. More untamed than the company's general fare, but that's why you work so well for this show."

Natalie took in the compliment. "Thanks. I'm trying to rein in my technique, work on form as well. Pull back the untamed a tad. Ana's helped."

"I've helped with what?" They turned then to find Ana standing in the doorway.

"Dancing," Natalie said. "Shelter over my head. A nemesis when I need one. All of it. You check lots of boxes."

"Well, I suppose that's true. Especially the nemesis part." Ana held up her phone. "My phone reads, 'There are people in need of ice or they'll die. Race to Audrey and Helen's apartment right now.'"

"That's us!" Audrey said. "We're the dying."

Ana nodded. "Sure. I can help. Three, uh, ice buckets on their way." Natalie sat up and watched Ana's progress to the kitchen. She wore jeans and a beige Henley, which greatly contrasted with the dark hair that fell down her back. Natalie swallowed against the tantalizing visual.

"Why don't I help?" Natalie asked. Helen stared at her as if working a difficult puzzle. "What? I'm feeling more energetic."

"Yes, all of a sudden you are. Got my eye on you," Helen said, raising one eyebrow. Natalie blew her off and joined Ana in the kitchen a few feet away.

"Hey, thought you could use a hand."

Ana eyed her skeptically. "I thought you were dying."

"I rebound nicely. So, hey. I get my apartment back tonight. Sal said they'd finish up by dinnertime. I haven't headed up to check, but it should be free and clear. New bottom cabinets and everything."

"Oh," Ana said and studied the bag of ice she'd pulled from the freezer, a dancer's necessity. "That's great."

"I know you'll be thrilled to have full use of your couch again."

"Yeah," Ana said meeting her eyes. The moment felt charged and thick, with a lot going unacknowledged. The near week she'd spent at Ana's apartment had been a catalyst to a palpable connection between them. Now that she was leaving, she felt...hollow. From the look on Ana's face, she did, too.

Natalie did her best to lighten the mood. "I hate to break it to you, but I'll still be across the hall. Ever present and ready to get on your last nerve."

"I don't know how I'll manage," Ana said simply.

"And our HGTV veg outs will have to continue. In fact, I might show up on your doorstep tonight."

Ana focused on the ice. "I might be busy tonight."

Natalie leaned in close. "No, you won't."

"Yes, I will. I have a lot going on with the show opening so quickly, and I need to take care of myself more but," she blew out a breath as if surrendering to something unnamed, "I might have a break in there somewhere."

"Benevolent. That's what you are."

"I can be other things, too," Ana said quietly, a comment that left Natalie's heart taking extra beats, and Ana, seemingly shocked by her own words, picked up the ice and headed back to Audrey and Helen. As Natalie stood there with half her brain concentrating on the number the workday had done on her body, and the other half on the number Ana Mikhelson was doing on it now, her phone buzzed.

"Morgan," the readout said. With one finger up to her friends, she excused herself to the hall.

"Baby!" Morgan said. Wherever she was calling from, it was boisterous. Music and loud voices in combination.

"Hey, you," Natalie said back. The phone calls between them had gotten fewer and farther between. Though Natalie admitted she sometimes called in the early-morning hours on purpose, knowing she'd be leaving a message for Morgan, who often slept until noon on non-diner days. "How are you?"

"Drunk. Very drunk. But in a good way."

"Oh...well, little early, isn't it?" She did the California time conversion and came up with just after seven p.m. there.

"Since when do you care about that?" Morgan said. She had to shout to be heard over the din in the background. "Anyway, got your message about coming for the opening. I will definitely be there. It's going to be off-the-charts fun."

Natalie laughed. "Great. I can't wait to see you."

"Put that drink down, Charlie. Huh? What did you say? Say it again."

"Me?" Natalie asked, squinting as if that was going to help her hear better. "Or Charlie?"

"Yes, you."

"Oh." Natalie decided to speak louder and enunciate. "I said I can't wait to see you. Send me the details of your flight and we can—"

"I'm serious, you guys! Baby, I gotta go. These people are crazy here tonight. We miss you! See you soon!" And then she was gone. Natalie stared at the phone as a pang of sadness hit. She'd been in New York for a couple of months now, and already the world she'd left felt light-years away. She missed it, but not in the way she imagined she would. The work she was doing felt more important to her with each day that passed.

When she walked back into the apartment, she found Ana doing her best, and surprisingly accurate, impersonation of Roger's latest meltdown, including an imaginary clipboard toss for Helen and Audrey, who ate up every minute of it. Natalie watched from the door, smiling proudly at the more outgoing version of Ana that had emerged of late. She really did seem to be coming out of her reclusive shell.

"You've got this guy down," Helen said, laughing as Natalie took a seat next to Ana.

Audrey pointed at Ana as she regained her composure. "That was awesome. You have to do that for Boomer and Marcus."

Ana covered her mouth and pink dusted her cheeks. "No. No. I couldn't. It was a spur-of-the-moment thing."

"They're back together, by the way," Audrey said offhandedly to Helen.

"Everyone's in love at the holidays."

"It's my plan to be, too," Audrey told them. "I have a date with Clark Kent in 2B on Saturday." She covered her mouth with both hands and waited for the reaction.

"Whoa!" Natalie shouted, and pointed at her. "You did it. You're a saucy minx over there."

"Wait. Who lives in 2B?" Ana asked quietly.

"The man who will bear my children," Audrey informed her.

Helen held up a hand and addressed Ana. "This buttoned-up guy that Audrey regularly drools over in the elevator. He's cute, in that businessman with glasses kind of way."

Audrey beamed. "We're going to Scarlatto in Midtown and then he's taking me to see *Cabaret*."

"That's a pretty major date," Natalie pointed out. "That's not just a get-to-know-you chat over pizza. He's trying to woo you."

"Woo away, I always say." Audrey fanned herself. "I'm not hard to impress."

"A friend of mine stars in that show," Ana told them.

"You're friends with Adrienne Kenyon?" Helen asked.

Ana nodded.

"I've wanted to be her best friend since I was a kid. I grew up watching her on *Highland High*."

Ana nodded. "That's where we met. My father did a guest spot on the show and I got to hang out on set with him. Adrienne was a little bit older and became kind of like a big sister during that time. When I was hired on at City, she was over the moon for me. She's come to quite a few of the shows."

"You're officially the coolest person in the room," Audrey told her. "And no offense, but I never would have guessed that."

"None taken. We only get to see each other here and there," Ana said, downplaying her connection to one of the most talked about and celebrated celebrities of late.

"I have to agree with Audrey," Natalie said. "You get cool points." Ana smiled at her. "I've not had many of those. I'll take them." She stood. "I'm also going to take my leave, as it's getting late." Natalie watched her progress to the door, wishing she'd stay, but knowing Ana had a big dance day ahead of her tomorrow and needed to rest up.

"Hey, Ana," Helen said.

"Yeah?" Ana replied from the door.

"We're going out next Sunday following *Aftermath*'s opening. We figured since Monday was dark, we could stay out late, celebrate. You should come."

Natalie watched the contemplation cross Ana's features, knowing the internal battle that was at play. "Okay. Sounds like fun. Good night, everyone." She made brief eye contact with Natalie before exiting the apartment.

The second the door closed, Helen turned to Natalie, eyes wide. "What in the hell was that?"

"What was what?" Natalie asked as nonchalantly as possible.

"So it wasn't just me?" Audrey asked Helen.

"Nope."

"What?" Natalie asked. "Is this an Ana thing? I think she's gathering social courage, so cut her a break. It's nice that she hangs with us more. No?"

Helen passed her a hard look. "It's more about all the lustacular looks crossing back and forth between you two. What the hell was that?"

"Noooo," Natalie said, drawing the word out. Even she knew it was a weak retort.

"Oh yes." Audrey inclined her head to the door. "You could just cover her in whipped cream and lick it off. Might be more subtle."

Natalie swallowed, a little surprised that she'd been so obvious. Okay, lesson learned. Something to work on. But at the same time, this was confirmation that maybe it wasn't just her projecting and it ran both ways. She decided to seize this opportunity and learn what her friends had observed. "Explain yourselves."

Helen fielded this one. "You're both all swoony looking and

hyperaware of the other person and where she is in the room. Is she into girls and we never knew it? Or is she just into *you*?"

Natalie balked. "Who said she's into either?"

Helen pointed back and forth between Natalie and an imaginary Ana on the couch. "Well, first of all, the little stares she snuck at you said you're her greatest fantasy come to life. That might have been the tip-off."

"That was my tip-off," Audrey tossed in to Helen.

Natalie covered her face with her hands and fell backward onto the couch. "It's one of those things I can't explain, okay? She's not at all my type. She's all serious and pretentious and maddening, but—"

"You want to kiss her face off because of it?" Audrey asked.

"A little," Natalie sighed. "Okay, a lot. But I'm not going to, because (A) I'm seeing someone else, and (B) even if I weren't, Ana's terrifying. Anything with her would be…intense. I don't think it's possible to do *casual* when it comes to Anastasia Mikhelson."

"No, I'm with you on that." Helen joined Natalie on the couch. "But she's different since you've been around. Less intense, actually. She's…blossomed into a…"

"Human being," Audrey supplied. "And a likable one, which is jaw dropping. I actually *like* Ana Mikhelson. Frozen and I are *friends* now. Words I never thought I'd utter."

Helen stared thoughtfully at Natalie. "This girlfriend of yours, how serious are we talking? Are you in love with her?"

Natalie marinated on the question. The same one Ana had asked her not too long ago. "We have fun together, and I care about her. It felt serious for a time. But truthfully? The distance has drawn a big arrow sign over the fact that we seem to be doing okay without each other."

"So what's the plan?"

Natalie stood, a little uncomfortable with the subject matter. "There is no plan. Morgan is coming for the opening next week, and Ana and I will trade off doing the show until it closes."

"That simple, huh?" Helen asked. "As in nothing could possibly go wrong with that plan?"

"Yeah," Natalie said, feeling less confident than she sounded. "That simple."

Chapter Eight

A na tossed her towel into her dance bag in frustration and pulled her hair from the knot at the back of her neck and gave her head an angry shake. What the hell was that? She'd had bad rehearsals before. They happened all the time, but this one set a new record and shined a spotlight on all the ways she sucked at this part.

Embarrassing. That's what it had been, and in front of the entire cast.

They'd focused on the climax of the piece that day, which begins with a tortured Mira's solo and then crescendos into a partnered dance where Titus joins her and the characters battle until their passion unites them as one.

"Try it again, Ana. The character has to feel something," Roger had yelled at her from his chair in the house. She could still hear his words echoing through the expanse of the theatre. "How was that any different from the time before?" he said when she'd finished. "Get out of your head, Ana. This isn't math, it's poetry."

She slammed her dance bag down on the bench and leaned against the cement wall.

"It's not that bad." She opened her eyes to see Natalie standing near her in the wings. She was packed up and ready to go, her dance bag slung over her shoulder, jeans on over her leotard.

"Did you just sit through the same rehearsal I did? He loves everything you do and hates me."

"That's only because you took the time to set me on the right track, show me all the ways I was screwing up. Maybe I can return the favor now."

Okay, so that was an interesting proposition. Perhaps Natalie could help. Regardless, Ana was out of ideas and willing to try anything. "What did you have in mind?"

"Meet me in studio four. Let's play around."

Seriously, what did she have to lose?

Ten minutes later, that was exactly where they were. Natalie took a spot on the bench in the corner and pulled out her phone. Ana watched as she scrolled through her music. "What are we doing exactly?"

Natalie looked up and smiled. "We're going to dance."

"Okay, but that particular variation—"

Natalie stood and placed one finger over Ana's lips. "We're not dancing the show."

"We're not?"

"God, no. Freestyle."

"I don't necessarily see how that's productive."

"You don't have to. Leave it to me. This is the fun part. I'm going to play a song and you're going to dance to it. Use what you're feeling right now and just go."

"I don't think I can do that. I don't freestyle."

"Bullshit. You just don't want to. You hate letting go and you overthink everything like it's your job. Want me to go first? Will that help?"

Ana made a sweeping gesture with her arm, inviting Natalie ahead of her because she wasn't comfortable with this whole exercise. "By all means."

Natalie nodded once, plugged her phone into the portable speaker, and selected a song with a touch of the screen. Ana watched as Natalie took off across the floor in a series of movements not at all reminiscent of ballet. Whoa. For the next three minutes she watched in awe of the woman in front of her, so fearless in everything she did. There wasn't any restraint, any self-awareness in the way Natalie circled from the waist and tossed her head back, leaping once and then again, spinning when she felt the need to spin. Ana's breath caught in her throat at the beauty, skill, and sheer inhibition in front of her now. What she wouldn't give to be that free.

The music cut out and Natalie walked back to her as if it were the most natural thing in the world. "You're up, Russian."

"I don't know how to do what you just did," Ana said defensively and crossed her arms.

"Of course you don't. That was all me. But you'll make it your own and the result will be all you. You're one of the best dancers in the country, aren't you? Time to prove it."

Ana stared at her, taken back by the comment, the challenge, but familiar enough with Natalie not to be totally offended. If anything, the thrown gauntlet had inspired her competitive side. "Wow. Okay. Fine. If that's how you want to play it, stand back." Ana moved to the center of the room, deciding to have fun with this assignment if it killed her. She struck a dramatic pose, which pulled a laugh from Natalie.

"Oh, now that's a 'fuck you' stance if I've ever seen one."

"Put the music on, California. I don't have all night."

"Yes, Queen." Moments later, Ana put herself to the test, doing everything in her power not to restrict her body, her mind, or her feelings. She let the music carry her and pushed herself further and further as the song, some sort of grunge rock, played to its conclusion. Ana was out of breath, but feeling lighter, as if she'd released a huge amount of tension. "How was that?" she asked.

"Color me impressed," Natalie said, joining her on the floor. "Where did you go? Tell me where your head was."

"I didn't *go* anywhere per se. In fact, I tried not to think too much."

Natalie nodded. "Did you know that George Balanchine once said that music was the most important thing in his ballets? Music first followed by artistry. Technique took a distant third."

"He did say that. What's your point?"

Natalie took a step into Ana, energized. "Think about it. He wanted the audience listening closely to the music and feeling something," she placed her hand over Ana's heart, "right here. I can feel your heart beating." Silence reigned in the studio, and Ana's eyes fluttered closed and she swallowed against the sensation of Natalie's hand on her chest. Natalie's voice dipped to quiet. "Now I want to know what it's saying. And so does everyone who watches you, Ana, because you're that good. You figure out how to tell them the story and there will be no stopping you. You're the best dancer I've ever seen."

"Do you really believe that?"

"I do. Now you just have to learn how to emote. There's a moment when you take your place on that stage when we're all on the edges of our seats waiting to see what it is you're going to do." Natalie dropped her hand and took a step back. Ana instantly lamented the loss of contact. "Do you remember that day in rehearsal where you slayed it? Got everyone all excited with how awesome you were?"

Ana ran her fingers through her hair. "And then never pulled it off again? Yeah, sounds familiar."

"Now, that was a performance. Something had distracted you. You said you're not sure what it was, but I think you know."

"You do, huh?" Ana reflected on the very specific thing that had carried her through that performance.

"I do. What was it? We can use it."

"I'd rather not go into it. In fact, it was very—"

"What are you afraid of exactly?" Natalie's eyes flashed and Ana took a defensive step back.

"I'm not afraid."

"Then tell me."

"It's not going to change anything."

"So it can't hurt to tell me."

"Fine. It was you. Happy?" Natalie's eyes widened, but only briefly as Ana continued. "Everything about you drove me crazy that day. You were late. You were chatty. You were...beautiful. You still are." Natalie's lips parted in surprise at that last part. Ana had no idea where she'd derived the courage to confess what she just had. Maybe this little exercise had loosened more than just her dancing inhibitions.

Natalie opened her mouth and closed it before settling on a sentence. "I didn't realize you'd—"

"Hey, it's okay. Let's not make it awkward. We don't have to talk about it."

"No, we don't," Natalie said solemnly. "Try it again. For me? The ending variation."

Natalie hadn't pulled away. She hadn't run screaming from the room at Ana's admission and that was something, wasn't it? Her dignity had survived.

"You want me to think of you while I dance?"

Natalie nodded. "It worked the last time."

"And you're going to watch?"

"If you'll let me."

Ana walked to the center of the room. She mentally removed each and every proverbial barricade and let her thoughts, feelings, and emotions, everything inspired by Natalie, flood through her. The end result left Ana feeling bare and on display. However, when the music started, she held nothing back. She didn't tap into the anger as she had for Natalie that first time. Instead she focused on the feelings that had taken root and only seemed to grow with each passing day she and Natalie spent together. That, coupled with the fact that she could feel Natalie's gaze on her while she danced, had the whole thing happening in a bit of a blur. One thing was for sure, she gave all of herself to the performance. As a result, she lost track of technique, pacing, and even what day of the week it was, which contributed to her surprise when she spun her way across the floor and into Natalie, who caught her and held her there, looking every bit as surprised as Ana felt.

"Whoa," Natalie said quietly. "I've got you."

The air around them hung heavy and Ana felt the flush hit her cheek. "Thanks."

Ana briefly registered faraway voices in the hall. Still, neither of them moved. Instead, they stood there. Shallow breathing, locked eyes, and the fast-paced thud of their hearts combined to create the most charged moment Ana could remember ever having experienced.

Her hands on Natalie's shoulders, Natalie's nestled at her waist.

Ana was transfixed. Natalie looked sexy as hell standing there, her hair tousled around her shoulders, her lips full and parted just a touch. Ana could barely stand it.

But it was when Natalie's eyes dropped to her mouth that Ana's stomach clenched in that uncomfortable, wonderful, thrilling way. That's when she knew: Natalie felt it, too. And that was all it took for her to incline her head and claim Natalie's mouth in a kiss every bit as gratifying as she'd imagined. More so. Natalie let out a low murmur of satisfaction before slanting her mouth over Ana's and kissing her back with a ferocity that had Ana grappling for conscious thought, equilibrium, anything to ground her. Instead, she reveled in the softness, the taste, the perfection of Natalie's mouth. Better than she had imagined. Better than she'd even thought possible. Natalie's hands moved from the sides of her waist to around it, hauling Ana closer, their curves melding in a manner that sent an erotic bolt right to Ana's center and had her aching for more. Natalie kissed her eagerly, skillfully, until her lips granted entrance, culminating in a delicious collision of tongues.

Finally.

How had they gone so long without doing this?

Ana eased her hands into Natalie's hair and heard a sweet surrendering sigh before realizing, distantly, that it had come from her. Upon hearing it, Natalie slowed her movements to stillness and stepped out of Ana's grasp. She gently took hold of Ana's wrists and didn't let go as they each struggled for air. Finally releasing Ana altogether, Natalie gave her head a little shake, as if waking from a dream. "What was that?" she asked.

"I just…I had to," Ana said, realizing it wasn't much of an answer at all. Natalie touched her lips as if to hold in the taste of Ana. "I guess I lost my mind for a minute."

"Well, it was quite a minute."

Ana had to smile. "It was." But she was a realist. This was Natalie she was talking about. Not only was Ana's showbiz rule number one not to get involved with people you worked with (she'd learned that the hard way), but Natalie was her complete opposite in every way, and involved with someone else to boot. Still, there stood Natalie, looking like everything Ana never knew she wanted, and logic didn't seem to stop Ana from the wanting.

Because God, she *wanted.*

Was it really that crazy, after all? The idea of her and Natalie?

"We should probably get going," Natalie said, answering that question. Her gaze brushed the ground uncomfortably.

"Oh, definitely. I'm sorry. I didn't mean to keep you." Her defenses flared, and she did everything in her power to distance herself emotionally from what she'd just experienced. After all, Natalie clearly wanted her to.

"Ana, wait. Don't pull away like that. This is not a rejection."

Ana blew out a breath because it sure as hell felt like one. "Okay. Then what is it?"

Natalie held her gaze. "This is us, taking a moment to regroup. I need a time-out, and maybe you do, too."

Ana nodded. "A time-out would be great."

Natalie sighed. "Your voice is doing that calm, polite, closed-off thing, and I don't want that from you right now. In fact, I can't stand it."

"What do you want, then?" It was a legitimate question that had Ana feeling every bit exposed.

"I think that's what the time-out is for. Do you understand?"

"I understand that you think I'm a horrible idea and need a time-out to figure out how to tell me. I can't fault you for that, because I probably am." She attempted to pass Natalie on the way to collect her dance bag, but Natalie sidestepped, blocking her path.

"Stop for a second, please?" She cupped Ana's face, and at the contact, Ana softened. Ached even. She was in serious trouble here. "That's not at all what I'm doing. I think we're…complicated. Give me a chance to sort it out. *Please*."

It was the "please" that got her. "Whatever you need."

"You've become important to me, and I want to be as honest with you as I can."

"And you want time to find that honesty," Ana stated.

"Something like that."

Ana nodded. "Okay."

"As for the ballet, that's all you have to do," Natalie said, gesturing to the floor. "What you did a few minutes ago was…overwhelming. In the best way." She moved to the wall where they'd dropped their bags. "You slayed it. Just remember to, uh…stay on top of your spacing." She was rattled, that much Ana could tell. This was new, as she'd never seen Natalie rattled about anything.

"I owe you one. That's for sure." She joined Natalie, retrieving her bag, and they headed out together as always.

"That's not true," Natalie said. "You did the same for me, remember? We're square."

"Square," Ana repeated, knowing things between them felt anything but squared off.

They made their way down the hall and to the front entrance of the building in silence. Natalie was avoiding eye contact, which had Ana doing what she could to right them again. "You've come a long way, you know that? You're different now."

"In what way?" Natalie asked.

"To start with, you're here an hour before the rest of us each day, which is just as shocking as it is impressive."

"Well, I keep hearing this one girl's voice in my head. Something about putting in the work and not relying on talent alone. So that's what

I'm doing, putting in the work. It's actually great advice. She's pretty smart, this girl."

Ana smiled. "I'll be sure to pass that on. I hear she's—"

"Baby!"

They turned at the sound of the shout. A girl with pink strands in her hair and a stocking cap moved toward them, waving frantically. She had to be, what? Twenty-two years old? Twenty-four max?

Natalie stared, seemingly shocked. But then a smile hit and Ana felt like she'd been punched. "Morgan? Wow. How are you here right now?"

Oh God.

Oh no.

The *girlfriend.*

The realization hit Ana like a speeding train and felt just as brutal. The ecstatic girlfriend flew into Natalie's arms, and Ana forced a smile. "This guy who always comes into the diner gave me his miles. And here I am. Live and in person." The girl, Morgan, wrapped her arms around Natalie's neck and moved in for a kiss that Natalie stepped out of.

"Oh, uh, probably not where I work," she told Morgan lamely and passed Ana a look. Realizing she was in the way there, Ana began looking for an opportune moment to sneak off. "Why didn't you tell me you were coming?"

"It was super last minute," Morgan said, "and oh, I came with Janelle and Harris. They went back to the hotel. But they want to go out with us, so I need to text Janelle that I found you." Morgan began to type into her phone.

Natalie dipped her head to catch Morgan's eye. "Hey. Wait a sec for me, okay? I want to introduce you to my friend, Ana."

"Nice to meet you, Morgan," Ana said, and offered her hand. But Morgan was texting and didn't see the gesture, prompting Ana to eventually abandon the attempt, feeling foolish in the process.

"Cool. Really nice to meet you," Morgan said, glancing briefly from her phone with a smile.

Natalie gestured to Ana. "Ana's a principal dancer with the company and will also be dancing the role of Mira in the show."

"That's the part you're dancing, right?" Morgan said. She took a short break from typing.

"Right. We split the role. I told you, remember?"

"Baby, you tell me a lot. It's hard to remember everything. What I do know is that you're amazing when you dance, which is the important part. Oh, hey," Morgan said to Ana. "O-M-G. You should come out with us tonight, Ana. Janelle and Harris have already found some awesome prospects in the Village, but maybe you guys know some killer clubs since you're here all the time."

First of all, going out with Morgan and Natalie? Because this whole thing wasn't awkward enough? Not going to happen. Second of all, there should be some cosmic rule that anyone over the age of fifteen who said O-M-G would be swallowed up by the Universe. Okay, so now she was entering the land of the petty. Perfect. Ana stole a glance at Natalie, who looked back at her apologetically, and in that moment she felt so unbearably small. "You know, I appreciate the invitation," Ana said to Morgan, "I do. But I think it's best if I head home and let you two spend some time together. I'm kind of an early riser."

"We understand," Natalie said, letting her off the hook.

"It was nice meeting you, Morgan. You guys have fun." She didn't stick around for further conversation, and no one seemed to mind. All Ana knew was that she needed to get out of there, and quick, because the idea of watching Morgan touch and moon over Natalie for one moment longer was about as enticing as swimming lessons in the shark-infested Arctic. She was smarter than that, and an astute practitioner of self-preservation, but damn it, tears were already gathering behind her eyes as she walked. The fact that her heart clenched uncomfortably on the train home was a circumstance she pushed aside. And the longing she felt for a woman already spoken for was best not indulged.

Ana had always been excellent at self-discipline.

So why wasn't any of it working anymore?

Chapter Nine

*P*unce it. *Punce it. Punce it. Punce it. Punce it.* The nonstop beat from the DJ booth bled through the club floor and vibrated through the bottom of Natalie's shoes. The sensation was one she'd often enjoyed and identified with good times from her past.

Not tonight.

Her emotions swirled, and the loud music and moving lights only added to the off-kilter sensation she couldn't quite shake.

To say Natalie was floored to see Morgan, to have her standing there on the steps at Lincoln Center, was an understatement. But the reunion also had her emotions warring. On one hand, she was over the moon to see Morgan, having missed her all this time. On the other, her life was wildly different of late and she didn't know how to be the person she was when she left LA. Too much had changed, and wouldn't Morgan notice that? And then there was Ana and the moment between them in the studio, which she hadn't yet fully processed. Ana had kissed her, something she never would have predicted from Ana's well-established aversion to risk taking. The kiss itself had been off the charts and affected her still, just playing it back. She gave her head an admonishing shake, knowing full well she couldn't go down that road right now. Instead, she tucked the memory away for examination later.

"So do you want to change before we meet Janelle?" Morgan had asked just after Ana left them.

Natalie glanced down at her jeans, leotard, and hoodie. "I have a shirt in my bag I can wear. But, hey, I don't know that I can hit up a bunch of clubs tonight, Morg. We open in a week and this show is a pretty big deal."

"I thought you hated ballet," Morgan said almost teasingly as she thumbed Natalie's zipper.

"Yeah, well, I'm not saying it's my go-to genre of dance, but it can actually be really beautiful. This ballet in particular is—"

"You're really cute when you get all dreamy looking like that," Morgan said, clearly not listening. "The opening sounds really cool, though."

"About that, I actually thought you were coming next week so you could be there with me on opening night."

"I know, but the timing didn't work out. I'm dying to see you dance all prim and proper, and I will soon, but there's this warehouse Ryan rented out for next Saturday. You remember him, right? From the diner? It's like this foam party and I volunteered to help out with it, work the door, and I didn't want to cancel on him last minute."

"No. I get it. Foam party."

"*Foam party*," Morgan repeated with emphasis, tugging on Natalie's hoodie. Well, how could she expect to compete with that? That's when it hit Natalie how far apart their lives were becoming, even after only a few months. What did that say for what lay ahead? How were they supposed to build on a relationship if they were on two completely separate paths? "We should get going," Morgan said. "Janelle is already at this one place she says is tight. Hot people everywhere."

Natalie drew a breath and made a decision. She should enjoy this time with Morgan, but not at the expense of the work she'd put forth. "Just one stop, okay? I need to be up early tomorrow for rehearsal, and my body is already on fumes."

"One club and then we're out."

Except they weren't.

They hit up Splash in the Meatpacking district where, true to Janelle's word, beautiful people danced to a hypnotic beat. A woman with green hair DJ'd from the tall booth in the corner, and at first, Natalie found herself kicking back and attempting to have fun. She allowed herself two drinks, two more than her new limit when working. She and Morgan kissed and danced and laughed. When Natalie finally checked out her watch, two hours had passed.

"We should head out now," she shouted, which was in fact the only way one could be heard above the music.

Morgan frowned at her. "Already? We just got here." She high-fived Janelle and downed another shot.

"I have class in the morning and then rehearsal, and the day will be a long one. Come back to my place with me? You can see where I live and meet up with Janelle in the morning."

"I just want to dance a little bit more, babe, okay? Then we'll go. I love New York!" And with that Morgan danced her way into the throngs until Natalie lost sight of her. With each passing minute, the fun fell away a little bit more. By one a.m., Morgan was flat-out drunk.

"Why aren't you having funnnn with us?" Morgan slurred in her ear. She hung on Natalie's arm and hopped a little to the now-obnoxious music.

"It was fun two hours ago, not so much anymore. Can we go?"

"You should go," Morgan said, pushing her away. "I'm staying here. How often am I in New York? I want to experience this."

"Over spending time with me? We haven't even had a real conversation yet."

"We can do that tomorrow. You go home. I'm gonna play."

"Are you mad at me?" Natalie asked, though she wasn't sure if it would stop her from leaving at this point.

Morgan balked. "Pshhh. No." And then laughter. Drunken laughter. "You need your dancer sleep. Me and Janelle want to hit up one last place that the bartender told us about. I'll crash at her hotel so I won't wake you or whatever. It's cool."

"Are you sure I can't convince you to—"

"You look hot tonight," Morgan said, dancing off into the masses once again.

Well, fuck. This was not how she wanted the evening to play itself out. Honestly, she was hurt that Morgan didn't want to spend time with her. But then again, Morgan had always been a pleasure seeker. It was one of the reasons they'd had so much fun together.

But fun only went so far, she was finding.

Natalie waited around another twenty minutes in the hopes of saying good night, but when neither Morgan nor Janelle ever emerged from the crowd, she reluctantly took her leave and hopped a cab home.

Natalie was exhausted, sad, and in possession of very few coping skills. Her limbs hurt, but her heart hurt, too. She paused outside Ana's door, knowing she'd be asleep at this hour. She smiled at Ana's strict adherence to living well and getting a good night's sleep. That smile faded when she thought of the way she'd held Ana earlier that night and stared into those luminous, and frustrating, blue eyes. The memory had her heart executing the strangest little beat, and when she waited for sleep to claim her at long last, it was Ana's face she saw when she closed her eyes, and Ana that she thought of as she drifted off into slumber.

❖

Natalie stirred her coffee and she stared out the window of Andrew's Coffee Shop for any sign of Morgan. They'd made plans via text to have breakfast before Natalie headed into work, but so far Morgan was twenty minutes late. As she waited, Natalie wrestled with the butterflies in her stomach and the confession that bubbled inside her. The feelings she had for Ana were not going away, and she'd be lying to herself and Morgan if she didn't fess up to them and to the kiss they'd shared. It was the right thing to do.

"You sure you don't want to order something while you wait, hon?" the sassy waitress asked. She had the gruff voice and the accent down pat. Very New York.

"No, she'll be here. Kind of a late night, I think."

The woman raised her eyebrow. "I'll put on some stronger coffee, then."

Another ten minutes passed, but then there she was, wearing leggings and a comfortable sweatshirt. Morgan slid into the booth across from Natalie and regarded her grumpily. "I don't know how you get up at this hour and manage to live."

Natalie smiled. "It's eight thirty-five."

"Exactly my point." Morgan wordlessly held out her coffee cup to the waitress.

"This is the strong stuff," the woman told her. "Drink that."

Morgan passed her a don't-be-creepy look and nodded. They placed their breakfast orders and sat in silence a few moments.

"You missed a memorable time last night," Morgan said.

"I'm sure I did."

She sat back in the booth, dejected at the fact that Natalie didn't seem interested in asking for more details. "So what's going on with you anyway? You're, I don't know, off in your own world."

"Right. I realize it probably seems that way, but it's more like I'm focused in a way I never have been. I wanted to see you, Morgan, but last night wasn't what I had in mind."

"What? You're too good for the club scene now that you've been officially discovered?"

Okay, ouch. "No. It's not that at all. But if I want my body to do all the things I'm asking of it, I need to get rest and try to not get shitfaced before an important rehearsal."

Morgan shook her head. "It's whatever. You used to dance and party back home. It was fine with you then."

"I need to tell you something." She met Morgan's gaze, and took a deep breath. "I kissed someone. It was just one time, but it happened. I shouldn't have while we're together. It was wrong of me and I wanted us to talk about it."

Morgan took a moment and Natalie waited for whatever anger or sadness would come her way. "I slept with someone," Morgan said instead. "A couple times. If we're doing the honesty thing right now."

"I'm sorry—you what?"

"You were gone, and…things happened. It's only natural. People aren't meant to be alone."

Natalie turned her head to the window and absently stared at the foot traffic as her mind struggled to catch up. Men and women dashed to their respective offices, some holding coffee, some expensive briefcases. All while she sat there trying to understand her own life. It should hurt, what Morgan had just said to her.

But it didn't.

Shocking? Yes. Disappointing? Sure.

But painful? Not really. Not in the way it should be.

That had to say something, right?

"So, what are you thinking?" Morgan asked. "Because maybe we should just chalk this up to long distance and life or whatever. Go our separate ways now."

"Wait. Are you breaking up with me?" Natalie asked, nonplussed. Morgan was breaking up with *her*? Seriously?

"I think it's for the best, babe. We're headed different places. It's going to hurt for a while. But eventually, you'll start to feel like yourself again." Morgan reached across the booth and patted Natalie's arm.

"Thanks," she said, still mystified.

"You'll bounce back." She raised her hand and signaled the waitress.

In the midst of this circus, Natalie smiled at the woman, who kicked her hip out and barked at Morgan. "You need something, hon?" She felt lighter somehow, as if she'd dodged a really scary bullet.

"I'll take that breakfast wrap to go. Oh, we'll need the check. You're good with handling that, yeah?"

Natalie laughed at the audacity. "Of course."

She replayed the whole series of events in her head as she walked the eight blocks to work, still not quite believing them. One thing she didn't do was allow herself to think about what this could potentially mean for her and Ana and the electricity between them. There would be time for all of that down the road. In the meantime, they had a ballet to perfect. In the face of that, they should focus on their friendship first, right? Table the rest.

Only, when she arrived onstage for the run through and saw Ana looking gorgeous in the slinky costume for the second movement, the slope got a little more slippery. "Hey," she said to Ana, as a costume mistress made work of the ten hooks down the back of the short dress.

Ana turned at the sound of her voice, but there was a softness missing in the way she looked at Natalie. Her guard was up now, and that stung. "Hi. Good morning."

"You look great."

"Oh. Thanks. You're next."

Natalie nodded and then nodded some more, not sure what words to assemble to make life feel natural and breezy. Should she bring up the breakup at some point? Or was that a presumptuous and weird thing to do? When normal banter failed her, Natalie took her leave. However, she was always aware of Ana's location in the room, a detail she couldn't ignore if she wanted to.

By the end of the day, it was clear. Yes, sir. Anastasia Mikhelson somehow commanded nearly all of her thoughts. And Natalie could project rules and best practices upon their relationship all she wanted, but the reality was, she was done for.

Chapter Ten

I'm not sure I get the point of the bar if I'm not actually going to drink," Ana told Jason as they arrived at McKenna's just after eight.

"It's five days before opening, and rehearsal is coming to a close. It's hard to be inside a theatre twelve hours a day," he told her.

"So?"

"So we need to do something other than rehearse. And I have to say, you're getting better at the whole social life thing. Gotta give you credit."

"Thanks."

"Anytime."

She put a hand on his arm as he moved to the door. "But before we go in, do we know who's going to be in there? Specifically?"

He studied her. "Is this one of those *Mean Girls* questions? Should I find Helen, because I'm a dude and not sure I'll live up."

Ana studied him. "What are you talking about? It was a simple question."

"Girl drama. I'm guessing you and Nat are in some kind of fight, because you're acting all weird around each other and you want to know if *she's* in there before we head in. Am I right? Do I need to find Helen?"

She walloped him in the stomach with the back of her hand. "No, Presumptuous, we don't need to call Helen. And we're not fighting. We're fine. Do I not look fine?"

"You look hot. You always do. And now that you mention it, let's get out of here. Go somewhere on our own."

"No way. I'm here to socialize and unwind like other people do. Let's go."

"Her majesty has spoken. After you." Jason opened the door for her and gestured inside.

Ana scanned the bar and found the section at the far end where the other dancers had congregated in a grouping of tables. Spotting the two of them, several hands raised, beckoning them over. "I spot a leading lady," Theo said. He was a principal dancer working on another of the ballets that would go up alongside *Aftermath*. He kissed Ana's cheek and offered Jason a high five up top. "So who's the better Mira?" he asked Jason boldly, beer in hand, clearly aware of Ana's presence.

Without missing a beat, Jason studied the ceiling, pointing at the tiny cracks as if he'd discovered the most interesting pattern in the world.

In an attempt to save him, she pointed at Theo. "You'll just have to watch both shows and make your own decision."

"Two beautiful ladies make that an easy request."

Out of the corner of her eye, Ana spotted Natalie across the way, chatting with some of the younger members of the *corps*.

"Plus, that means you get to see me twice," Jason said. "I'm pretty easy on the eyes myself." He went up on his toes as best he could, imitating a traditional ballerina.

"Well, you can't win 'em all." Theo grimaced, earning himself a jab in the shoulder from Jason, who found himself in a headlock as a result.

"Maker's Mark, Everclear, Diet Coke? What am I buying you?" Jason asked her, once freed.

"Actually, I'll get this round." He raised an eyebrow and she smiled proudly, flashing a twenty. A couple of the company members whistled at her playful sashay to the bar. Okay, so the drink display was a pathetic move to see if she could slap a Band-Aid on things between her and Natalie, who sat at a table not too far from the bar. It had been a few days since Morgan had made her appearance and then headed home. She and Natalie had tiptoed around each other since, speaking politely in the course of rehearsal and even trying to land a joke now and again. The joke thing hadn't really worked, which was a shame because she missed the laughs they'd shared.

The friendship felt...broken. And she, for one, needed to do something about it.

As she waited for service, she glanced back at Natalie, who was caught up in a conversation. She had her hair pulled back on the sides today, which offered an extra glimpse of her neck. *Damn it.* There should be no neck-looking if she wanted to fix things. She rolled her shoulders. Friendship Mode in effect. A second glance showed that Natalie was now laughing at something one of the guys said, and this time Ana couldn't look away. Natalie really did have the most amazing smile, and when she leveled it on you, all bets were off. That was something a friend was allowed to think about another friend, right? That's all they were, friends. All they would ever be. Natalie hadn't so much as looked at her since she'd walked into the bar.

"Uh, hello?" the bartender said, loud enough to suggest that this probably hadn't been the first time.

"Oh, sorry." Ana snapped to attention. "A Diet Coke and Old Fashioned, please."

"Coming up," the bartender said. He was an older guy—most likely the owner.

She watched as he mixed Jason's drink and she slid the twenty onto the bar after he delivered the final product. She turned to go and found herself face-to-face with Natalie, who smiled.

"Do you think his last name is McKenna?" she asked quietly.

Ana smiled. "I was just wondering the same thing myself."

"I'll find out," she said, stepping up to the bar. "Take one for the team."

"The team will be, uh, waiting for a verdict." *Smooth, Ana. Really smooth.*

Natalie nodded, but she looked about as unsettled as Ana felt.

What was happening right now? Why were they so *on* with each other?

"Indulging a little tonight?" Natalie inclined her head toward the Old Fashioned.

"Not until we're open. This is for Jason. You know me."

"I do," Natalie said in all seriousness.

Silence. Ana had no idea what to say, and decided to abandon ship before it got any more awkward. "I'll let you get a drink."

"A ginger ale." She shrugged. "Since we're not open yet."

"I'm impressed. Enjoy."

"You, too."

She returned to Jason and Theo, who were now deciding whether the Cowboys or the Bills were worse. She smiled and chimed in, just as Audrey arrived and chastised them for being boring and clichéd. But all the while, she never really lost track of Natalie, including her departure from the bar a short while later. While part of Ana wanted to walk home with her, find a way to make conversation, she knew her efforts at normalcy would once again fall flat.

An hour later, when the bar started to get rowdy, Ana took her own leave.

"I'll walk you," Jason said, and shook hands with his buddies. Theo whispered something conspiratorially in his ear and Jason nodded, glancing in Ana's direction. Sooner or later, she should probably have a talk with him. Make things clear. Tonight, she didn't have the energy.

"You doing okay?" he asked as they waited on the light to change.

"I've had better days," she told him candidly.

"This is the Natalie thing again, huh?"

She shoved her hands into her coat pockets in frustration and stared at the Do Not Walk sign. "It is. This is most definitely a Natalie thing."

"If it helps, I think it's on her and not you."

She paused as they made it to the other end of the street. "What makes you say that?"

"She's moodier, quieter. Audrey says the breakup is most likely weighing on her. Give her time. She'll come around."

"What breakup?" She asked. He had her full attention now.

"Apparently, she and her girlfriend broke up. Something about not really clicking the way they should."

Ana took a moment, wondering why Natalie hadn't said a word to her about it. *Because she doesn't want you getting the wrong idea after your kissing ambush*, her brain supplied. "I'm sorry. What?" He had said something, but she couldn't hear over the roar of her wounded pride.

"Lunch. Tomorrow. Want to grab some with me?"

"Yeah, sure," she said distantly as her gaze landed squarely on the steps in front of their building. Natalie looked up from where she sat as they approached.

"Hey, you two," she said a little wearily. "Long day, huh?"

"Killer," Jason said.

Ana only nodded and met Natalie's gaze.

Jason looked from Ana to Natalie and back again before making a decision. "I'll leave you two to...chat. Good night."

"Good night," they each said absently.

Not knowing whether it was better to sit or stand, Ana held her ground. Neither one of them said anything, so Ana decided to just jump in. "You didn't tell me about Morgan."

"I didn't? Been a busy week, I guess."

"You know you didn't," Ana said gently, knowing this was potentially a difficult topic. "Are you doing okay?"

"About the breakup? Yeah, I'm good. Morgan's good. Just wasn't really one of those meant-to-be things."

Ana nodded and smiled politely at a couple passing on the street. "And otherwise?"

Natalie blew out a breath and stared straight ahead. "That's trickier."

"Why is that?"

"Because I miss us."

Relief flared and Ana took this opportunity to have an honest exchange. "I miss us, too. It's been so strange the last couple of days. I've tried to be your friend again, but it's different now and awkward and—"

"Totally agree."

"I'm glad. You don't understand how glad."

"So I guess what I'm saying is that I don't think it's a good idea."

"That what's not a good idea."

"Our friendship. It doesn't work, and I'm tired of trying to force it."

"Oh. Okay." The words hit her hard. Ana squeezed the railing and climbed the stairs leading to the building. She was done. She had to be. She'd put herself out there and actually opened up to someone and what had it gotten her? Crushed. Beyond. "If you don't want to be friends, we don't have to be. I understand."

"Would you wait a sec?"

"For what? All you had to—"

But she didn't get to finish, because Natalie grabbed her by the wrist and pulled her in for a kiss she would spend the next week reliving…all authoritative and demanding and sexy as hell. When they came up for air, Ana gave her head a little shake to clear it.

"You're so damn stubborn," Natalie said, quieter this time.

"But you said—"

"I said we couldn't be friends anymore, because I tried, Ana, really hard to be your friend. But now that I know what it's like to kiss you, friendship wasn't really an option any longer."

Ana blinked at her, taking in the words that lifted her up to a new and terrifying height. "So there might be more…um, kissing?"

Natalie leaned in and hovered just shy of Ana's mouth before softly answering the question. "I hope so. It's up to you, I guess." As close as she was, Natalie didn't kiss Ana, but instead she waited, so very close. Ana's stomach twisted in anticipation, not to mention other parts of her. She dipped her head slightly and met Natalie's lips again, tentatively this time, until the rush of heat that came with kissing Natalie assaulted her. All things halted—sound, awareness, life as she knew it. As she stood on those steps kissing the girl she'd been dreaming of kissing, Ana floated somewhere close to heaven.

"We should probably get off the street," Natalie said, smiling against Ana's mouth.

"Yeah. I guess we should."

Natalie led the way to the elevator, but as they stood there, waiting for it to arrive, the impatience overtook them and they were kissing again. She wasn't even sure whose fault it was. The door to the elevator at last slid open and Natalie walked her into it. With Ana's back against the elevator wall, the make-out session continued. Fireworks. That's what the whole experience felt like. Something powerful climbed steadily within her and made Ana feel like she just might explode in the most awesome way. She couldn't get enough. Kissing Natalie should come with a warning label, "potential addiction ahead." And God, Natalie herself had a wild streak, and Ana loved that about her. Normally, Ana would *never* kiss someone in public, on the street or in an elevator. She wasn't sure she recognized herself, and that was surprisingly okay. Natalie's kiss became more insistent, deeper, hotter, and Ana matched her every step of the way.

Distantly, she registered the sound of a bell, but it was in the way and she shoved the recognition aside. Natalie's hands slipped beneath the back of her sweater and touched the skin there, and the sensation did crazy things to Ana.

"We seem to be interrupting," a male voice said, followed by a female chuckle of appreciation. "We can wait for the next one."

"Like hell we will," said the female.

Ana pulled her mouth away and found the elevator door standing open with Audrey and a guy she recognized from the building gazing at them in amusement. Natalie turned and smiled at the pair as if running into old friends at the supermarket.

"Hey, Audrey," she said. "And you must be Superman?"

"This is Tad," Audrey told her. "He lives on the second floor."

"Nice to meet you," Ana said.

"Likewise." Tad pointed at the panel on the wall. "Is it possible that you two forgot to push the button for your floor?"

Ana looked to the panel on the wall. That they had. She gingerly selected the seven and stepped to the side as Audrey and Tad joined them.

"Nice night," she said as the elevator climbed, and then cringed at how ridiculously contrived she sounded.

"You two seemed to be enjoying it," Audrey said gleefully and elbowed Natalie in the ribs while never taking her eyes off the climbing numbers on the readout. "We're at seven," she reported as the elevator came to a halt. "Unless you guys wanted to ride around some more."

"No, we're good. Aren't we good?" she asked Natalie. Why was she talking so fast?

"We're good," Natalie said, sounding so much cooler than she did. "See you tomorrow, Audrey. It was nice meeting you, Superman-Tad. You two have a nice night."

"Yours will be hard to top," Audrey called through the closing elevator doors.

They walked in silence down the hall. Ana noted that everything still felt uneven, strange, but in a hopeful, the-world-has-possibilities-now kind of way. However, Mayday! She didn't know the protocol here. Was there a chart she could consult about whether or not to invite Natalie inside? Did Google provide that kind of on-the-spot insight? They should just say good night and go their separate ways, right? That was more than likely what Google would say, or that irritable woman on her phone. Yep. That was what they should do in order to maintain control of this thing.

"We should make hot chocolate with marshmallows," Natalie said to Ana when they arrived at their doors. "I'm a big fan of cocoa when it's chilly out." Her hands were on Ana's waist and her thumbs subtly moved up and down over her ribs. Torturous and unfair!

She was already losing her resolve. "You seem to like my coffee cups."

What?

Who says that?

Why was she the lamest person in New York?

"Well, they have little dancers on them," Natalie said, stepping farther into her space.

"How can one resist little dancers?"

"It would be hard."

"Harder than resisting you right now?" She placed a kiss on Ana's neck that almost had her sinking to her knees. Holy Mikhail Baryshnikov.

"This is the problem," Ana managed to murmur.

"Tell me," Natalie said, refocusing on Ana's neck, taking one hot nibble at a time. Ana was on fire and caught between her head and libido, which seemed to be in a war for the record books, and she didn't know which the hell to root for. But, no, she had to stay strong here.

"You know I'm attracted to you. That's not a secret," she began.

"The feeling is mutual," Natalie said, straightening. She smiled, and that was so not fair, because Ana loved her mouth.

"But you're also my friend," Ana explained, "And, um, I don't have a ton of those, which means I want to do this right."

"Then we will."

"Thereby, I can't invite you in tonight as much as I may want to. God," she said, kissing Natalie one more time. "And as you can tell, I would want to."

"So inviting me in is code for sex?" Natalie asked with an amused eyebrow raise.

Ana gave her shoulder a little shove. "Stop it. You know that if I took you in there—"

"That I'd have you naked in under ten minutes."

Ana closed her eyes against the rush of desire that crashed into her at those words. "Yes," she managed after a purposeful swallow. "That's exactly why."

"You would rather wait," Natalie stated simply. "As in minutes? We're talking minutes, aren't we?" She was grinning that overconfident Natalie grin that Ana had grown rather fond of. "I'm kidding," Natalie said, finally holding her palms up in surrender. "And I get it. We can reconvene at another time for…inviting in."

"Understand this is a decision I'm probably going to regret as soon as I walk into that apartment."

Natalie nodded. "I'm not sure it's my vote, but it makes sense with everything I know about you. A cold shower, and I'm good." She took a step back, looking like a sad little puppy.

"This is not a rejection," Ana said, smiling at the adorable display happening in front of her.

Natalie laughed softly and covered her heart with her hand. "I see what you did there. That was good, the callback."

"I thought you might like it."

"Can I at least kiss you good night?" Natalie asked. "Just a little kiss and I'll go in there. I promise." She gestured to the door to her apartment.

Ana looked skyward as if there were even a decision to be made, when in fact there was not. "I think that will be okay."

Whether the kiss Natalie left her with was designed to make her regret her decision even more than she already did was unclear. The reality of its effect however, was crystal. As Natalie pulled her lips away, Ana held on to the doorway for support while her skin thrummed and her thighs vibrated. That kiss had her aching for more. Instead of asking for just that, she looked on in rapt interest as Natalie strolled the ten feet to her own apartment door and disappeared behind it.

"What just happened?" Ana whispered to the hallway. She touched her very swollen lips and marveled at how quickly things could change.

"I can still hear you," she heard Natalie say from inside her apartment, followed by quiet laughter.

Perfect. Ana shook her head at herself, always the epitome of cool—that was her. It didn't matter, though. She let herself into her own apartment and took a seat on her sofa to continue marveling. Things like tonight didn't just happen to Ana. She'd never been that girl. But tonight she was, and it was an evening she'd never forget.

Chapter Eleven

I'll take the cheddar bacon burger," Jason told the waitress at Five Napkin. "Extra sweet potato fries and a side of the vinegar slaw." They'd snagged a table by the window at the trendy burger joint frequented by a handful of company members at the lunch rush.

Ana handed her menu to the waitress. "Chef salad with chicken for me, dressing on the side."

The waitress nodded and disappeared into the kitchen as Jason balked at Ana. "I don't know how you can do that. This place receives rave write-ups for their burgers, yet you still hold strong."

"Welcome to being female in the professional world of ballet. I'd kill for your metabolism, Jase, but I wasn't born with that kind of luck. I eat like you and I'm back in the *corps*, at best."

"Whatever. You look great. Beyond. You could indulge in a cheeseburger now and again. The ballet gods will allow it."

"I can. And I will. But it won't happen until after we're open, and then I will enjoy every damn bite in celebration."

"Fair enough." He grinned at her and sat back against the booth. "You didn't remember we were having lunch today."

"I did, too," she told him in defense. "Just not entirely, is all."

"I asked you last night, just as we walked up to your building."

Ah, yes. The moment she saw Natalie sitting there, lost and confused and gorgeous. No wonder she'd gone into automatic conversation pilot. She smiled, reflecting on what had been a great day of rehearsal thus far. She'd gotten to watch Natalie dance the show, and watching Natalie dance had become one of her absolute favorite activities. Not to mention, it gave her left foot a rest. The stolen looks she and Natalie passed here and there were a bonus on the day that had her a little bit on cloud nine. Plus the teasing was back. God, she'd missed the teasing.

She gave her head a shake. "I must have been distracted or something. But I'm here now and happy we're doing this. We should do one-on-one stuff more often. Like, partner maintenance."

"That's actually what I wanted to talk to you about."

"Scheduling lunches?"

"Go on a date with me."

Wait. That sounded like a different thing entirely.

"As in a real date. I pick you up. We go out on the town. You can choose where, and we see where it goes. No pressure."

The way he was staring at her now had her heart in her throat. She didn't want to hurt Jason. He was her friend, and her work husband, but at the same time, she had to be honest. "You mean a romantic date?" Ana asked. She wasn't stupid. She knew what he was asking, but the question bought her a little time.

"Well, yeah. Probably not a secret that I've had a thing for you since the beginning of time. I happen to think we'd be good together, Ana. We are in every other aspect of life. You trust me. I trust you. See? Good for each other." He slid his hand into hers, which rested on the table. "So what do you say?"

"We are good for each other. You're right." Oh God, how was she going to say this? Here went nothing. "But I'm not sure that the same... spark is there for me."

He blinked back at her, and her heart squeezed painfully in her chest. "You're not sure?" He said the words as if they didn't seem quite possible.

She shook her head. "You're great, Jase. The best. And I know you're going to find the perfect girl for you, but I don't think I'm her."

"You don't *think*," he said, seizing the lifeline. "So there's a chance. That's all I'm asking for, Ana. A chance to show you what we could be like together."

"It's not that. I *know* I'm not the perfect girl," she said delicately. "It's early, so I hesitate to even say this, but I'm sort of involved. In a way."

A combination of mystification and annoyance crossed his features in succession. "Since when?"

"I guess if we were going to pinpoint the exact moment—"

"I heard someone got some face sucking done in the elevator last night," Helen whispered, passing their table with Audrey, followed shortly by Boomer and Marcus, who were apparently back in love for the ninth time. To oblige Helen's comment, they made saucy kissy faces in a move that reminded Ana of the sixth grade. They meant well, though, and she wasn't going to let anything kill her buzz.

Except maybe breaking Jason's heart. That part, she could do without.

She turned back to him. He looked struck by this newest information, and then a thought seemed to flash through his mind. "No way," he said, struggling with the timeline of events. "You were with Natalie last I left you. You didn't have time to suck face."

"Right," Ana said purposefully, even pointedly. "I was *with Natalie.*"

"You made out with *Natalie* in an elevator?" He said it as a joke, but it only took a moment for understanding to settle. When it did, he didn't seem thrilled, but she didn't expect him to be. If anything, she hoped he'd find a way to understand.

Ana studied him with sympathy. "I don't want to hurt you, Jason, but she's starting to matter to me. I didn't see it coming any more than you did."

"You two drive each other crazy. I've watched it on the daily."

"That hasn't changed. She still drives me crazy, but there's something to that, I think. It's part of it. I wish I knew how better to explain."

He shook his head as if to say *unbelievable.* "You know what? You didn't *hurt* me. We're fine. Let's just talk about something else."

"Okay," she said, drawing the word out. "What shall we talk about?"

"How's your dad?"

And it went from there. She and Jason discussing anything and everything as they always had, with the exception of the one topic they probably should be talking about. Ana decided to let Jason make that call. Set the pace. In the meantime, she stared longingly at his burger and hoped that in the end, they'd be okay.

❖

Natalie walked offstage to reset herself for the same cue combination they'd run what felt like a hundred times. Technical rehearsals had started on *Aftermath* that afternoon, which, for the dancers, meant a series of long days made up of hurrying and waiting. Technicals, while not Natalie's favorite, were a necessary evil. Because she was less familiar with the process at City Ballet than Ana, Bill Bradshaw thought it would be a better learning experience if she was the one to tech the show. On the plus side, the long waits in between cues did give the two of them some downtime, as Ana was there to learn the timing of each cue as well.

As Natalie exited the stage to the wings, she paused and looked to where Ana had been executing a series of stretches, but instead found her examining her foot. "How's it feeling?" she asked.

Ana looked up at her. "How's what feeling?"

"Your left foot. You're preoccupied with it, and when you think no one's watching, you allow yourself to limp."

"I do not."

"You do so."

But then the music started and Natalie heard her cue, pausing the conversation she intended to revisit. Ana was one of the most stubborn people she'd ever encountered, and it was frustrating as hell. After a few leaps, and a pose-step-pose, followed by the complicated *pas* with Jason, in which she totally botched the flying shoulder sits, Natalie exited one way and he the other.

"Please hold," Priscilla, the stage manager said, pausing the sequence once again while the creative team made some decisions in the house.

Ana was on her feet now and smiled as Natalie approached her in the wings. "I meant to tell you, Jason asked me out earlier today."

"Seriously?" Natalie asked. "What did you say?"

"I said, yes, definitely. I've always wanted to have your babies. When can we start?" Ana passed her a look.

"Touché. How easily did you let him down?"

Ana glanced over her shoulder and lowered her voice just in case. "As easily as I could. He knows about the elevator escapade of last night, though. Audrey has a big mouth."

"Fantastic. That explains why he's super businesslike and short with me today."

"Yeah, I'm sorry about that."

"You know what?" Natalie said, shifting to a whisper when several stagehands passed them admonishing looks. "I'm not. I have no elevator escapade regrets. In fact, I'd escapade in an elevator with you right now."

Ana laughed, but her smile then dimmed to the sexy kind. "Right now. Really?"

Natalie moved until her mouth was very close to Ana's ear, and slid her arm around Ana's waist from behind. *"Right now."*

"We're going again, everyone," came the voice from the heavens. The music started and Ana closed her eyes. "Right now, you have to dance."

"Fuck my life. Excuse me." She danced the sequence yet again, meeting Jason center stage and pretending that he was her mortal enemy, which maybe after everything, he was. Who knew? She also sent up a silent prayer that they could nail down these cues and move forward in the show, because God, this particular section was taxing.

"That was really good," Ana said when Natalie returned. She gestured with her head to the stage. "You kept your chest back like we talked about. You're looking killer out there. Better each day."

"I listen when you tell me things. So, tell me about your foot. I'm all ears."

"There's nothing to discuss."

"Lies. I feel we've avoided it long enough."

Ana sighed. "Fine, Dr. Frederico. It's tender and painful. Nothing I haven't dealt with before."

"How tender are we talking?"

Her face sobered and she seemed to make a decision. "Very."

"Do you need to say something before we open?" Natalie asked, her concern escalating. "You don't want to do serious damage."

"I think the damage is done. It's just a matter of getting through these performances and then I can rest, lay up during the winter season and let it heal."

"I can do more of the shows if it will help. We can talk to Bill."

"No way," Ana said in playful mode. "As if I'm letting you steal more performances. All part of your evil plan."

"And we're going again," Priscilla said over the God mic. *Damn it.*

"This isn't over," she told Ana as the music struck up again.

And it went on like that into the evening, the start and stop, the repetition of sequences until finally just before nine p.m., stage management thanked the company and sent them on their way. By the time Natalie changed and picked up a few notes from Roger, Ana was gone. Though when she returned to the dressing room, she did find a note on her mirror, folded and with her name on the outside.

Have a headache. Headed home early.—Ana
P.S. You looked hot today.

Natalie smiled and tucked the note into her jacket pocket, though worry pricked at the back of her neck as she made her way home. Ana shouldn't be dancing on that injury. Natalie could tell it was more serious than even Ana was letting on. She went through her memory and added up all the winces, extended breaks, and extra wrapping Ana did in relation to her left foot. Things Natalie had written off as routine dancer wear and tear now took on new meaning.

This injury was a big deal.

Her gut was rarely wrong.

Chapter Twelve

This is your thirty-minute call for third ballet of the evening," Priscilla's voice said over the loudspeaker. "This is your thirty-minute call for *Aftermath*." Ana faced herself in the mirror, adjusting a tiny strand of hair that seemed to have a mind of its own. "Don't do this tonight," she told her wayward strand. "I need you to cooperate. There are some very rich people out there who paid big money for their seats, and they're not interested in a ballerina with Don King hair."

It was a big night for Ana. She'd danced in countless ballets with City, but never the lead. There would be write-ups in the paper that night. The critics would review her performance over Natalie's, as she had been the dancer selected to perform on opening night. They were the final ballet of the evening, following two twenty-minute pieces all under the thematic heading of "Underworld."

"Get it together," she said under her breath.

Ana never got nervous. Opening-night jitters or even generic stage fright were conditions that other people dealt with. Certainly not her. She was a pro and always arrived for a given performance at ease and looking forward to seeing the work come together in front of an audience.

Until today, that is. Also known as her worst nightmare.

Ana took a seat at her dressing table, hardly recognizing her own face beneath the stage makeup that had every feature overdrawn and colored in to reach the fourth ring of Lincoln Center. Her stomach fluttered to the point of distraction and her breathing felt shallow, a surefire sign that she was scared. She'd never danced a part like Mira before, and in all truthfulness, wasn't sure she could fully deliver. Not only that, but the pain from her foot hadn't subsided at all, despite the anti-inflammatories she'd taken. She'd popped a second dose, just for good measure. While she'd become an expert at dancing through the discomfort, the pain was beginning to eat away at her and strip her concentration while performing.

A major problem.

Three sharp knocks on her dressing room door and Ana turned just as Natalie entered. Her eyes were bright and she smiled at Ana, which really did help. No other smile had anywhere near the same effect.

"Sorry about crashing in on you, but I couldn't seem to help myself. I just wanted to stop in and see how you were. Got my house seat ready to go." She held up a ticket proudly.

"You didn't have to do that," Ana said, but just having Natalie there seemed to right her lilting ship. Natalie was dressed for the theatre, more conservative than her normal attire. Sophisticated even, which captured Ana's attention. She wore a simple form-fitting black dress, black heels, and a thin red scarf that added a pop of color to the whole look. That was one part of the ensemble that screamed Natalie.

"I did have to. It's in my contract that I have to be within four blocks of the theatre whenever you're performing." That part was true. Ana had the same clause in her contract, just in case they needed her to go in for Natalie.

She shook her head. "I meant you didn't have to pop in. But can I confess that I'm happy you did?"

"You look killer," Natalie said, taking her in. "They're gonna eat it up. It's a beautiful piece. You know that, right? Roger knows what he's doing."

"He does. As much as I fought the idea, he did the right thing bringing you here. Without everything I've learned from my time spent with you, I wouldn't have half my performance."

"Now you're just being nice," Natalie said, standing behind Ana's chair and placing her hands on Ana's shoulders. "It's like you want to get me into bed or something. God, you have to stop pursuing me so vehemently."

"Vehemently?" Ana laughed. "Is that what I was doing? Stalking you?"

Natalie nodded in the mirror. "It's exhausting how much you like me and want to make out with me."

"Now, that part I can agree with."

"Aww, do you say that to all the girls?"

"I do," Ana said, laughing. "All of them. That's me. So many girls, so little time."

The smile faded slowly from Natalie's lips and her voice softened. The mood had definitely shifted. "So, how are you feeling really? Tell me about your foot."

"Foot's fine."

Natalie studied her in the mirror. "Is it?"

"Uh-huh. Feeling much better actually."

"Okay. That's good news. What about the rest of you?"

Ana decided to level with her. "Between you and me? I'm a little all over the place. Nerves. Which is new for me. I don't quite know what to do with them."

"Do you know what I do for nerves?"

"I would love to know."

"I tell them to go fuck themselves."

Ana laughed at the irreverence. "I'm not sure how they'd take the language."

"Doesn't matter. They're gone."

"While I love that you do that, I'm not sure it will work for me."

"Well, of course you're not. You haven't tried it. Here. Stand up." Natalie took a step to the side and Ana followed her instructions. "I want you to look in that mirror, and despite the fact that I've never heard you properly curse, tell your nerves to go fuck themselves."

"I'm not really someone who swears a lot."

"Then it's time you give it a try."

"I don't really think—"

"Do it!"

Ana turned to her reflection in the mirror. "Go fuck yourselves," she said with authority.

Natalie nodded seriously. "That was very good. And how did it feel?"

"Really amazing actually."

"Now, come on. We're going to stand like superheroes for two minutes." Natalie inflated her chest, placed both hands on her hips, and looked skyward à la Superman. It wasn't as if Natalie's first suggestion had been a bad one, so Ana complied, mimicking the ridiculous pose.

"And this is effective how, exactly?"

"If you pose like a superhero for several minutes, it's chemically proven to manufacture confidence. Is it working? Are you crazy-confident?"

"Let's give it the full two minutes," Ana said, focusing on her pose.

"Good call."

So they stood there in silence, both posing for all they were worth.

"Ms. Mikhelson, ten minutes until—oh, I'm sorry," the assistant stage manager said, her eyes doing their best saucer impersonation at the sight of what she'd just walked in on. "I didn't realize you were... otherwise engaged."

"I think you mean saving the universe," Natalie said without moving a muscle beyond her mouth. "Because that's what we're doing."

"That's okay, Henrietta," Ana said, also not breaking her pose. "Almost ready."

"I'll leave you alone, then," she said and backed out of the room slowly, as if her movement might disrupt the mojo.

When she felt the allotted time was up, Ana relaxed and turned slowly to Natalie. "I can't believe I'm going to say this, but pretending to be a superhero works. I feel like a superhero. A *fucking* superhero!"

Natalie shot a fist up in victory. "Look at you. A two for one! Told you. Now I'm going to go and find my seat, Supergirl. Is it possible I'll see you after? Because I was really hoping to see you after."

Ana smiled at the clear flirtation, and her stomach fluttered for an entirely new reason. They hadn't spent much alone time together since the elevator escapade, as the show had taken its toll on their stamina. Now that the ballet was in performances, however, Ana hoped that dynamic might change. "I would like that. Afterparty?"

"I will find you there. *Merde*," Natalie told her and kissed her cheek for luck.

"Natalie?" Ana stopped her just before she closed the door.

"Yeah?"

"If you hadn't stopped by, I don't know what would have happened to me out there. So thank you."

"You would have been awesome. That's what would have happened. I just helped you realize it. You're a pro, Ana. The best there is. Now, show everyone."

Ana heard those words repeated in her head a hundred times over as she walked to the stage. For the next forty minutes, she put her heart and soul into her performance in front of 2,500 people. This, for her, was the culmination of so many things. And instead of concentrating on each precise movement, she trusted that her body innately remembered how to dance the combinations.

Instead, she allowed herself to feel, just as Natalie had taught her. When Mira faced adversity, she borrowed from her own personal frustrations as a dancer being passed over again and again for promotion. When Mira felt triumphant, she remembered what it was like picking up the phone to call her father to tell him she'd been cast in the show. When Mira lusted after Titus, her thoughts fell to Natalie and all of the sensations being near her inspired. Before Ana knew what had happened, the ballet was over. The stage lights dimmed on their final lift and she and Jason, alone onstage, were met with thunderous applause that enveloped and embraced her like the warmest of blankets. Tears sprang to her eyes as Jason lowered her to the stage deck and held her close. They moved into position for final bows, the emotion overwhelming, all encompassing.

This was the kind of moment she'd worked so hard for all of those years. Sacrificing creature comforts, a social life, and her physical well-being.

Standing onstage now, she knew it had all been worth it.

Natalie had never seen anything like the elegance on display at the opening-night party—correction, gala. Three ballets had performed that evening, culminating in the world premiere of *Aftermath*. In celebration, the promenade of the David H. Koch Theater had been transformed into a fantastic odyssey, akin to the journeys taken by many of the main characters onstage. Round tables, each surrounded by ten high-backed white chairs, dotted the promenade floor. Gigantic white balloons floated seamlessly two stories above, giving the room an otherworldly look and feel. The party was given not so much for the cast, but instead for the wider world of ballet. Board members, important donors, and celebrities shared the space with the company and creative teams at City Ballet in a lavish and splashy PR event.

Roger had already taken her on a semi-tour around the room, hitting up the VIPs. He introduced her as not only one of the lead dancers in his ballet, but one to watch. It was flattering and kind of exciting to feel important. On one hand, she reminded herself how much she hated art for commerce, which was kind of what this whole party was about. On the other, she told herself to shut the hell up and enjoy the evening. She landed somewhere in the middle, snagging a glass of champagne as it was whisked by and sighing at the pretense of it all. But then again, it was cool to meet Sarah Jessica Parker.

She checked her watch and eyed the door.

Ana should be out of costume, into her dress, and on her way down. Any minute now she should—

"Looking for someone?" a voice said quietly in her ear. She smiled in recognition and turned to congratulate the woman who'd stolen her heart with the performance she'd given. Instead, the words died on her lips at the sight of Ana in a floor-length pale peach gown that some designer must have created especially for her. Her hair was swept up, exposing the elegant lines of her neck. A simple necklace with a modest drop diamond fell just above the subtle dip of her cleavage, a spot Natalie's eyes fell to and lingered.

"I'm up here, tiger," Ana said quietly, but her face held amusement when Natalie finally did snap her gaze to it.

"I'm sorry. I was a little…captivated," Natalie said apologetically. "Still am. You're beautiful."

"Thank you." A pause. Ana looked to her tentatively. "So what did you think?"

"I wish I had the right words. But I'll go with superbly danced, intricately performed. You were a smash. I had tears in my eyes at the end, and I know the damn show backward and forward. You really brought it. Your best yet."

"Really? You're not just saying that?"

"I will never lie to you. That's one guarantee I can make. And if you still don't believe me, just take a stroll through this room and hear the chatter. It's *Aftermath* everyone is talking about and, more specifically, you."

"Ana," Bill said, and kissed her on both cheeks. "Groundbreaking performance tonight. There are some donors I'd like you to meet." He turned to Natalie. "Looking forward to tomorrow night, my dear."

"I'll be there." Natalie widened her eyes at Ana as she was whisked away by Bill. Natalie surveyed the room and located Jason. Feeling the need to maybe…smooth things over with him before they danced together the next night, she headed his way.

"So you were awesome tonight," she told him, once his conversation with an older couple concluded.

He eyed her carefully. "Thanks. Ana and I work really well together."

"And it shows."

"What, are you jealous?" He smiled at her, and it felt like a challenge.

"Of Ana?"

"Of *me*. I get to dance with her in a way you never will."

Okay, so Jason was a little angrier than she realized, and maybe more of a prick. "Do you want to talk about this civilly? Because this isn't some sort of contest for me." They both paused to smile and say hello as a line of patrons walked past.

"Yeah, okay." He straightened as if remembering himself. "Maybe that last comment was out of line, but you're a bad idea for her," he said quietly when they had a moment alone. "You're reckless and unreliable. Not to mention, you had a girlfriend just a few weeks ago, and now all of a sudden you have a thing for Ana? Super convenient. What's on the menu for next week?"

"You don't know me nearly as well as you think you do."

"Sleep with whoever you want, Natalie. But can you just leave Ana out of it? Hell, I'm not sure she's even really into girls. For all I know, that's all your doing, too."

Natalie raised an eyebrow and leaned in. "You're gonna have to trust me when I tell you that it's definitely not my doing."

He shook his head, dubious. "Yeah, okay. If you say so."

"Listen, Jason." She softened and decided to take a new approach and just level with the guy. He was clearly hurting. "I genuinely care about Ana. I'm not playing any sort of game, and I have no plans to break her heart."

He scoffed. "Famous last words. Have you met yourself? From what I hear, you quit things *a lot*." He let the statement land. "If you'll excuse me, I see a friend of mine." He stalked away in annoyance and Natalie stared after him, not sure how that could have gone much worse.

"Hey," Ana said, touching Natalie's elbow as she returned. "I want you to meet a friend of mine."

"Of course." Natalie forced herself to brighten, shaking off the previous conversation, and followed where Ana led, which happened to be in the direction of a very beautiful and very familiar face.

"Natalie Frederico, meet Adrienne Kenyon, a supporter of City Ballet and a good friend of mine."

"Oh, wow. Really nice to meet you," Natalie said, offering her hand to the woman she'd seen on screen for years. Adrienne smiled and accepted the handshake. "I'm an admirer of your work."

"I appreciate that. Ana says lots of really nice things about you. The show tonight was breathtaking. Really proud of the honorary kid sister here." Adrienne bumped Ana's shoulder.

"Well, that makes two of us."

Adrienne turned to Ana. "Jenna would have absolutely loved it. I'm sad she missed it."

Natalie looked to Ana in question.

"Jenna's is Adrienne's girlfriend. As in Jenna McGovern."

"That's right," Natalie said. She remembered now that they were a couple. Suddenly, there was uncontrollable gushing. "I'm a huge fan of hers. I saw *Elevation* last summer on a short trip to the city and my head practically exploded. I stayed an extra day just so I could see it again. She's a gifted dancer. I was inspired for days after."

"I *like* her," Adrienne said to Ana, and couldn't have seemed more touched if Natalie's compliment had been directed at her. "I agree with you one hundred percent and will certainly tell her what you said. Though Ana says you're quite the gifted dancer yourself. I'd love to hear about your work in LA. Maybe we can all get together sometime."

"We should," Ana told her.

"Then we will." Adrienne kissed Ana's cheek. "You were on fire tonight. I'm so glad I got to see it. Natalie, a pleasure meeting you. I have no doubt you will slay tomorrow when you debut. *Merde.*" With a good-bye wave, Adrienne was on her way.

"So that was Adrienne," Ana informed her. "She's pretty great."

"And warm. And kind. God. Living in LA, you never know what to expect from celebrities, but she really lives up."

"Agreed entirely."

"She called you her honorary kid sister."

"Yeah. It's always kind of been that way. She looks out for me."

"Excuse me, ladies," Bill said. "I don't mean to interrupt, but there's a photographer from *New York* magazine who wants to get a shot of the two of you. If you'll follow me."

The rest of the evening was much of the same. Lots of chitchatting, mingling, and an abundance of congratulating. They stayed until it felt like a good portion of the crowd had dwindled and their PR responsibilities had been fulfilled. Natalie looked on as Ana said good night to a longtime board member, still looking ridiculously hot in her gown. The visual was torturous for Natalie and had her staring at the ceiling so as not to appear too obvious to anyone paying attention. That damn gown mocked her, offering just a glimpse of Ana's skin here, a bare shoulder there. Natalie's thoughts were those of a teenage boy, and she wondered when a woman had last captivated her the same way Ana did.

Never, she informed herself. Never had anyone affected her this much. This woman was different.

In a way, the attraction was a double-edged sword. Her feelings for Ana came with an exhilarating rush, the kind of adrenaline that junkies chased. It also left her feeling vulnerable and terrified all at the same time. Natalie preferred being in charge of her own emotions and responses, but when it came to Ana, her heart and libido seemed to have minds of their own. She was merely along for the ride.

"What?" Ana asked, as she returned to her. "What's with that very focused look?"

"I think when we get out of here, we need a celebration of our own," Natalie whispered. Ana's cheeks dusted with pink at the barely veiled suggestion. It was beyond cute, and Natalie wanted to kiss her then and there. Who had dubbed this woman an ice queen? The concept seemed so foreign to her now. Ana, as Natalie knew her in this moment, was anything but.

"I will grab my coat and my bag and meet you on the steps out front."

"Is that a yes?"

Ana turned her face to the side and shot Natalie a heated look, sending a delicious chill through her stomach and downward.

Feeling extra deserving, she and Ana decided to take a cab home. They sat in silence on the ride, but Natalie had never been so aware of another person's proximity. Sitting next to Ana, she could register the scent of watermelon from Ana's lip gloss and feel the heat from Ana's body against the chill of the night air. Everything about Ana inspired sensations in her body that she didn't know what to do with.

Except she did.

God, she'd never wanted another human so badly.

Two blocks from their building, Ana turned her face against the seat and met Natalie's gaze. Everything about it carried heat. The dark, hooded intensity spoke volumes as to what was on Ana's mind, and that meant Natalie was not alone.

"My place?" Ana asked quietly.

Natalie nodded.

They were barely through the door when it all erupted. They met in a clash right there in the entryway of Ana's living room. Before they could have counted to three, her mouth was on Ana's or Ana's was on hers. She wasn't sure which. But God, did it feel good. She pulled back and stared at Ana, whose breathing was ragged and sexy. Natalie needed to see her, to look at her, to drink her in. She slid her hands into Ana's thick hair, found her mouth once again, and plundered. Exploring, savoring, tasting. Ana's murmur of approval only increased the sense of urgency, and Ana kissed her back with just as much authority.

Yeah, this was what she needed. *This.*

As they kissed, Ana's hands were on the move. Natalie's scarf was gone. On the floor. Ana snaked a hand behind her and she felt her zipper start to go. She smiled against Ana's mouth. "You want this off?" she asked. "Is that what you want?"

Ana nodded.

Natalie could oblige.

She took Ana by the hand and led her to the couch. Most of the lights were still off, but Ana had managed to turn on a small lamp on the end table before everything went a little hazy. As Ana looked on, Natalie stood before her and unzipped her dress the rest of the way, stepping out of it once it fell. The little gasp Ana let out at the sight of Natalie in her black bikinis and bra caused her to steady herself a moment before walking to Ana and slowly straddling her on the couch.

Ana's hands were on Natalie's hips before slowly moving upward. She tossed her head back as they moved up her stomach, over her breasts, to her neck until they cradled her face. At the intimate touches, her body throbbed and she undulated her hips ever so slightly against Ana's stomach.

"God, you're beautiful," Ana breathed. "I've never seen anything like you." She then pulled Natalie's face to hers and captured her mouth in an achingly hungry kiss. Natalie continued to push against Ana, signaling the need that was about to overtake her. As they kissed, Ana eased a hand between Natalie's legs, on the outside of her underwear, and closed her eyes. "You're so wet," she whispered. "I haven't even touched you yet."

"This is what you do to me," Natalie managed to say.

Without taking her eyes from Natalie's, Ana unclasped the black bra and pulled the straps slowly down Natalie's shoulders, revealing her breasts. "Look at you," she said reverently. Her hands were on Natalie's breasts instantly, and this time it was Natalie who murmured with pleasure as little arrows of desire pulsed through her. Ana caressed each breast, squeezing softly, her thumbs circling Natalie's nipples. Natalie had never considered her breasts particularly sensitive, but as Ana kissed them and played and focused so intently on each one, Natalie thought she might come undone.

"We have to slow down," she said. "Ana. Wait."

"I don't see why," Ana said, pulling a nipple into her mouth, raking her teeth gently across it and then not so gently. God. "I like our pace."

Natalie rocked her hips desperately, pushing against Ana, anything that would give her purchase. "I don't think I can hold on."

"Who said you have to?" Ana whispered. She wrapped one arm around Natalie's waist to steady her and slipped the other into Natalie's underwear and stroked her softly. Natalie's hips bucked at the intimate contact and she bit her lip in an attempt not to cry out. But what was the point really? She'd lost any semblance of control. The back-and-forth motion of Ana's hand between her legs had her climbing, climbing, climbing.

"Let go for me," Ana whispered, tracing her thumb over Natalie's most sensitive spot. But she didn't dwell there, which was a shame, because Natalie needed her to. Ana, she was finding, liked to tease.

"Ana," she said. It was a request, and one that Ana apparently wasn't ready to honor. Instead, she slid inside Natalie, who moaned and gripped Ana's shoulders for support. She didn't know how she was going to survive the wonderfully torturous intensity she felt building each time Ana withdrew and then entered her again. The built-up pressure was too much. She moved against Ana's hand, searching urgently for relief, hearing herself cry out along the way. Finally, Ana had mercy and pressed her thumb firmly where Natalie needed it most, sending her into an oblivion of sharp, hot pleasure. She rode out the intense waves that hit her again and again and again in glorious payout. She couldn't remember the last time she'd come so hard.

In recovery mode, Natalie blinked in an attempt to regain focused vision and the use of her brain. The world floated back to her slowly. Details clicked into place. She was plastered against Ana, who still wore the damn gown that started it all. Ana still had hold of her and was still touching her intimately, easing her back down with the slow and soft touches of her fingers.

"Hey. You with me?" Ana asked quietly, and kissed the top of her breast. Natalie nodded, not quite trusting her voice. She sat back in Ana's lap and found her gaze. Ana tucked a strand of hair behind Natalie's ear. "Good, because you? Just now? That was something to behold."

"Yeah, well, I don't know what you did to me." She closed her eyes and bucked her hips as Ana's fingers hit an overly sensitive spot. "Are *doing* to me," she corrected. "But it was…memorable." She leaned down and kissed Ana, slowly at first, but then the fire took hold again and she couldn't stop herself or the passion that rained down on that kiss. She'd let Ana be the aggressor for a while, had handed her the reins, but Natalie was done with that now. And she was also done with that annoying peach gown.

She stood and offered Ana her hand.

"Where are we going?" Ana asked, looking up, her blue eyes now darkened with desire.

"To your bed. And we're going now."

Wordlessly, Ana accepted Natalie's hand.

Natalie didn't bother to turn the light on. The moon was bright and streamed through the window, offering a soft blue layer, all the visibility that Natalie needed. She unzipped the dress immediately, because it had to go. Natalie gasped at the realization that Ana wasn't wearing a bra. Ana smiled nervously at her, but that smile dimmed when Natalie moved to her and ran a hand across her breast. The sound of Ana taking in air at the touch only served to increase Natalie's need for her.

She wanted Ana.

Craved her.

And felt that craving, tight and hard and coiled, all over.

She kissed one breast and then the other before dropping to her knees in front of Ana. She pulled her underwear down her legs and gazed at what was exposed to her now. She leaned in and kissed Ana intimately, unabashedly, reveling in the taste of her. Ana, she noticed, placed a hand behind her against the wall for support as she murmured sounds of pleasure. With a swift hand around Ana's waist, she guided her to the bed, laid her head down on the pillow, and slid on top.

"Off," Ana breathed, and tugged on the side of the bikinis Natalie still wore.

"Demanding, but okay," Natalie said playfully, obliging the request.

"Can't help it," Ana said, her eyes combing over Natalie's now-naked body as she settled back on top. Natalie moaned reverently at the feel of them together at last, skin on skin, nothing between them now. She couldn't help but grind into Ana, her own heat level rising yet again. Ana arched her back against Natalie and met her there. Ana slid a hand between them and lower, cupping Natalie, almost sending her over the edge once again.

But this was Natalie's show.

She took Ana's hand and guided it to the spindled headboard. "Hold on," she told her. When Ana complied, Natalie repeated the action, placing Ana's other hand next to the first. "Don't let go." Ana's lips parted at the implication, but she did as she was told.

She kissed her way down Ana's stomach to her inner thighs and settled her mouth right where she'd left off. Natalie took her time and meticulously went to work. She found Ana's rhythm easily and settled in, loving the little noises she heard from above her. The squirming. The ragged breaths as her need increased. She stole a glimpse of Ana, who still held on to the headboard, her head tossing against the pillow in urgency. With one thrust, Natalie pushed her fingers inside Ana and then pulled her fully into her mouth. With a loud cry, Ana's hips pushed off the bed and held as the orgasm tore through her. For someone as reserved as Ana on the day-to-day, she didn't hold back now, calling out in what could only be described as one of the sexiest sounds Natalie had ever heard. She climbed on top and settled a thigh between Ana's legs as she rode out the last surge. She hadn't seen it coming when Ana slipped a hand between them and expertly caressed Natalie. With just that one touch from Ana, she gasped and tumbled over the edge again, helpless to the wonderful shock waves that rippled through her. It was too much and not enough at the same damn time.

It was everything.

She slid off Ana, exhausted and reveling. Ana stared up at the ceiling, her arm tossed over her forehead making her look like the beautiful subject of a Renaissance painting. Tiny beads of sweat dotted her chest and Natalie had to restrain herself from licking them off.

"Good?" she asked finally.

"There are bound to be stronger words," Ana said, still captivated by the ceiling. And then she turned to Natalie with an upshift in energy. "People should have sex more."

Natalie laughed. "They should. They *do*."

"Then I've seriously been missing out."

Okay, that was it. Natalie couldn't take it anymore. "You're being entirely too adorable." She rolled over and kissed Ana, gently this time, savoring the taste. "And that wasn't just sex. That was what you'd call *good* sex."

"It was, wasn't it?" she marveled. "Not just me?"

"Definitely not just you. It turns out we fit."

"Lucky us."

They drifted off together on the same pillow, their limbs intertwined. When Natalie awoke a couple hours later with her body on fire, she smiled as the reason became clear: Ana's mouth on her breast and her hand between Natalie's legs.

"I think you're making up for lost time," Natalie whispered. She then hissed in a breath, moving into the touch.

"Is that bad?" Ana asked, smiling against Natalie's skin.

"Are you kidding?"

Chapter Thirteen

A na smiled and blinked against the sunlight streaming in through her window. There was a woman lying across her body, which she realized was the reason for her automatic smile. Natalie, it occurred to her fondly, was a deep sleeper who enjoyed sleeping in the center of the bed.

But she looked really, really sexy when she did it.

She removed the strand of Natalie's hair across her own face, taking note of the way Natalie's breathing, in soft rhythmic puffs, tickled her neck. She lay completely on top of Ana, their bare breasts pressed together. Natalie had tucked a hand between them, and the other rested on Ana's shoulder. They'd stayed together all night, which was new for Ana. She'd never really partaken in the sleepover thing before. And though one part of her wanted to leap from the bed at the new and unnerving experience, another wanted something very different. She pulled Natalie into her and closed her eyes, reveling in the warmth and how sated and heavy her body felt.

In that moment, Ana forced herself to let go of her inhibitions and experienced happiness in a way she never had before in her life. She'd had a fantastic opening the night before, and what was happening between her and Natalie, while early and terrifying, had her looking forward to life and everything that lay ahead.

Natalie stirred in her arms then. "Good morning," Ana said quietly, as Natalie had never really struck her as a morning person. A deep sigh of contentment was her answer as Natalie snuggled into her even further.

"Isn't it though?" Natalie asked finally, and then nuzzled Ana's neck.

"It's your opening today," Ana told her, bracing against the flutters Natalie's mouth seemed to cause her. "Are you excited?"

"A lot of things have me excited lately." Natalie pushed onto her elbows and met her eyes. Her untamed hair and swollen lips made her the sexiest person alive, and she was right there in Ana's bed.

"Me too. My father's coming next week," Ana blurted. "Sorry. That was kind of a non sequitur. I think I'm bad at pillow talk."

Natalie smiled widely. "That's okay. It was cute. So your pop's gonna pop in and see you perform?"

"Yeah." She felt the smile dim on her face.

"And that has you a little nervous."

"No," Ana said, as if it were the craziest thing in the world, when in reality it was her exact life. "Okay, yes. He makes me incredibly nervous."

"Understandable. You guys get along?"

"We do. It's not a terribly deep relationship. But we respect one another."

Natalie inclined her head. "Okay, what aren't you saying? I'm naked and vulnerable in your bed right now, so you owe me your utmost honesty."

"You are not vulnerable in the slightest. You're the most confident person on the planet, and that extends to the bedroom, we now know."

Natalie laughed and kissed her. "Fine," she murmured against Ana's mouth. "But I still wanna know. You're beautiful in the morning, by the way. Proceed." She leaned her head back onto her hand and looked down at Ana expectantly.

"My father's good at what he does."

"Right, the world knows this. Beloved by all."

"But I don't think he believes I am. Or at least, not as good as he would like me to be."

"Why? Because you're not the household name he is?"

"Something like that." And then, "No, *exactly* that."

"Well, that's bullshit. You're awesome onstage and I don't say that with bias. I've watched you daily for months now and continue to marvel at how you do what you do."

"You mean that, don't you?" Ana said, starting to believe her. She was also coming to understand how important Natalie's opinion was to her. A scary thought.

"Look at my face." Ana did and what she saw there vanquished any lingering doubt, because the eyes looking back at her were solemn, sincere. "You amaze me on the regular. You're easily the most talented person I've ever worked with, and you've been generous enough to teach me what I didn't know. He should be nothing but proud of you."

"Thank you," Ana said. She had to look away because the emotion that threatened was too powerful a foe for her typical resolve. Hearing those words from someone who mattered to her slammed her hard with overwhelming gratitude and joy. How pathetic was she?

"Hey," Natalie said, turning Ana's chin back to face her. "Since your eyes are all watery, I think I should choose this moment to say that you also amaze me with your clothes off. I might like the clothes off part even *more* than the dancing part. But we should continue the investigation just to be sure."

Ana laughed, the comment lifting her instantly. Natalie had a way of knowing just what she needed. Scary, really, but this time in a good way. She only hoped she could find a way to do the same for her. "I've never let anyone sleep over before." She covered her mouth, realizing that she'd once again blurted. What was with all of the off-the-cuff admissions? Had sleeping with Natalie completely annihilated her filter? And if so, what else was going to come flying out of her mouth?

"Seriously? No sleepovers?"

"It's true. I slept at her place for half a night a couple of times. Roxanne, I mean. But there were no mornings and she never slept here."

"Why not?"

"I guess I wasn't comfortable with it."

"Does that mean you're totally freaking out right now because I'm in your bed staring at your gorgeous body and it's morning?"

Ana tilted her head from side to side. "A little bit, yeah. But at the same time, I'm also very, very happy. And if it's all right with you, I plan to kiss you some more before you're whisked away to the theater."

Natalie looked skyward. "If that's the price of morning admission at Ana's place, I suppose you've twisted my arm." She slid on top, and the kissing session they engaged in turned out to be only the opening act.

❖

"Three orgasms?" Audrey asked, and absently popped a yogurt-covered raisin in her mouth. "You're not telling the truth right now."

"That's not even counting this morning," Natalie said, nabbing a yogurt-covered raisin of her own. She had an hour before she had to be in costume and makeup, so she lounged with Audrey on the comfortable couch next to her dressing table, alongside Ana's, which sat empty that night.

"There were more orgasms this morning?"

Natalie didn't answer with words; instead, she chewed her raisin and regarded Audrey with a pointed eyebrow raise.

"There were," Audrey said, pointing at her. "There were more orgasms! Who knew you guys would be so hot and heavy right off the bat? I mean, work up to it, people."

"Oh, I knew. More." She held out her hand and Audrey poured her a few more of the awesome raisins. "The sparks were bouncing off us from the moment we met. Not that they were all good sparks, but sometimes the bad sparks transition into really *really* good sparks. The kind of sparks that give you three orgasms."

"Right! I should be writing this down." Audrey made a grabby gesture with her hands. "You guys had that fiery tension right off, which surely fanned the flames of your uninhibited passion. All that conflict. All that angsty build-up. The fighting just…" Audrey fanned herself in lieu of any real word.

"Fantastic," Jason said flatly from the doorway of the dressing room.

Natalie turned at the sound of his voice, and her heart sank knowing what he'd just heard.

"I was just stopping by to—never mind."

"Jason, wait. What did you want to say?" Natalie asked.

He took a deep breath. "We're dancing together tonight and despite our…*differences* lately, I want you to know that I have your back out there. We need to be able to trust each other."

Natalie nodded. Jason was a pro. She knew this. "Thanks, Jase. I feel the same way."

"Great. Okay, then," he said, still zero inflection in his voice. And just as quickly as he'd appeared, he was gone, dragging his broken heart on a sad little rope behind him. As into Ana as Natalie was, she hated this particular side effect.

But Jason stayed true to his word, and once he and Natalie met onstage, all of that awkward tension seemed to float away. They connected and they danced. Natalie gave everything she had to the performance, and though she felt she could have been more polished, she was pleased with her work.

There was no fancy afterparty like there had been the night prior, but Roger was waiting for her backstage with a double-cheek kiss and a bouquet of flowers. "You were exquisite tonight, Natalie. You've come a long way, my dear. Congratulations. You're a true leading lady."

She beamed up at him, but resisted the urge to punch him in the shoulder. "Thanks, Rog. I owe you for bringing me here. As much as I fought it, and as awful as I was to work with at points, you stuck with me. So, thank you."

As conservative as he normally was, Roger blushed at the sentiment. "I hope you'll stay with us in the coming seasons."

But would she?

It was a question Natalie asked herself a lot.

Was she now a full-fledged ballerina for life? The answer tugged at her.

As much as she'd enjoyed working on *Aftermath*, and as much as she'd learned, the idea of staying with the company long term was daunting. What about her own work? Her own vision? There'd been a time when she'd had big plans for herself. And yet…how could she walk away from something so steady, so prestigious, so shockingly rewarding?

After a quick transformation back into Natalie-of-the-real-world, she flipped off the light to the shared dressing room and headed into the hall, where she found Ana waiting with a foot kicked against the wall. She straightened when she saw Natalie and inclined her head and smiled.

"Hey, you," Natalie said. "I thought we were meeting outside."

"I wanted to see you sooner because you were just that brilliant tonight. I couldn't wait."

"Stop. You know I screwed up the second variation." It was a minor mistake, but Ana would have caught it easily.

"Didn't matter. You owned that stage."

"Thank you. But I think you're just being nice."

"Have you met me?"

Natalie chuckled. "*Touché.* What shall we do now?"

"Um, ice cream," Ana said without hesitation.

"You're going to take me out for ice cream?"

"It's what my father always did for me after a stellar performance. And now I'm going to do it for you. There's really no better celebration." She looked at Ana out of the corner of her eye. "The opening-night party yesterday was pretty awesome."

"Doesn't hold a candle to where I'm about to take you."

"And where is that?" Natalie asked, intrigued.

"A heavenly place on Earth. It's called Shake Shack. Follow me."

They arrived at the Shake Shack close to eleven p.m. There was a line on the street outside, but then there was always a line at Shake Shack. As they waited patiently on the sidewalk, Ana bounced on her heels a couple of times in order to stay warm. It was turning into an unseasonably cold fall, and temperatures had dipped into the uncomfortable zone.

"Give me your hands," Natalie said.

Ana stared at her suspiciously. "What are you going to do with them?"

"Only you would say that. Watch." Natalie covered Ana's hands with her own, rubbing the outsides before breathing into them. Her warm breath did cut the chill, and Ana smiled at the sweetness of the gesture. "Any better?" Natalie blew into their hands again.

Ana nodded. "Much."

"Good. Any ice cream tips as we wait? You seem to be the pro."

"Tip number one: they call it custard here." Ana held up her hand to halt any argument. "I know. It's barbaric, but we forgive them when they hand it to us because it's awesome ice cream in disguise."

"Got it. We forgive the custard moniker. What's your favorite flavor?"

Ana looked skyward. "Well, I don't allow myself to indulge too often."

"Shocking," Natalie said and rolled her eyes. Ana had no choice but to shove her playfully.

"But when I do indulge, on an important day such as this one, I feel that Jelly's Last Donut is the only way to go."

"Explain."

"I can try. We're talking vanilla with little donut pieces, topped off with a strawberry jam and this amazing cinnamon sugar that will have you falling on your knees."

"That's a bold endorsement."

Ana looked at her emphatically. "It is. Yet I stand by it."

"Do you realize you're adorable when you talk about ice cream? I mean you've had adorable moments before, but this one takes the cake."

"You mean the donut?"

"And there's a rare joke from Ana. Nice! You're slaying me with cute right now. I might be on overload. You have to refrain from any more endearing ice cream wit."

"Stop it," Ana said, laughing. "I'm serious over here. I happen to love Shake Shack."

Natalie stepped into her space. "Then I'm supremely honored you brought me here. To one of your time-honored traditions."

"Well, you earned it," Ana said, savoring the closeness after they'd been apart most of the day.

Natalie dropped her tone. "Are you referring to the events of your apartment or the stage?"

Ana felt the pink hit her cheeks at merely the reference to the night prior, when Natalie had combusted in her lap and then owned Ana in no time flat. She'd never been so responsive to someone else's touch before, but somehow Natalie rendered her helpless in that department. It had only been their first time together, and already they had shattered any record of Ana's. "I think we can include both," Ana said shyly, recalling the question at hand.

"I was hoping you felt that way."

After they at long last ordered and received their ice cream (custard), Ana followed Natalie to a table as a question tugged. They sat along the window, which offered excellent people-watching potential. "So, last night," Ana began, her stomach tightening with nervous energy.

"Yeah?" Natalie asked, smiling at her in amusement.

The thing was, Natalie knew Ana well enough to know when she was out of her comfort zone. But something about that calmed Ana because there was very little pretense here. "It was...good?" She shifted focus to her ice cream and took a bite, simply because she couldn't look at Natalie after asking such an intimate question.

"You don't think last night was good?" Ana raised her gaze and watched as Natalie took a bite of her ice cream (custard) and licked the last little bit of it off the plastic spoon. It was a visual that stopped Ana short. "What's with the hot-dark look you're sporting over there?" She took another slow lick of her ice cream.

Ana blinked at her before giving her head a little toss to clear it. "No, it's *really* good. I mean last night was really good...is all...and I wondered just...what you thought. It's not a big deal."

Natalie set down her ice cream, folded her hands on the table, and regarded Ana. "Let's just say that last night, I came to the realization that you have really good hands and that your talent extends beyond the stage."

"Oh," Ana said, feeling bashful and, at the same time, a little bit eager to reprise her role in last night's post-show. Natalie thought she was good in bed, which had her wanting to...spend some more time there. Hone her skills.

"You also have amazing taste in ice cream. I'm in heaven over here."

Ana grinned and sat back in her chair. "I don't know whether to enjoy mine or watch you eat yours. The show is a good one." This time it was Natalie's turn to blush, which was a rare occurrence indeed. Little Miss Confident had her vulnerable moments, and Ana found those short glimpses highly attractive.

An hour later, they stood on opposite sides of the elevator, staring at each other with the kind of pent-up tension Ana found excruciating. Natalie took a step toward her and Ana held up a hand. "We can't. We have an elevator reputation."

"Yeah, and it's kind of a good one," Natalie said, all sly and reckless. Ana loved her reckless streak. So not helping. "I see no reason to trade it in."

"Patience," Ana said, placing a hand on Natalie's chest, "will get you everywhere, Ms. Frederico."

"I think I like it when you call me that."

"You saying provocative things to me is only making this elevator move slower."

"All the more reason to make out in it."

Ana shook her head and blew out a steadying breath, counting the moments until they'd be alone, because she really, really wanted to be alone with Natalie.

By the time they made it down the corridor, Natalie's hands were on her, and her hands were on Natalie. In a hot clash of lips and tongues, they stumbled down the hall like blissfully drunk people. "My place," Natalie murmured between kisses. "I'm taking you back to my cave and having my way with you. And I'm not going slow."

Ana laughed and grabbed ahold of the lapels of Natalie's jacket. "You don't have a cave."

Natalie raised an eyebrow, opened the door to her place, and much to Ana's surprise picked her up and carried her inside. "Wanna bet?" With Ana laughing and protesting the whole way, Natalie carried her to her bedroom and deposited her on the bed with a bounce. Before Ana could even take a breath, Natalie was on top of her and kissing her and oh, that was more than good, because Natalie was warm and sexy and wonderful with her curves pressed up against Ana. She blazed a trail down Ana's neck to her collarbone, igniting each spot she touched.

And now Ana wanted things.

She wanted things she didn't even have names for.

They spent that night in pursuit of those things and so much more. The sensuous acts they performed on each other were outside the realm of Ana's limited experience, and she thrilled to them. They were still awake when the sun came up.

Exhausted, but wonderfully content.

Ana glanced around Natalie's room for the first time. There hadn't been any opportunity for examination the night prior. Her bedroom was the mirror version of Ana's, but it seemed to come with a lot more stuff. On the exposed brick wall hung a black-and-white photo of Kermit in a director's chair, and across from that a dancer leaping from one rooftop to another with sparks trailing behind her. "That reminds me of you," she murmured to Natalie, who'd closed her eyes and had begun playing with Ana's hair. "A risk taker." Natalie sleepily glanced at the photo in question.

"That's because it *is* me. My friend Antonio is a photographer in LA and conceptualized the shot. It was part of his gallery show on modern dance. The original sold for a lot of dough. That's just a printed poster."

Ana pushed herself up onto her elbow and stared at the silhouetted female dancer, and sure enough, she recognized the shape of Natalie's body. "It is you," she breathed, now in love with the photo for a whole separate reason. She turned in Natalie's arms and stared up at her. "What's it like to be you?"

Natalie inclined her head, considering the question. "Right now it feels pretty awesome."

"No," Ana said, as she trailed her fingers softly across Natalie's stomach and back again. "To be so fearless. You take chances in life and in your work. I could never do that. I play it safe."

"Not true. You're taking the biggest risk of your life dancing on that tendon, and you know it."

The mention of her injury had Ana deflating from the high she'd been on. "That's different."

"No, it's not. You think you're dancing through an injury to keep your career afloat, when in reality you're gambling with the thing you love most."

Natalie was right. She *was* gambling, but she didn't see any way around it. "I'm just trying to get through this show."

"And what if it's your last?"

She shook her head. "Don't say that."

"Promise me something," Natalie said, sitting up in bed, the covers pulled to her chest.

"I'll try."

"If it gets any worse, you'll pull yourself from the show." There were another three weeks on the run. The plan was that she'd go straight into dancing in the Sugar Plum Fairy rotation for *The Nutcracker* during the winter season, a detail she hadn't discussed yet with Natalie.

"I won't let it get worse. But if it does, I will talk to Bill."

Natalie slid down the bed so they were face-to-face. "You need to make peace with the fact that you can't control the world, Ana, and you may not be able to control this injury."

Ana nodded, but couldn't make herself agree. "Easier said than done."

Natalie shook her head in defeat and placed a kiss at Ana's temple. "Try and get some sleep. You have a matinee today. I'm gonna go seek out some breakfast for us." Ana watched in appreciation as Natalie walked, naked and confident, across the room before slipping into a pair of jeans and a hoodie.

"Oh! Can I have a bagel with—"

"Fat-free cream cheese. I'm familiar with you." Natalie shimmied her way into her second shoe and headed for the door.

"Thank you," Ana called after her.

"Get some sleep!" she heard from the hallway. "That's an order."

Once alone, Ana closed her eyes and snuggled into the sheets that smelled so much like cucumber and cotton, a combination she'd come to identify as uniquely Natalie. Slumber claimed her quickly and she slept long and hard, as the most wonderful dreams descended on her.

Maybe it *was* possible to have it all.

Chapter Fourteen

Two weeks later, the holidays had firmly fallen on New York City, and Natalie was ready to explore. Skip down the sidewalk even if necessary, though skipping was not exactly her style. Hot chocolate, holly, and holiday music had her geared up for Christmas. This city knew how to do merriment right, and Natalie loved Christmas.

"We have to go to Rockefeller Center," she told Ana, who buttered her toast with the precision of a Renaissance painter as she stood at the counter in a T-shirt and underwear. This was one of Natalie's favorite images in her years on planet Earth. "Now."

"Now?" Ana said, narrowing her gaze. "We just woke up."

"Yes. It's called We're Missing Out on the Fun in Rockefeller Center. The tree is up and we need to see it."

"It looks the same as it did last year. But your lovable factor is kicking in, so it's possible I could be persuaded."

"Got it. Persuasion I can handle. First persuasive argument: Today is a day off and we rarely have those at the same time."

"Valid point. I'm listening."

"Second persuasive argument: What if I told you that you were the cutest toast butterer I've ever met and if you don't come do Christmassy tasks with me in midtown, I'll die of a broken heart? I will, too." She wrapped her arms around Ana from behind and placed a kiss on the visible skin of her shoulder blade just outside of her shirt.

"You think you're pretty smooth, don't you?"

"I am smooth. Admit it." Another kiss, slower this time and up the column of Ana's neck.

"I don't know what you're, um, talking about."

"Do so." Natalie slipped a hand under the T-shirt and palmed Ana's breast. At the murmur of satisfaction, Natalie knew the toast would be abandoned soon. To her delight, she wasn't wrong.

Two hours later, after a fulfilling morning spent in and out of bed, they were right where Natalie wanted them to be, staring up at the biggest, grandest Christmas tree she'd ever laid eyes on. Tourists snapped candid photos and waited in line for the official photographer. Natalie was content to sit on a nearby bench with Ana and some hot cocoa, and marvel. "Where do they find trees that big?" she asked Ana.

"Iceland. It's where all the tall trees come from."

"Wow. I had no idea."

"Actually, I just made that up, but it's encouraging to know that you trust me so implicitly."

The comment struck an unexpected chord. "I do, you know, trust you."

Ana stared at her, softening, her voice quiet when she spoke. "I know. I trust you, too."

Natalie shook her head slightly. "You're so different, Ana, from everything I first decided about you." Natalie thought back to her first day with the company and then before that, back to school. She'd placed Ana in a box marked "boring" and left her there, when there was so much more to discover.

"Let me guess. Unapproachable. Unfriendly. Unexciting."

"Yes, and don't forget uptight and stuck up."

"Ouch."

"We're keeping the uptight moniker," Natalie said with an affectionate grin. "But we'll lose the rest. We already have."

"And now?" Ana asked, her vulnerability on the subject apparent in her gaze. "You can be honest."

"Now I think you're funny, smart, talented, and kind. Don't even get me started on the sexy." She looked skyward and shook her head. "Because that part makes me a little weak in the knees, as clichéd as that sounds."

"I can't imagine anything making you weak in the knees. You're so unaffected, so strong."

"It is my goal generally. But there are exceptions, and you, Ana

Mikhelson, affect me in the most potent sense. I'm sitting here on this bench with you and there's nowhere else in the world I'd rather be. Well, unless you were there, too. Then I'd want to be in *that* place. It says a lot. I like a lot of people, but it's rare that I lose myself in someone this way."

Ana took a moment, seemingly lost in thought. "Who would have predicted this, you and me? We're as different as they come and we clashed hardcore early on."

"Oh, there'll be more clashing, I guarantee it. But now we know there's more underneath."

"Hot chocolate in front of a giant public Christmas tree?" Ana asked.

"Exactly that. And post-clashing makeup sex is pretty awesome."

"It is. At least, I imagine it is." Ana blushed and Natalie took her hand and gave it a squeeze.

"I love it when you blush. Even more so when I inspire it."

"I'm not sure anyone else can."

"God." Natalie leaned over and kissed Ana right there on that bench because there was no way she couldn't.

"What was that for?" Ana asked, smiling and touching her lips.

"You. That's what it was for. Because you're sitting next to me being *you*, looking like *you*. That's why."

"I don't think I've ever been kissed in public before. As in, with actual public around."

"Yeah, well, you might want to get used it."

"I'll add it to the lengthy list."

Natalie laughed and intertwined her fingers with Ana's, which happened to be freezing. "I think you should tell me all of what's on the list. What else will take getting used to?"

Ana took a sip of her cocoa and considered the questions. "A beautiful woman stretched out across the center of my bed each morning. Or sometimes completely on top of me, depending on the day. You're the definition of bed hog."

Natalie scrunched one eye. "Guilty. I apologize."

"Don't."

"What else?"

"Little packets. Empty ones on the counter. You're a fan of

sweetener and there's evidence all over my apartment in the form of wrappers and loose granules of sugar."

Natalie shook her head. "Man, I'm racking up the points right now."

"Then there's how I'm feeling. That's new." Ana settled her gaze on Natalie's.

"Annoyed that a woman sleeps practically on top of you and then sprinkles sugar substitute all over your kitchen?"

"More like how I've never been so excited to wake up each morning. How I get this little upshot in energy when I know I'm going to spend time with you. The tiny bits of sugar are purely bonus."

"Wow," Natalie said, and let the declaration settle. It had to be one of her favorite series of sentences ever. "That's…"

"What?"

"The most perfect thing anyone's ever said to me." She leaned very close to Ana's ear and dropped her voice. "Tell me how I stop myself from falling head over heels for you. Because, Ana…I feel it happening."

Ana turned her face to Natalie's and touched her cheek. A soft smile tugged the corners of her mouth. "If you figure it out, let me know, because I'm losing the battle, too."

"So what do we do about that?"

Ana stared at the Christmas tree in search of the answer. "Hold on tight? I know that I, for one, am beyond scared of this new, unknown territory. So while I'm white-knuckling it a bit, I also want to enjoy every second because I've never felt more alive."

Natalie grinned and inclined her head in the direction of the tree. "Take a photo with me in front of this guy. I don't ever want to forget today."

"Anything," Ana said, and Natalie knew she meant it.

❖

My father is in the audience.

It was the only cognizant thought coming to Ana as she stepped off stage and into the rosin box. She was in an immense amount of pain but *her father was in the audience.* Damn it, she had to get a hold of the situation. She had roughly ninety seconds before making her next entrance, and she used the time in the rosin box to apply the non-slip substance to the tip of her pointe shoe.

And she was off again.

Twirling en pointe as pain, the most excruciating imaginable, shot from her foot and upward through her calf. What made it worse was that her shoes seemed to be dying, the shank beginning to give way. This put even more pressure on her feet, causing her to work that much harder to stay on her toes, and secondly, *her father was in the audience.*

She used breathing exercises to push past it, though Jason seemed to pick up on the fact that something was wrong. "Mik, you okay?" he asked in her ear, his lips barely moving to give nothing away to their audience.

She offered him the slightest of nods as they came to the most complicated portion of the ballet, the last *pas de deux.* She prepared herself for what was to come, and though the pain was blinding, she was doing it. She was hitting each step and she would make it to the end of this thing if it killed her.

While the performance felt like an eternity to Ana, it at long last came to a close and she was met with the same hearty applause this ballet always seemed to command. Once again the last ballet of the evening, she smiled through curtain call and held it until the curtain fell. Her breath came in shallow spurts, and she felt Jason's hand on her back.

"Mik, talk to me. What happened out there? Are you okay?" Jason asked as they exited the stage.

She shook her head and walked a few steps to the wings, limping fully now. "I'm fine."

"You're not fine. Do you need a doctor?" He looked to Priscilla for help.

"Ana, are you injured?" Priscilla asked gently.

Ana straightened and got it together. "I'm not. My shoes died early and made it a rough performance. But I got through it. I'll talk to Henry about it." For good measure, she offered up a smile. Once Priscilla seemed satisfied, Ana limped her way back to the dressing room, closed the door, and sank onto the couch as the tears came in hot streams. She freed herself from the shoes and stared at her offending left foot, doing everything in her power to will the problem away. She had two days until her next scheduled performance, which was not enough rest for the caliber of injury she was dealing with. Not even close.

There was a knock on her door followed by her father's unique accent. "Anastasia, come out and hug your papa."

She stared at her features in the mirror and cursed her tear-streaked face, a sign of weakness in her family if there ever was one. "One moment, Papa." She grabbed a Kleenex and with quick motions dabbed away the tears, followed by a quick pass with makeup remover to rid her face of the show's dramatic design. "Here I am," she said finally, opening the door and smiling up at her father. He was slightly heavier than the last time she'd seen him and his beard held a few more gray hairs, but the blue eyes twinkling down at her were so familiar that the tears nearly sprang into her eyes again, this time for a whole separate reason. He held his arms open and she fell into them just as she'd done as a child.

"Kotik, you were magnificent," he said to her softly. "So proud, I am."

"Thank you, Papa."

He placed a firm kiss on her cheek and squeezed her just a little too hard as always, though she wouldn't want it any other way. "I will find Roger and say my congratulations on his work."

"I'm not sure he's here. We're weeks into the run."

"He reserved my ticket. He is here. I will find him." In actuality, that was probably true. When her father made his impending presence known, people tended to show up. He held one finger in the air and dashed down the hall. For the next twenty minutes, Klaus Mikhelson held court as company members, crew, and staff took turns clamoring over him, asking for autographs and photos. Ana waited patiently in the hallway, looking on and smiling, all the while swallowing against the ever-present pain. The role of "less important daughter" was one she could play expertly.

"Shall we go to restaurant?" he asked, once they were outside. He had a car waiting and opened the door for her.

"Yes, let's," she said, sliding into the backseat. "And remember my friend is joining us. She'll meet us there."

"Yes, yes. My assistant made reservations for three at your request. She is another dancer, yes?"

"She is. I believe you refer to her as the competition."

He slid into the backseat next to her and chuckled. "Well, well, I look forward to meeting this competition. Her name?"

"Natalie Frederico."

"Yes. An Italian."

"I believe so, yes."

"No, she is of Italian lineage. I read her bio in program."

"Right." Ana should have predicted that.

"She is here? Should we wait?"

"She was. She's required to be close by when I'm on. But I asked her earlier to head to the restaurant once the curtain fell. That way you and I would have a little time to chat on our own. Papa, there's something else you should know about Natalie."

"And what is that? Take Ninth all the way," he said to the driver in a commanding voice. Once she regained his attention, she smiled against the nervous energy that descended. *Here goes nothing.*

"She's started to matter to me a lot."

"She keeps you on your toes, you mean." He laughed at the obvious ballet reference.

"What I mean is that we're involved."

"You are doing another show together?"

She laughed. "Maybe someday, but that's not it either. We're *involved*," she said, overstating the word. He stared at her hard, what she referred to as his Russian stare. Fine. Forget it. "We're dating, Papa."

He straightened and studied her with interest. "You are dating the *competition*? No, no, no. Unwise to date competition. Never."

She found wry amusement in the fact that his focus fell squarely on Natalie's relationship to her career, rather than the fact that she was a *woman*. So very Klaus Mikhelson. But she could roll with it.

"We happen to share a role. We're not competitive. Well, at least not anymore."

"And you like this Natalie? To do romance?"

"I do."

"Interesting. And you say she is talented?"

"Very."

"We shall see about that." He relaxed against his seat, staring out at the passing scenery in silence for the rest of the ride. She wondered what he was thinking about, though his face was carefully closed off. He had a way of withholding, and it drove Ana crazy. Always had.

When they arrived at Sardi's, his favorite restaurant in New York, Natalie stood out front. Ana took a deep breath and prepared herself for what was very new territory. When she saw them approach, Natalie smiled radiantly and Ana's heart skipped. She moved ahead several steps on the sidewalk to greet Natalie first, careful to mask her limp, an art she'd refined.

"How was the show?" Natalie asked as Ana approached.

"It was fine. Really good," Ana lied, internally wincing as she recalled the agony of the performance itself.

"Why are you limping?" Natalie whispered. "Did something happen? Is it your foot?"

"I'm not limping." Damn it. Natalie was good at this.

"You are."

"I'm not."

"Can you just—"

"Ana, introduce us," she heard her father say loudly from behind her.

"Yes, yes, of course. Natalie Frederico, meet Klaus Mikhelson, my father."

"Pleased to meet you," Natalie said and extended her hand.

"Likewise," he said accepting. "You are dating my daughter. In romance." It was an announcement more than a question, and Natalie looked from her father to Ana and back again.

"Yes. Oh. I didn't know she'd—"

"Of course she told me. I'm the papa. Let's eat the dinner." With that, he stalked into the restaurant.

"Come on," Ana said, employing her best Russian accent. "It's time to eat the dinner."

"Is he going to kill me?"

Ana smiled. "Well, we're about to find out."

❖

Halfway through dinner, Natalie felt like she was sitting before an inquisition. She focused on her chicken curry as she entertained yet another question from Klaus Mikhelson.

"And where did you, how do you say? Hone your technique after you *quit* the School of American Ballet?" He raised a judgmental eyebrow.

"Oh, um, various places," she told him candidly. "Garages, random studios, an occasional theater if we were lucky."

"Garages? For ballet? No. No." He seemed appalled and signaled the waiter for more wine, as if he would need it to survive her. "Anastasia had best training in the world from the time she was four years old. Best only."

"And it shows." She and Ana exchanged a private glance across the table, but Klaus wasn't done.

"What did you do in these garages made for cars?"

She sat back in her chair and considered the question. "Create, I guess is the best way to put it. Generally a fusion of styles, ballet included, but heavily mixed with modern dance."

Klaus snorted. "Modern dance is for fun only."

"It's not," she said. "It's a perfectly valid art form." He studied her and seemed to soften, making her wonder if standing up to him had earned his respect.

"Do you love my daughter?"

"Papa," Ana said, stepping in. "We're not there yet."

"And why not?" he practically boomed. "Why would you not love her? She is wonderful."

Natalie nodded to Ana to signal that she was okay and turned to Klaus. "I love spending time with your daughter. I think the world of Ana. Even when she's stubborn."

"Oh, she is that," he said emphatically, pointing his fork at Natalie. "When she was six, she refused to take off pointe shoes for two days. And the crust had to be gone from the bread. The crust off or no eating!"

"Oh, I can imagine."

"You have experienced this as well?"

"I have. Not with the crust or shoes specifically, but stubborn in general? Oh yes."

With that, Klaus picked up his wineglass and touched it to Natalie's. "We have something in common. But it is not enough."

Natalie looked from Ana to Klaus. "I'm sorry?"

Ana shook her head at him. "I'm right here, you know."

"I'm speaking to your friend," he told her. "Ana's never introduced me to anyone she had romance for before today," he said to Natalie matter-of-factly. "Not even stage manager."

Ana practically spat her wine across the table, and instead began to choke on it. Natalie coolly passed her a glass of water.

"You knew about that?" Ana asked, clearly floored.

"You're my daughter. It is my job to know the things."

"So spies," she stated. "That means you employed spies to check up on me. Who was it? Bill? I don't even think he knew."

"He knew nothing. Useless. Henry is good man, though."

"Henry from shoes?" Natalie asked, struggling to keep up.

"Henry from shoes," Ana affirmed. "He always was very intuitive and apparently a spy."

"So," Klaus said, taking the reins back and looking to Natalie, "she must think you are very special. Me? I am not so sure." His stare was hard and laser sharp when he said the words, and Natalie knew that this was going to be an uphill battle. Klaus Mikhelson was gruff and imposing with an air of entitlement. He wanted the best for Ana. He just didn't seem to think the best was Natalie.

Perfect.

She drew a breath. "I hope one day I can find a way to change your mind."

"No. Doubtful. Ana needs person who understands her drive. A person who can mirror her, how you say? Ambition. No blessing!"

Natalie looked to Ana, not sure where to go from there.

Ana raised a finger, a fire in her eyes. "I didn't ask for your blessing."

"I am the papa. I give the blessing."

"If this were 1943 maybe," Ana countered, standing up to him. "But you can't just—"

"No more arguing. No blessing." He raised his hand to the passing bus boy. "The check, please! On me, of course," he said to them both.

The dinner had been a roller coaster that Natalie, for one, couldn't wait to disembark.

Later that night at Ana's apartment, she looked on with acute concern as Ana iced down her feet. She was quieter than usual, content to live in her own head, but Natalie wasn't ready to let her deal with whatever was going on alone. "So do you think he'll come around? Your father, I mean."

Ana's eyes were sorrowful when she raised them to Natalie. "He's pretty stubborn, but never say never."

"I know his opinion matters to you."

"It does. More than it should."

Natalie's throat felt tight. "So after tonight, does that make you want to—"

"Change my mind about you and go screaming for the hills?"

Natalie nodded, waiting to hear the words that could clobber her in every way. Better to know now, however. "Yeah, I guess that's what I'm asking. Be honest. Does your dad's opinion of me make you want to rethink things?"

Ana stared at her a moment before shaking her head. "He may be stubborn, Natalie, but I am, too. You're not getting rid of me that easily."

The magnitude of relief that hit rivaled a last-minute stay of execution, and the comparison was eye opening. "But the dinner made you sad. I can tell."

Ana took a moment. "The dinner didn't go as well as I had hoped, but it's not just the dinner. There's just been a lot of difficult going on lately."

Natalie understood that Ana had been masking her injury more than she'd originally let on.

Once Ana finished icing her foot, Natalie held out her hand to her. "Come talk to me. Please?"

Ana took a seat next to her on the couch and Natalie pulled Ana's legs across her lap, which brought Ana close to her. "Tell me about tonight. What happened?"

The telltale tears that touched Ana's eyes told Natalie her intuition hadn't been wrong. "It was awful," Ana said, allowing the tears to fall freely. "And as I'm sitting here, I don't know what I'm going to do. The pain tonight was overwhelming, like nothing I've ever experienced, and my shoes started to die midway through the ballet, making it that much worse." She shrugged. "I was helpless to the situation. The pain markedly affected my performance, and I was modifying steps just to get through it."

"No one noticed. I guarantee it."

"My father would have. He barely said three words about the show, if you hadn't noticed."

"I'm less concerned about him and more concerned about you."

Ana nodded, lifting her arm and then helplessly letting it drop. "I've never been this scared in my life. I guess that's the only way to say it. I don't know what's going to happen and I don't have a solution."

"Okay," Natalie said, mulling this over. "You have two days off. You'll rest that foot and see where you're at."

"I have rehearsal for *Nutcracker* tomorrow."

"No way. You call out. You have to."

Ana nodded, looking more defeated than Natalie thought possible. It was heartbreaking to witness. She pulled Ana the rest of the way into her lap and kissed her cheek, her chin, and with her thumbs wiped away the tears. "I've got you, you know that?"

Ana took a moment with the sentiment. "I've never had that before."

"Well, now you do." Ana stared at her hands, seeming to contemplate the concept. "Do you want to sleep? Are you tired? Tell me what you need."

"Can we veg with the TV first?" Ana asked in the softest, most adorable voice possible.

Natalie nodded and tucked a strand of hair behind Ana's ear. "I was hoping you'd say that." They snuggled up on the couch and zoned out to HGTV, occasionally making fun of the really rich homebuyers. When their eyes were too heavy to continue, they headed to bed. Natalie held Ana and played with her hair as she fell asleep. While her own thoughts about Ana's injury were less than hopeful, she did everything in her power to make Ana feel safe and cared for that night.

They would deal with the rest one step at a time.

❖

The next morning Ana awoke warm and cozy in her own bed, and smiled as the sunlight streaming in from the window touched her face. She realized when her senses floated back that the covers had been tucked intricately around her, as if someone had truly taken the time. But a glance to her right showed her that that someone was gone, which was total shame. Ana reached across the bed to where Natalie had slept the night prior, but found the space cold, signaling that Natalie had been gone a while. After a quick shower and cup of tea, Ana stared at her cell phone knowing what she had to do. Her foot was still incredibly tender to walk on, and Natalie was right. Dancing on it now, on a non-show day, would be a bad idea.

Before she could change her mind, she called the designated company line and let the assistant who answered know that she was under the weather and needed to use a sick day. It meant she'd have some catch-up to do later, but she'd danced the Sugarplum Fairy many times in the past and could rebound easily enough.

With time on her hands now, she decided to explore Natalie's possible whereabouts. She knocked softly on Natalie's apartment door, but was greeted with a rather loud, exasperated, "Come in!"

Ana entered and paused because it looked like a flour bomb had gone off in Natalie's apartment. Billowy white flour dusted the floor, the countertops, and the cabinets and all but completely covered Natalie herself, who stood over a mixing bowl looking like she might kill someone. "Hey, there, Julia Child. What in the world happened in here?"

Natalie regarded her with wild eyes. "There's a potluck before the show tonight and I signed up for chocolate chip cookies, which I figured couldn't be that hard, right? But apparently they *are* because my first round was a bunch of flat and hard paperweights and my second was a gooey mess of awful and I might cry."

Ana inclined her head in sympathy, but bit her lip to hold back her smile. "Have you never made chocolate chip cookies before?"

"Would you believe no?"

Ana took in the wreckage that used to be Natalie's kitchen. "I *would*. Want some help?"

Natalie stood a little taller. "Actually, no. I can do this. It's a matter of principle now. Me versus the cookies."

"You versus the cookies?"

"Uh-huh. We're in a standoff. A chocolate duel, and I'm not going down like this. Do you feel me?"

"Right. Okay. I'll be over here." Ana took a seat nearby at the kitchen table. "Reading this magazine. Hey," she said, holding up a copy of *Pointe Magazine*. "I'm a little surprised to see this here."

"Why?" Natalie asked as she measured a teaspoon of vanilla, spilling extra into her bowl.

Ana winced, but refocused. "Because it's super conscientious of you to study ballet on your off time."

"I'm not a total slacker, you know."

"I never said that. You got up early to make cookies for your colleagues, which is hardly slacking." Natalie cracked an egg and Ana frowned as tiny pieces of shell crumbled into the mixture. "So how would you say it's going over there?"

Natalie glanced up. "Fine."

"Really? Because it looks a little concerning from where I'm sitting, and I say that with only support in my voice. See?"

Natalie shrugged and Ana watched as she blinked back tears. *Natalie* was near *tears* and it was over *cookies*. How was that possible? She learned more about this girl every day. She was anything but predictable. Ana leapt to her feet and covered the short distance to the kitchen counter. "Do you know one thing I'm really good at?" Natalie shook her sad little head, and flour plumed around her as a result. Ana laughed and swatted the cloud into submission. "Making cookies. In fact, I happen to excel at it. You see, when you don't grow up with tons of friends, you occupy yourself in other ways."

"You're brilliant at baking, too? Of course you are. You're good at everything. You should run the world."

Ana took Natalie's chin and turned her face toward her own. "Do you remember what you said to me last night? You said you had me. And that goes both ways, okay? So let me grab my apron and we will knock out some delicious cookies for the potluck." She headed to the door. "We won't even need that many. These are dancers. They're all watching their weight."

"More for me, then," Natalie said. When Ana glanced back, Natalie's smile had returned, and that was everything.

Five short minutes later, and they were under way. Ana had selected her green Christmas Tree apron, and though she brought an extra for Natalie, it was refused. "Aprons are for wusses," Natalie told her.

"Says the girl covered in flour from head to toe."

"You can't make valid points to me right now. I'm super-vulnerable."

"Suit yourself, you delicate flower. You see what I did there?"

Natalie raised a sardonic eyebrow. "So Frozen has a few jokes up her sleeve." Ana dusted one shoulder, then the other in confident victory. She turned to Natalie and rubbed her hands together. "Now let's get this little lesson started." Ana took the lead and, for the next forty-five minutes, instructed Natalie in a step-by-step tutorial of all things cookie. Natalie, it turned out, was an excellent student, but a horrible chef. She wound up wearing half the ingredients she mixed and splattered the walls with cookie dough when the electric mixer got the better of her. Luckily, Ana was there to shepherd the cause, saving her from her confectionary self, time and again.

When the first batch dinged in the oven, Natalie looked to Ana expectantly. "Don't worry," Ana told her. "Third time's a charm."

And it was.

When they cut a warm cookie in half and sampled the merchandise, Natalie's eyes widened in appreciation. "This is my cookie best friend," she said, her mouth still full. "Oh my God, it's so good. We'll probably be eloping."

"You and your cookie?"

"Yep. To Puerto Vallarta."

"That's specific," Ana said, enjoying the candid childlike happiness in front of her.

"Don't be jealous," Natalie said. "You can visit us."

"Puerto Vallarta it is. Now, you get the next batch on the tray and I'll start cleaning up." She gestured around the room. "Because it looks like Hurricane Chocolate blew through here and took no prisoners."

"On it," Natalie said, now in excellent spirits.

They put on some music and Natalie joined Ana in her cleaning quest, dancing as she did it. With flour still covering her ass, she shook it for all she was worth. And what a fine ass it was. Ana had to stop and stare because the flour was like a giant arrow sign. "Don't objectify me while I'm cleaning," Natalie said, continuing her booty pops.

"So when you're finished?"

"Absolutely."

But when they did finish, and the kitchen gleamed once again, smelling of amazing chocolaty goodness, Natalie's appearance placed her in a game of "One of These Things Is Not Like the Others."

"What?" Natalie asked. "Why are you looking at me like that?"

"Well," Ana said, advancing on her, "because you have cookie dough on your cheek." With a kiss to the spot in question, she took care of it. "And a spot of chocolate on your lip." Again, she was happy to help. "Flour in your hair," she said, as she pulled Natalie's ponytail free and watched her hair tumble. "And you're still the hottest woman I've ever seen in my life." Natalie's eyes flashed dark, a look Ana had come to learn signaled desire.

"Well, the hottest woman you've ever seen should probably change clothes," Natalie said quietly. "Do you think you can help with that?"

"I mean, I could try," Ana said innocently. "If you want."

"You've been such a big help so far. I'm just saying that maybe there are a few other tasks you could help me with."

Ana didn't need any more invitation than that. She lifted Natalie's sweater over her head, leaving her standing there in her red bra, which shockingly also showed traces of flour. "Well, look at that," Ana said, gesturing to the marks. "Maybe that should come off, too."

Natalie shrugged. "You're the expert."

Ana undid the front clasp and looked on as Natalie's breasts filled her palms. She pushed against them, squeezing firmly.

"Fuck," Natalie breathed, and closed her eyes.

"I can do that," Ana answered softly, kneading her breasts, captivated by how intensely it affected Natalie. She teased her nipples, loving the weight of Natalie's breasts in her hands. But then the shape of Natalie's exposed neck was too inviting to pass up. Ana placed an open-mouthed kiss there, wringing another gasp from Natalie, who was trapped against the bedroom door. Ana kissed her way up the column and turned Natalie's face to hers, hovering just shy of her lips. "Why are you so irresistible?" she asked. "We can't even get through a simple task like making cookies without my hands needing to touch you."

"You're the one saying that to me?" Natalie asked and crushed her lips to Ana's. The bedroom, Ana thought distantly. They should find their way to the bedroom. Ana reached for the knob, and Natalie pulled her mouth away. "No. Right here," she said, her breathing ragged.

Ana nipped at her jaw. "Here? But shouldn't we find a bed and—"

"No," Natalie said. "Take me right here." Her hips pushed into Ana's thigh. "I like it when you get all instructor-like. You do it a lot."

"You do, huh?" Ana asked and unbuttoned Natalie's jeans. "So that day in the studio—"

"When you kept putting your hands on me—"

"Had you hot?"

"You have no idea." Ana slid her hand into Natalie's jeans and closed her eyes at how wet she already was. Natalie stifled a moan, and with her hand Ana began to explore every dip and crevice until Natalie's fingers were white-knuckling their grip on her shoulders. "Stay with me," Ana said, when Natalie closed her eyes. Natalie blinked hard but obliged. She was staring straight into Ana's eyes when she slid into Natalie. It was Ana who gasped this time, struck at the feel of Natalie enveloping her. She gave her a slow circle with her thumb and Natalie strained against her touch, letting out an inarticulate murmur of pleasure. Her breathing was shallow now, and it was clear she was strung tight. Ana kissed the underside of her jaw and then her neck and she moved in and out, applying pressure with her thumb. When she drove hard inside, Natalie shattered and stilled, her cry muffled into Ana's neck. She would have collapsed onto the floor had Ana not been there to steady her with a firm arm around her waist.

"I'm dead right now, you know that?" Natalie said finally. "You killed me."

Ana smiled against her skin, her hand still down the front of Natalie's jeans. "Not the goal. I'd rather keep you around."

"Try getting rid of me," Natalie said to her quite seriously. And she meant it, which sparked a pang of something powerful within Ana. Things were moving quickly between them, and her feelings for Natalie grew exponentially by the day. As scary as that felt, Ana craved more.

Natalie straightened from the door and slipped her hands up the back of Ana's Henley. "Do you have an hour? I have this idea."

Ana took a step back and stared at her sideways, because with Natalie you never knew. "What's the idea?"

"We climb into that bed," Natalie said and opened the door behind her. "I take your clothes off and do exactly what I've been fantasizing ever since you put that damn apron on."

"I may have an hour," Ana said casually as Natalie tugged her into the bedroom.

Chapter Fifteen

On Ana's second day of calling out of rehearsal, she found herself with very little to occupy her time. Natalie had a rehearsal of her own for a ballet that would open in the winter season, and Ana, given that she couldn't dance, was feeling frustrated with the empty time on her hands and wildly at sea.

This was why she didn't take days off. Ever.

She dully surveyed her apartment, making mental notes of ways to spruce it up and give it more color like Natalie's. Next she made a grocery list, then followed it up with a session of people-watching (as much as one could from the seventh story). She then retrieved the heat wrap for her foot, and finally, curled up on the couch with a novel she'd selected from her modest collection, *A Farewell to Arms*. She'd never been a huge reader, but then again she'd never had much time on her hands. Seconds passed into minutes and minutes passed into hours as she read about Henry and Catherine and their passion-filled love affair.

The sound of a knock followed by the door opening ripped Ana from the tale just as Natalie burst into the apartment.

"Hey, you," she said and placed a kiss on the side of Ana's temple. "I don't know about yours, but today kicked my ass."

"Ditto. What was today?"

"First stumble-through for the Balanchine deal."

"*Symphony in C* can hardly be referred to as the Balanchine deal."

Natalie slid onto the couch next to Ana and gave her chin the tiniest shake. "Fine, Miss Traditionalist. Final dress for *Symphony in C* kicked my ass, and my part isn't even that big."

"At least you got to dance today," Ana said.

Natalie ignored the comment and picked up the book. "What's this book about?"

"Hemingway's version of romance in the midst of a really depressing war. Not bad, actually."

"You read Hemingway?"

"Today I do."

"I don't know if I mentioned this, but I have kind of a thing for smart girls."

"Well, I read a lot of Hemingway," Ana said simply, which earned her a laugh and a kiss.

"I missed you today," Ana told her truthfully. She leaned her head against the couch and let herself float a little, adrift in Natalie's big green eyes. Ana touched her cheek softly. "I never get tired of looking at you, you know that? How do you manage it?"

"I can't give away all my secrets," Natalie said quietly, and stole a lingering kiss.

"I'm lucky to have you," Ana said. They stared at each other for a long moment.

"Nope. That would be me." She tucked a strand of hair behind Ana's ear. "Want to join me in the shower? Could be fun."

Ana laughed at such a blatant leap. "The *shower*? We'd never make it to dinner." But Natalie was already on her way to the bathroom, and moments later Ana heard the sound of the water.

"A total shame," Natalie called to her.

As tempting as it was, they'd made dinner plans with Adrienne and Jenna, and it would be rude to show up late, especially since Adrienne was cooking. "We need to stop for some wine to take," she called to Natalie, who returned to the living room in her bra and underwear.

"I'll let you do the choosing," Natalie said. "Not much of a wine kind of girl."

"Deal."

"And stop checking out my ass," Natalie said as she sauntered back to her waiting shower.

Ana laughed. "I can't agree to that."

An hour later they stood in Adrienne's kitchen, Natalie opening the wine they brought as one amazing aroma after another wafted Ana's way. "I forget how accomplished a chef you are," she told Adrienne, her hip kicked against the counter as Adrienne stirred a decadent-looking mushroom cream sauce on the stove.

"Cooking is one of my most favorite things ever," Adrienne told her with a smile. "I just rarely get to do it." She had her hair pulled into a twist and wore a green sweater that matched her eyes. Ana had always admired Adrienne's sense of style. She'd attempted to copy it when she was younger, but failed dismally. "When I have a lot on my mind or I need to decompress from the world, I head to the kitchen."

"I like the way you think," Natalie said.

"Says the girl who burns toast," Ana told Adrienne dryly.

"Guilty," Natalie said, handing Adrienne a glass of the 2012 Montepulciano d'Abruzzo the wine shop owner had told them was "to die for." "I'm a work in progress. I can admit this."

Adrienne touched her glass to Natalie's. "There's plenty of time for proper toast preparation. Speaking of," she glanced at the clock on the wall, "I apologize about Jenna. She so wanted to be here, but her flight was held up in Chicago."

"What was she doing in LA?" Ana asked.

"Taking a meeting with the Weinstein Company. They're interested in her for an action flick set in the future. It's outside of what she's done before, but if she can add action superstar to her résumé, then there really isn't anything she can't do."

"What about *Elevation*?" Natalie asked, referencing the Broadway dance show Jenna starred in. She took the spinach salad Adrienne handed her and set it on the table.

"That's the tricky part. Her contract with the show is for another six months, so she'd have to negotiate at least four weeks off to shoot the film. They'd most likely bring in someone temporarily and then she'll finish out her run after the film wraps."

Natalie shook her head in reverence. "That show is everything. I've never seen anything so innovative. It's all the things I love about dance packed into ninety amazing minutes."

Adrienne looked as if an idea struck. "If you love it so much, you should audition. Like I said, they're going to need someone to fill in. Plus, you said your true love was modern. It's possible Jenna could get them to take a look at you. No promises, of course."

Natalie passed Ana an "oh my God" look. "I don't want to be presumptuous," Natalie told Adrienne. "But I'd kill for that chance."

"Well," Adrienne said, ruffling Ana's hair as she headed to the table with the bowl of sauce, "let's see how her meeting went and go from there."

"Whose meeting are we talking about?" said a voice from the living room just prior to the sound of the door closing. As they turned, Jenna McGovern appeared in the archway separating the living room and kitchen. Her blond hair was down and she carried a bag slung over her shoulder. She smiled widely at Adrienne as if drinking her in.

"Baby, you're here," Adrienne said, moving to her immediately. She took Jenna's face in her hands and kissed her long and good. "I thought your flight was delayed."

"It was, but I got creative and talked my way onto another one leaving half an hour later. So here I am. Hi," she said, dipping her face to Adrienne's for a kiss.

"Hi," Adrienne said back. "God, I've missed you." And there was more kissing. And then some more.

Ana and Natalie exchanged a smile at the sweet display. Ana had always admired Adrienne and Jenna's relationship. They fit together in the most harmonious mash-up ever. She couldn't help but wonder if she and Natalie were on their way to something similar, and it gave her heart a squeeze. Always intuitive, Natalie slipped her hand inside Ana's and threaded their fingers.

"Ana's here!" Jenna said finally, and moved to her. "I'm so glad we're finally doing this. And I was not at all ignoring you. Just needed to say hello to that one."

Ana hugged Jenna tight. "I understand entirely. And it's good to see you, Jenna."

As Jenna released her, she turned to Natalie and passed Ana an expectant glance. "Well, introduce us."

Ana laughed. "Of course. Jenna, meet my girlfriend, Natalie Frederico."

❖

Her *girlfriend.*

As starstruck as Natalie was to meet one of her idols, she took a moment to let the enjoyment wash over her. It was the first time she could remember Ana using that word. *Girlfriend.* Sure, they were a couple. How could they not be after everything? But she'd yet to hear Ana say the word. So if she was beaming, she didn't mind.

"A pleasure," Jenna said and extended her hand.

"Likewise. I'm a fan of your work. A big one."

"I hear you're quite the dancer yourself." Jenna snagged a grape from the tray Adrienne had laid out on the counter.

"I'm working on it. That's the goal."

"She's being modest," Adrienne said. "They don't cast you as the lead at City Ballet unless you're at the top. Much like Ana."

At the comment, Natalie watched the confident smile dim on Ana's face. It hadn't escaped Natalie that Ana had selected her most comfortable pair of shoes and even then couldn't totally hide the limp, at least from Natalie.

"Speaking of, how's the show?" Adrienne asked as they dug into the amazing food she'd prepared.

"I'm enjoying myself. Because of the rotation with Natalie, I got to luxuriate in a couple days off."

"Enjoy them," Jenna said, obviously in need of a day off herself.

"Back at it tomorrow," Ana said and delicately cut her chicken.

"Unless you call out," Natalie said innocently, and focused on her own dinner, just letting the comment hover. She knew the move was a bold one, exposing Ana's injury to her friends, but the feeling of dread she carried at the concept of Ana dancing on that foot the following day had her consumed and preoccupied. Maybe a couple of seasoned performers, like Jenna and Adrienne, could help Ana see reason.

"Why? What's up?" Adrienne asked, concern creasing her brow.

Ana blew off the question with a wave of her fork. "Nothing. A tendon in my foot has been giving me trouble. But it's feeling much better." Back to her dinner.

"Is it?" Natalie asked, further poking at the lion.

Ana met Natalie's gaze, her blue eyes steely and focused. "It is. Thank you."

Adrienne stepped in. "Ana, if you're hurt, you need to give yourself time. I know how frustrating it can be when you're sidelined from what you want to be doing, but it's for the best in the long run."

Jenna turned to Natalie in explanation. "Adrienne tore her ACL a few years back and had pretty extensive surgery, which took her out of a show we did together."

Natalie nodded. "I had no idea. But you're better now?" she asked Adrienne.

"It took time and there's still some residual stiffness, but yeah, back in business."

"You were lucky," Ana said quite seriously. She looked as if the weight of the world rested squarely on her shoulders, and it probably did. Natalie was doing what she could to ensure that things wouldn't get worse. Surely Ana could see that.

"I was," Adrienne said. "And if you take care of yourself when your body asks you to, you will be, too."

"Understood," Ana said. "That's really good advice. Thank you."

"Anytime. You know that." Adrienne must have decided the room was uncomfortable enough and moved them past it, turning her attention to Jenna. "Tell us about your meeting. We're dying."

"Yeah, tell us how it went," Natalie said.

"It went really well." Jenna sat back in her chair with her wineglass. She looked to Adrienne. "If you're on board, I think we're a go for the film. All parties were in agreement. It shoots for four weeks in Austin, Texas."

"I hung out with a girl there once." Adrienne winked at Jenna. "I think I can do it again. Congratulations." Adrienne picked up Jenna's hand and kissed the back of it. "And what about *Elevation*? Any word there?"

"The producers agreed. I cleared the dates with them first. So I'll step away from the show for four weeks and then step back in."

"So how does that work?" Natalie asked, not wanting to blatantly mention Adrienne's prediction. "Will they use your standby?"

"Possibly. Sometimes they like to bring in someone new so they can write up a fancy press release and act like it's a big deal so people will rush out and buy tickets."

Adrienne raised a conspiratorial eyebrow. "What if the person they brought in was from somewhere prestigious, like say, the New York City Ballet?"

Jenna studied Adrienne when understanding seemed to strike. "You'd be interested?" she said to Natalie. "It's an awesome show, but it kicks my ass nightly."

"I would. I'm in love with the show. It's everything I'm passionate about."

"Well, I will be happy to pass that information along to one of the producers. See if they might want to set something up. You never know. I mean, if you're serious."

"I'm serious."

She squeezed Ana's hand under the table, not really believing this could be a possibility. The squeeze she received back was halfhearted, but Ana passed her a small smile.

They spent the rest of the evening lounging in the living room, drinking wine and swapping stories from the performance trenches. Natalie really enjoyed herself. These girls were down-to-earth and tons of fun, surreal as it was to hang out with them. Even Ana seemed lighter as the evening wore on, laughing freely and leaning in to Natalie.

"I will call you this week," Jenna told Natalie as she pulled her into a tight hug. "Fantastic meeting you." She then wrapped an arm around Adrienne and placed a kiss on her cheek.

Natalie shook her head. "I can't thank you enough."

"You can thank her another time," Ana said playfully. "I think we should give these two some time on their own."

Jenna and Adrienne were now smiling at each other, and though it wasn't overt, Natalie could tell that Ana was right. "Good night, you two."

"Good night," Adrienne said absently.

"Yeah, good night," Jenna called. "Be safe."

Once they were alone in the elevator, Natalie turned to Ana. "I like them. You called it."

"I knew you would. And you were great tonight." Ana lightly grabbed the front of Natalie's shirt and pulled her in. She smiled at the show of affection and the tingles Ana always sent her way. They kissed until the elevator dinged. "We're really good at making use of our time in these things," Natalie said, glancing up at the ceiling.

Ana laughed. "You have a valid point. But I'm mad at you and I forgot."

As they spilled onto the street from Adrienne's building, Natalie feigned shock. "How could you be mad at me? I'm so sweet."

Ana briefly smiled at Natalie's attempt to win her over, but it wasn't the full wattage Natalie had hoped for. "You shouldn't have brought up the injury. I confided that to you and no one else."

Natalie took a moment as they walked. "I get that. I do. But I'm worried."

"Don't be. I'm fine." She said it with finality, like the subject was now closed.

When they climbed into bed that night at Ana's place, Natalie asked the question that had tugged since dinner. Ana hadn't said much at Adrienne's suggestion that she audition for Jenna's role.

"So, what do you think about the *Elevation* possibility?"

Ana studied Natalie, her cheek against the pillow. "So you're actually considering it? That wasn't just the wine talking?"

"Yeah, of course I'm considering it. It's the chance of a lifetime. Don't you think?"

Ana didn't answer right away. Instead, she seemed to gather herself. "You have a contract with City Ballet and you want to just walk away? Natalie, think this through. You don't really want to do that."

And this was where they were different.

Ballet was everything Ana held dear. Natalie was well aware that Ana couldn't for one second imagine how she didn't feel the same. Natalie struggled to explain. "I don't look at it that way. City Ballet has been an awesome training ground but, Ana, this opportunity comes with the kind of work I want to do."

Ana shook her head. "I just can't fathom how you would throw away what someone else would kill for. Don't you see that? There will be more shows down the road for you to branch out."

And there it was.

Natalie slid down the bed until she was face-to-face with Ana. "I just think that we're approaching this from two different—"

"We probably are." Ana sighed deeply. "And I don't want to cut this discussion short, but can we talk about it later? My mind is a mess and I think I just need some sleep before tomorrow."

"Sure. Yeah."

Ana must have sensed her downshifting and raised Natalie's chin, kissing her softly. "Hey, look at me. You are going to be killer at anything you do, whether it's with City or somewhere else That's how good you are. Sweet dreams."

Natalie lay awake, letting Ana's words wash over her. It was a Band-Aid on a disagreement that probably had staying power. In the end, the course of her career would be her decision. Ana would just have to find a way to understand.

Chapter Sixteen

I don't have a good feeling about this. I think it's a bad idea," Natalie said to Ana as they made their trek to Lincoln Center the next day. They'd been going back and forth about the performance most of the day, and now that it was close to call time, Natalie couldn't sit idly by anymore. "I realize you're a stubborn person. I get that, and I'm doing my best to be supportive, but you still limp when you think I'm not looking, and I know you're still dealing with more pain than you admit to."

Ana hadn't looked at her. Instead she'd concentrated on the sidewalk ahead of them. With her dance bag on her shoulder and a purposeful stride forward, Ana was more determined than ever to put herself back in the show. "Natalie, I'm fine. Please stop. I realize you have to be at the theatre, but I don't want you in my head when I'm trying to prep for a show."

"A show you *shouldn't* be dancing," Natalie said, as they crossed the street. Ana passed her a long look and Natalie held up her hands. "Fine. You're an adult, and I've said what I think on the subject."

As dusk shifted to night, they walked in silence for several blocks as they neared the theatre.

"I get that you're coming from a good place, but I'm in control of this situation."

"Sure you are." Natalie shook her head as her annoyance peaked. "So ridiculously stubborn."

"Yeah, well, that goes both ways. You haven't let up for hours now."

It felt horrible to be at odds with Ana, the girl who pretty much owned her thoughts of late, but there was a larger issue here. There were just under two hours until curtain, and Natalie was determined to find a way to make sure that it was her onstage that night and not Ana. She rolled her shoulders against the feeling of foreboding that had prickled her neck for the past twenty-four hours. Somehow she knew that if Ana danced in this performance, the result would be catastrophic.

"I need to talk to you," Natalie said to Jason, in the doorway of his dressing room.

He turned and regarded her without much interest. "Is it important? I still need to warm up."

"She shouldn't dance today. Ana. The tendon in her foot is frayed to nothing. She doesn't want people to know about it, but her doctor says it's serious. If she dances on that foot and the tendon snaps, she's done."

"What?" He swiveled, now fully invested. "She didn't say anything."

"Would you expect her to? You know what she's like."

Realization flared and he sat forward. "That's what was going on during the performance the other night. She wasn't herself."

"Because she was in excruciating pain, Jason. That's what I'm saying. She's in bad shape and she's not listening to her body because of the opportunity she's been given here. I've tried talking to her, but maybe if she heard it from you also."

He nodded. "Yeah, of course. Where is she?"

"She's in warm-up." Natalie followed him there, where they found close to sixty dancers stretching and preparing themselves for performance in a large space adjacent to the stage. Ana was toward the back of the room, but from yards away, Natalie recognized the telltale wince on Ana's face when she executed a leap. Ana shook her head and tried again, lifting her left foot from the floor on the landing and reaching for a barre to steady herself. Just watching made Natalie cringe.

"Hey, Mik. Got a second?" Jason asked as they approached.

Ana looked from Jason to Natalie and back again. "What's up?"

"If you're injured, you know the best thing to do is call out, right?"

Ana's facial expression hardened and sealed off as she flicked a glance to Natalie. "My left foot is tender, but it's much better than it was a couple of days ago. If I felt like I couldn't do my job, I would definitely have Natalie take my place." Ana returned to her warm up and placed her right foot on the freestanding barre and bent to it.

Jason turned to Natalie and shrugged his shoulders. "She seems to know what she's doing. She's a pro. It's not for you to question her." He moved into warm-up himself and Natalie stared at him, incredulous. "Wait. So that's it? You say two words to her and give up?" He looked at her hard. "It's her call to make. Not yours."

Natalie nodded a few times, understanding that siding with Ana placed Jason firmly in her good graces, on her team, which was the only place he ever wanted to be.

She was on her own with this one.

"This is your half-hour call for *Aftermath,*" Priscilla said over the loudspeaker. "Half-hour call, please." Ana caught her reflection in the mirror and recognized the expression: fear. She was scared. She could admit that much. But this opportunity was a huge one for her, and there was only a week left in the run. If she could get through the remaining four performances that belonged to her, *Aftermath* would go down as a triumph on her résumé and not one with an asterisk for attendance.

Still, her warm-up session had about killed her, and doubt crept in. There was a knock at the door and Natalie let herself in. Her face was a crease of worry, and she sat on the couch behind Ana and stared at her in the mirror. "You're sure about this?" she asked. "It's not something you can undo."

Ana met her gaze in the reflection and shook her head slowly. "Honestly, I don't know."

It seemed to be the only opening Natalie needed. She was instantly on her knees in front of Ana. "Look at me, and know how terrified I am right now. Tell me to get dressed, and I will. Please. Don't do this to yourself. It's too risky."

"And what will Bill think of that? And Roger?"

"That you're a world-class dancer with an injury. They run a professional company, Ana, they get it. Plus, you've sat out entire seasons due to injury before. You said so yourself."

"Yeah, and what did that get me? Years stuck in a rut as a soloist. I'm not falling back into that cycle."

Natalie's eyes seemed to plead and she took Ana's hands in hers. "If you won't do it for yourself, will you do it for me? You said that you care about me, that you might be falling in love. If that's true, you'll do this one thing for me."

The sentiment hit Ana hard because there was so much she was willing to do for Natalie.

"I just have this horrible feeling. Ana, if you trust me at all, you'll listen when I tell you that dancing on that tendon is the wrong decision."

Ana squeezed her eyes shut, willing herself to make the right decision. But this was her career she was talking about. She didn't buck that for anyone. She had to do the performance. But Natalie wasn't just anyone. She took Natalie's face in her hands and locked her gaze with Natalie's. "For you?" she asked.

"For me."

After a long moment, she sat back in her chair. "That's about the only thing you could have said to make me agree to this." She gently ran her fingers through Natalie's hair and caressed her cheek.

"Is that a yes? You'll call out?"

Ana nodded, feeling a combination of relief and disappointment hit. "I can't believe I'm saying this, but I'll let Priscilla know I can't do the show. You better get dressed."

Natalie stood and pulled Ana to her feet. "You're doing the right thing. I know it sucks, but it's the wise choice." Natalie kissed her and pressed her forehead to Ana's.

Ana nodded, feeling somehow lighter. "I can't believe I'm about to say this, but you're probably right. Now get to wardrobe and make sure this is a killer show. It's one of mine, so it better be good."

Natalie grinned. "I will do my absolute best to represent your good name."

"Fine. And then come home to me and tell me all about it."

"Deal. And, Ana, thank you. You're doing the right thing." Natalie kissed her one last time before hurrying off to get in costume.

Twenty minutes later, Ana was on her way home in a cab. She couldn't sit there while a performance of hers went on without her. Priscilla had been the consummate professional and immediately went to work making the last-minute changes for Natalie to dance the show. Ana's heart hurt as she sat in the backseat of the cab, watching as they whizzed past nameless, faceless individuals with no idea that she'd just thrown in the towel.

But Natalie was right.

She had a larger career to think about. A bigger picture. She couldn't be willing to give it all up for one performance in one ballet, no matter how noteworthy. She closed her eyes and leaned her back against the seat, willing herself to calm down and accept her situation. The sound of screeching brakes brought her out of it as she was slammed into the back of the passenger seat with such force, she lost her breath. They were spinning, that much she was aware of, as she gulped for air. She tried to grab ahold of something solid in the cab, anything to anchor herself, but the force was too great. Metal crunched. Something awful jammed into her, pinning her between the floor of the backseat and the driver's seat, which seemed to have been bent back and leveled on top of her. The pain hit, sharp and hot, and she screamed as it sliced through her. She couldn't move, that much was clear. Her left arm was trapped beneath the metal undercarriage of the driver's seat. She blinked hard as silence descended, the screeching and the crunching and the screaming now gone. She looked around for any way out of the twisted car around her. She could see the cab driver's hair from above her.

"Sir," she managed to whisper. "Are you okay? Sir, can you talk to me?" But the pain came back full force, and it was excruciating. She screamed, blinking against the agony, wishing it all away. Too much. The pain was too much, it was hard to get air. Her lungs were compressed in the tiny space and it hurt too much when she tried to move. She wasn't going to survive this. She'd been crushed. It was only a matter of time now until it was all over.

What had happened again?

Where was she?

There were people nearby. She could hear them, and then a man's face looked in at her thought the shattered glass. That man would help them, she thought, as blood ran from her forehead into her eyes. Please, God, someone help her.

Make it stop.

Make it stop.

❖

What in the world was going on?

Ana still wasn't answering her door and Natalie's text messages had all gone unanswered. She knocked again and waited. "Ana?" she called into the apartment. "If you're in there, I need you to let me know." It was close to midnight, and after coming home from the performance, Natalie was surprised to find Ana MIA. It was possible she was still upset about having to pull out of the show, which was why Natalie had made a detour on the way home and picked her up a to-go quart from Shake Shack, hoping to find a way to cheer her up. "Okay, well, I'm going to go back to my apartment and text you five thousand more times until you answer me. You're starting to freak me out."

Something didn't feel right.

Instead of texting Ana, Natalie went on a calling spree. She checked with Helen, Audrey, Jason, and anyone else who might have seen Ana after she left the theatre. Yet no one knew anything. She tried banging on the door again and, feeling out of options, slid down the wall in the hallway to the floor. She'd just sit there and wait then. What else could she do? Forty-five minutes later, her phone buzzed in her back pocket from a number she didn't recognize.

"Hello?"

"Natalie, it's Bill Bradshaw. I apologize for the late hour."

"That's okay. Is everything all right?"

"It's not. I received a call tonight from Klaus Mikhelson, who asked me to alert you to a situation we're dealing with. Ana Mikhelson was unfortunately in a serious car accident earlier this evening when her cab swerved to avoid a wrong-way driver and careened into a brick wall at a high rate of speed."

Natalie felt the cold shiver move up her spine as she covered her mouth, sending up silent prayers. *Please don't do this. No, no, no.*

"Is she okay?"

"Her prognosis is uncertain at the moment, though she's listed as critical. She's in surgery at Sinai."

"Sinai," she repeated, making sure she had it correctly. "What kind of surgery?"

"While she has multiple injuries, her arm sustained the worst of it. Her elbow practically shattered, according to her father."

"Oh my God, no," Natalie said, pushing herself to her feet. She needed her bag and then she needed a cab to the hospital.

"Her father's plane should be landing soon. Natalie, do you think you can cover some extra performances? We'll begin rehearsing the designated understudies to get them ready, but it will take a day or two."

"Of course. Whatever I can do. But I have to go." Her mind wasn't on the show at all. It was on Ana and what horrible thing had happened to her. When Natalie emerged from her apartment with her bag, she stared at the door to Ana's, knowing now that her apartment stood eerily empty. A feeling of dread like none other washed over her, cold and still, nearly paralyzing her there in the hallway. She took a deep breath and willed her mind to calm itself and instead focus on the tasks in front of her.

She needed to move her feet now. One in front of the other. That would get her to the hospital.

That would get her to Ana.

CHAPTER SEVENTEEN

Natalie had been at the hospital for eight hours as she waited for Ana to regain consciousness following surgery. She was sleep deprived, hungry, and scared, but there was no way she was going anywhere. The beep, beep, beep of the machine next to Ana's bed kept time in an eerie serenade. The sound, coupled with the sharp smell of disinfectant, had Natalie a little nauseous.

When she'd arrived at the hospital, she'd been relegated to the waiting room where she sat in a cold plastic chair, waiting hours for any sort of update. It hadn't been until Klaus had arrived, and reluctantly listed her as family on the intake form, that she'd been allowed into Ana's hospital room. And thank God, because she hadn't been getting anywhere with the tight-lipped nurses. After a few barked questions, Klaus had them providing whatever information they could on Ana, which still hadn't been much. He'd turned his gaze on Natalie next and regarded her the way one would a bug indoors. However, she reminded herself that he had been the one to get word to her of the accident, so she remained grateful in spite of the chilly reception.

Seeing Ana in her current state had been terrifying. Even now and with hours to adjust, Natalie still had trouble recognizing her. Her face was pale and swollen and carried a myriad of frightening bruises and lacerations, the one on her forehead deep and requiring stitches. She'd come away from the accident with a concussion they'd need to monitor, and her body appeared battered with a variety of injuries Natalie couldn't even name. However, it was Ana's left arm that caused the most concern. She'd severely broken the ulna bone in her forearm, and her elbow had required detailed reconstruction in a lengthy operation. Currently, her arm was immobilized in a brace that came with complicated metal joints and hinges, all of which terrified Natalie. More than anything, she just wanted to stroke Ana's hair and whisper to her that it was going to be all right. On one hand, she was afraid of hurting Ana. And on the other, she knew that it wasn't going to be all right. The doctors had confirmed to Klaus that her arm would heal with time and physical therapy, but with the nature of her injury, she would never regain full range of motion.

Translation: Ana was done as a professional ballet dancer and she didn't even know it yet.

"I need coffee. Strong coffee," Klaus announced to the room, though Natalie was the only one there.

"Sure. Go ahead. I'll be here if she wakes up."

"Do you want the coffee?" he asked, at last making eye contact with her, his voice softer now.

"No, thank you."

He nodded and left her alone with the beeps, the whirring, and the worry that ate away at her. She slid her chair closer to Ana and took her good hand, interlocking their fingers. "Hey, you. I don't really know where to start. I'm so very sorry this happened, Ana. So sorry. I know I tease you a lot, and we may argue about silly things, but you've come to mean more to me than any other human. So we're going to get through this together, you hear me? You and me. We got this. So how about you wake up so we can start?" Ana didn't stir. "You should be warned now that there will probably be lots of kissing along the way. I mean, have you met us? C'mon. I would love it if you would open your eyes, Ana, because I'm really scared about now."

But apparently Ana wasn't ready to wake up just yet.

As she waited, Natalie laid her head on the side of the bed next to Ana's shoulder and waited. Klaus returned after not too long, and they sat in silence as once again, the beeps reminded them of the horror that brought them to this spot.

"There she is," Ana heard a voice say distantly. The sound floated to her as if she were underwater and being called to the surface. She blinked in an attempt to right herself, but everything was blurry and the voices still seemed far away and strange. There was a woman standing over her, that much she could tell. "Anastasia, my name is Wendy. I'm the nurse who will be taking care of you today. Are you able to speak?"

Ana tried to say something, but her mouth was dry and her throat hurt.

"Here you go," the woman said and placed a straw against her lips.

The water was cool and refreshing even if it did hurt going down. "Thank you," she rasped. Her voice didn't seem to be there.

"Anastasia," the nurse said, "you just had surgery, but you're doing just fine, okay. You just rest. Can you do that for me?"

Ana stared at her blankly, blinked a few more times, and nodded. She swallowed again, and it was easier this time. A quick check-in with herself revealed that her body felt thick and heavy, as if it weren't totally hers.

"Your family is here." The nurse gestured to two people at the foot of Ana's bed: her father and Natalie. They were there with her, so it was going to be okay. They would make sure.

"Kotik, it is good to see you," her father said. Maybe she was dreaming, but it seemed as though there were tears in his eyes. Was that possible?

"Hey, you," Natalie said, standing so that Ana could see her better. She looked tired, as best as Ana could tell.

She attempted to speak, but it took her another moment to gather the strength. "What happened?" she asked finally.

Natalie sent her father a look. "You were in a cab on your way home from Lincoln Center. There was a wrong-way driver and you crashed. You're okay, but pretty banged up. Try to stay still, okay?"

Ana took a moment. "You did the performance," she stated, trying to piece it all together.

"I did."

"I don't really remember much after that."

"That's okay. That's probably a good thing. You were brought here in an ambulance and the doctors are taking great care of you. Bill called me, and I came right over. Your dad flew in right away."

"Of course I come," her father said. Those *were* tears, Ana realized as he wiped one away. That didn't bode well.

"We can get you caught up to speed later," the nurse said,

intervening. "Right now I'm going to take your vitals while you rest. That's the best thing you can do for yourself." The request wasn't a hard one to honor, as Ana's eyes were heavy and seemed to close again of their own volition. She drifted away easily, and maybe when she woke again, everything would be back to normal.

❖

The hospital cafeteria left much to be desired.

Natalie picked up one half of the burned grilled cheese sandwich, flipped it over and examined the pattern of the black markings, and set it down again. And repeat. Damn it. Taking a deep breath, she refocused. She needed to eat, as she would have to find the strength to dance the show that night. After pep-talking herself, she took a halfhearted bite of the now-cold sandwich and forced herself to chew the rubbery bread and cheese combo. She choked down half of the horrific sandwich and called it a victory before heading quickly back to Ana's room on the third floor.

Ana had been asleep for the past six hours. Natalie had left to allow Klaus some time on his own. He hadn't said much, though it was clear to Natalie that he was struggling a great deal with his emotions. When she arrived back at the room, however, it wasn't Klaus she found waiting there, but a wide-eyed Ana.

"Well, look who's up," she said and moved to Ana's bedside.

Ana searched her face as if desperately trying to figure out a difficult puzzle. "What happened to my arm?" she asked. "Natalie, my arm."

"Where did your father go?" Natalie asked instead.

"To find my doctor. He wouldn't answer my question. Please tell me. *Please.*"

Natalie didn't have a clue how to answer because as she understood it, Ana's arm was in horrible shape. But she couldn't avoid the question, with Ana wide-eyed and begging. She was out of her depth with how to tiptoe around that, but she had no choice but to give it a shot. "You had surgery to repair the broken bones in your arm and elbow. That brace keeps your arm from moving so it can heal."

Ana stared at her as understanding seemed to settle and then flare. Ana's eyes got wide. "How bad is it?"

"Bad," Natalie told her. Ana wasn't going to let her get away with anything but brutal honesty here. "It's bad. You're going to be just fine, though, and with therapy, you're going to get your arm back. It's just going to take some time."

"Fully?" Ana asked.

"We can worry about that later. Let me go find your father and that doctor."

"No. Tell me now! Natalie," her voice cracked with emotion, "I need to know. Fully?"

It was the question that would make all the difference, and Natalie braced against what she was about to say. This would be the moment Ana learned that her career, or at least the career she knew, was over. "No, sweetheart. Not fully. The doctors don't think the range of motion will return to what it was."

Ana shook her head against the pillow as tears pooled and fell. "Please be a dream. It has to be a dream."

"Ana, you have a concussion. You have to lie still."

"The cab crashed," she said, incredulous, in full panic mode. "Then what happened? After it crashed?"

"The best I can understand is that they had to work to get you free. The metal from the car, it was twisted around you."

Ana stared at the wall as if studying the detail. "There were people there. I remember the EMTs talking to me."

"You were very lucky."

She looked at her arm. "Doesn't feel lucky. God, it's like my mind won't work either, to work it all out. Everything is numb. I can't think."

Natalie smoothed her hair gently. "You don't need to think about it now. Let me think about it. I've got you, remember? Close your eyes and get some rest."

There were tears of terror in Ana's eyes as she looked around the room. "You won't leave me? Promise?"

"I have *Aftermath* tonight, but I'll be here until then. Everything is going to be okay."

"It's not. It's not okay," Ana said sorrowfully, just as she seemed to drift off again. "I never should have been in that cab."

Natalie swallowed against the blunt force of that statement, refusing to examine it too closely. She left Ana for the first time that night and did what she could to focus on dancing the way Ana would have, giving it her all. Unfortunately, her all was now diminished by her own emotional state, laced with fear and worry, not to mention the guilt that threatened to overwhelm her if she let it.

When she arrived back at the hospital late that night, Ana's bed had been raised so that she could sit up a bit. Her gaze fell dull and lifeless on the beige wall across from her.

"Hi," Natalie said quietly upon entering.

Ana shifted her focus to Natalie and her whole demeanor shifted. Gone was the lifeless stare, and in its place, she looked at Natalie with hurt in her eyes. "Why couldn't you have let me dance?"

"What?" she heard herself say, her voice barely audible.

"I should have been onstage last night, not in a cab."

Natalie swallowed against the words she'd feared most. "I didn't want you to hurt yourself. I was trying to do what I thought—"

"My career is over, Natalie. There's nothing left for me."

"That's not true. You can still have a career. It just might not be—"

Ana shook her head sadly. "The surgeon says if I work hard enough, I'll regain basic function. Basic. That's it. You can't be a professional with the word 'basic.'"

"I know, I just…I'm so sorry, Ana." Natalie's gaze fell to the floor. The spotted pattern of the tile swirled as she allowed herself to feel the full extent of what had transpired. Intentional or not, her actions had robbed Ana of the one thing she treasured over all else. "We're gonna get through this."

"We?" Ana's eyes flashed a combination of anger and sorrow. "You danced a show tonight. You didn't have anything to get through. I'm the one."

Natalie blinked against the unexpected assault of words. "I'll be here with you every step of the way."

"No."

Her insides went icy. "No?"

"You should probably leave."

"I can give you space, but I'm coming back tomorrow."

"If you care about me at all, Natalie, you won't do that. When I look at you, I just see the reason I'm in this bed. Maybe that's not fair, I don't know, but it's the reality of my world now, so…"

Natalie stood there paralyzed. Ana wanted her to go. She blamed

Natalie for the accident, and hell, maybe she was right to. "Ana." It was a plea.

"Please go, Natalie."

"I don't want to—"

"Go!" Ana shouted.

So she did. Hollowed out and broken inside, Natalie walked slowly from Ana's hospital room. The color drained slowly from the world around her until everything hung gray and heavy as she made her way home. She'd hurt the one person she cared for most in the world and lost her forever. Numb and empty, she crawled into her bed that night and replayed the events of the past forty-eight hours over and over again until she rushed to the bathroom, physically ill. She held her head in her hands as tears descended, falling thick and hot onto the bathroom floor. She'd give anything to take it all away.

Anything.

❖

The second week in the hospital brought with it a shift from difficult to unbearable for Ana. Her body was weak from so much time spent in bed, and her injuries, though healing, still had her in quite a bit of pain. A steady stream of visitors kept the days from dragging on too terribly, but even her friends had a difficult time cheering her up.

For Ana, life was now devoid of all meaning, and each day she struggled served as a harsh reminder that she'd lost everything.

"Mik, I need you to smile," Jason told her well into one of his visits. The day hadn't been a good one for Ana, and her frustration had peaked. He'd stopped by every couple of days and had apparently noticed the lack of improvement as far as her spirits went.

"See, that's the thing," she told him flatly. "Not feeling like there's a ton of things to smile at about now. If you were me, you'd feel the same way."

Jason pivoted from the touchy topic in typical Jason fashion. He wasn't a fan of conflict. "Any idea when you might be sprung from this place?"

"My doctor thinks end of the week is likely. Just waiting on some of my levels to bounce back." It was then that the respiratory therapist popped her perky head in the room. Ana winced inwardly. She so didn't need the perky right now. It took all of her restraint not use her good arm to throw a pillow at the sprite-like creature.

"Whose lungs are ready for their afternoon Jane Fonda?" the young woman asked, and reached for the little floating ball contraption.

"Not sure," Ana told her. "No one here. Try next door."

The young woman laughed like she'd just told the joke of the century. "Well, someone has their sense of humor back."

"Actually I don't, and I really can't do the lung thing right now. My friend is here."

"I can move you to the end of the rotation," the lung girl said, stricken now but still rallying, "but we need to work those little guys this afternoon."

"Fine. Come back later, please."

"Will do." She offered a crestfallen little salute and exited the room.

"That was hardcore," Jason told her once they were alone. "She's only trying to help."

"I'll write her an apology letter when I get out of here." She started to cough then, a result of breathing too deeply. The bottom portion of her lungs had diminished performance, and time spent in her hospital bed was only making them worse.

"Have you given any thought to your father's offer? Spending some time in Miami while you get better might be awesome."

"My home is here."

"I know. I just worry about you once you go home, you know. You'll need help."

"I'll be fine."

"What about Natalie?"

Ana went still. "What about her?"

"Any change of heart on that front? Listen, you know I'm not a huge fan, but she's a wreck, Mik. We close the show this week and that's probably a good thing. I think she might need a little break."

Ana swallowed against the information, pushing it to the side in the interest of self-preservation. "No, nothing has changed between us," she said quietly. In actuality, Ana didn't allow to let herself think about Natalie and what they'd had because at just the mention of her name, something painful and sharp hit and lingered. If she acknowledged the acute loss of that relationship, she'd come undone. The accident hadn't just stripped her of her ability to dance, it had sliced away at her entire life, and Natalie was part of the collateral damage.

It didn't matter, though.

There was no way for them to move forward.

Though she could see now that Natalie's intentions had been honorable the night of the accident, it didn't matter. That knowledge simply didn't take away the resentment she carried and couldn't quite shake. She would forever associate Natalie with what had happened to her whether she wanted to or not.

"She wants to come and see you."

"Not a good idea." An image of Natalie cradling her face and smiling at her in Rockefeller Center flashed and Ana shook her head against it, shutting out the image. Rejecting it and the feelings that came with it.

No. Not gonna happen.

"Have it your way," Jason said. "I gotta head out. Meeting with Bill about the upcoming season."

"Fabulous."

"Everyone misses you. Sends their love." He kissed her on the forehead and headed off into the world that seemed so very, very far away.

Alone in her room, she stared at the wall and, for the thousandth time, replayed the events of the night that had changed everything.

Chapter Eighteen

L et's try two more," Eugenia said. Ana stared hard at the physical therapist who had been assigned to her after leaving the hospital. She was not at all feeling it, after already having done the three extra reps Eugenia had talked her into beyond their normal session concluded. This woman was a slippery one and had to be watched. "I can't. My shoulder is killing me." And it was. With her arm completely out of commission in the T-scope brace for the past few weeks, it took a lot to stimulate the muscles again. After manually forcing the joint to open and her arm to extend—to enormous pain, she might add—they'd done a plethora of rotator cuff exercises that only added to the excruciating factor. Ana was frustrated, hurting, and ready to be done for the day.

Eugenia dipped her head and met Ana's eyes. "I need you to push yourself. You're a fighter, Ana. I can tell."

She had been a fighter. That part was true, right up until this accident. She thought back to the last time she'd been in rehab, following surgery on her ankle. Back then, she'd had plenty of reasons to get herself back in prime shape. She'd been highly motivated, pushing herself harder and harder so she could get back to work and back to doing what she loved. But that wouldn't be happening this time, so what was the point in putting herself through all the unnecessary pain? "I'm sorry," she told Eugenia. "But I need to go. Same time on Tuesday?"

Eugenia nodded reluctantly and stood as Ana did. "Don't forget your daily heat wraps. Let's stimulate those muscles and get them working again."

"Will do," Ana said halfheartedly on her way out the door. On the brighter side, all these weeks away from dance had moved the pain in her foot from astronomical to manageable. The irony was something she was trying to push past.

She glanced at her watch. If she hurried to the train, she could maybe beat the work rush of people who were out in the world doing things. Unlike herself.

The information slashed at her, the sting of her new fate still so very raw.

Everything felt different now. *She* felt different. *Life* did. So much of her identity had been tied to ballet. Now that she was removed from it, she wasn't sure how to exist anymore. Her purpose, a concept she ruminated on often, now eluded her.

When Ana arrived home to her apartment building that afternoon, she searched for her keys with her good arm, focusing on the newly difficult task, which was why she didn't notice Natalie exiting her own apartment and heading quickly down the hall until their near collision.

"Whoa," Natalie said, pulling up short. "I'm sorry I…" The words died on her lips when she raised her gaze to Ana. "You're home."

"Yeah. A couple days now." They'd been bound to run into each other sooner or later; they lived across the hall. Still, Ana hadn't been fully prepared for the impact of seeing Natalie again. Right there in front of her. Big green eyes. Hair pulled back in a ponytail. Dance bag over her shoulder.

"How are you?" Natalie asked.

"Better. Thank you."

A pause.

The uncomfortable kind.

"I called the hospital too see if I could stop by, but—"

"I said no. Yeah, I know. Just…wasn't a good idea."

Natalie nodded, but her eyes were sad. "I…understand."

Ana gestured to her door with her head. "I guess I better…"

"Right. Of course." Natalie headed down the hall, before pausing and turning back. "For what it's worth, Ana, it's really good to see you."

Ana nodded, swallowed against the onslaught of emotion, and let herself into her apartment. Once inside, she leaned against the door and let it come. The sharp tightening in her chest, the tears that touched her eyes, and the pang of longing for everything that once was and would never be again.

There was no going back in time.

Don't give it that kind of power, she reminded herself. She gave her head a determined shake and harnessed what strength she had to move past it.

Forcing herself to focus, she dropped her keys on the kitchen counter and checked for messages. Nothing. But really, what messages would there be? Friends calling to check up on her? Nope. The initial wave of well-wishers had all returned to regularly scheduled programming. They'd gone back to their lives. A job opportunity? Unlikely. The extent of her recovery was still very much in the air and no one knew where her head was. She was on the no-call list as far as the dance world was concerned, leaving her adrift on her own, with no real clue how to fix it. Her father had reiterated his offer to bring her out to Miami, giving her a chance to recuperate in the sunshine, which he swore had healing powers. But he looked at her differently now, too. He had to. She didn't carry the potential to do great things in the ballet world anymore, the way he always dreamed she would. The last time she'd seen him had been in the hospital. He'd smiled at her, but his eyes carried sadness, a sadness she'd placed there.

Her life felt like a bad dream she couldn't wake up from.

Ana found that January and its dreary bluster was the perfect companion to her mood of late. She'd been in the stupid brace for over three months now and counting the days until she was free of it. Another four weeks according to her doctor, though her physical therapy would persist a bit longer. But for Ana, the world had lost its color, and the edges of life had dulled into a boring gray mass.

She turned another page in her *Better Homes and Gardens* magazine and stared uninterested at the page. Apparently, blue was making a comeback. She hadn't been aware of its decline, but then she'd had other things to concentrate on. Now she could focus on things like blue and its phoenix-like rise from the ashes. *Go blue*, she thought blandly, just as a loud series of knocks stole her focus. Who in the world could that be? she wondered.

More knocking. Incessant knocking.

"Open up in there, you ridiculous rock star!" said a voice Ana recognized as Audrey's.

"We have Champagne, and damn it, we're not afraid to use it."

Helen was with her, Ana noted, from the second voice. Confused, she pushed herself from the couch and opened the door to investigate. What she found was that it wasn't her door being beaten down, but rather Natalie's.

"Congratulations!" the friends shouted just as Natalie swung open her own door. She was smiling widely and holding her hands up, palms out.

"You guys are awesome!" And that's when she noticed Ana. "Hi," she said, her smile dimming a tad.

"Hey. I didn't mean to interrupt. I just heard the noise."

Audrey and Helen turned and smiled at Ana. They'd visited her in the hospital, but seemed happy to see her standing there.

"Ana!" Audrey practically shouted. "Toast with us!"

"What are we toasting?" she asked absently as Helen wrapped her arm gingerly around Ana's shoulder and ushered her into Natalie's apartment.

"We're toasting Natalie's fantastic success," Helen said.

"She booked *Elevation* for the four weeks Jenna McGovern is out."

"She did?" Ana asked. "You did?" she repeated, turning to Natalie.

"I did." Natalie met her eyes. "I got the call this afternoon." She turned to her cabinet and pulled four glasses as Audrey opened the Champagne with a pop. Given everything that had transpired in the past six weeks, it somehow felt wrong for Ana to participate in the toast. As if she didn't belong there among this group of dancers. At the same time, it felt cold to back out of the apartment now. Then there was a third part of her that was actually happy for Natalie, as strange as that somehow felt.

"To Natalie and her kick-ass success," Helen said, raising a glass.

"Cheers," Audrey echoed.

Ana touched her glass to the center of the glasses and sipped lightly as Audrey and Helen peppered Natalie with questions. It seemed she'd met with one producer, danced for two others, and on Jenna's recommendation was offered the four-week stint.

"Jenna was right," Natalie told them. "They want to run a whole ad campaign surrounding City Ballet. Because it's good PR for the company, Bill is willing to give me the time off and collaborate with *Elevation* on marketing."

Helen nodded. "So you start rehearsal…"

"Monday for three weeks. It'll be a crazy-fast turnaround. I'll do the four-week run while Jenna's away, and then we'll see."

"We'll see about what?" Audrey asked.

Natalie searched for an answer. "What's next, I guess?"

"You go back to City Ballet," Ana said before thinking.

"Or…maybe I don't. I'm in the midst of my second ballet with City and I've learned an enormous amount, which has provided me with this awesome opportunity. But I'm not sure that holding on to classical ballet is the best career move, given where I want to be."

"But the opportunity," Ana said, shocked Natalie didn't recognize what she had. What she herself would give anything to have back.

"Is huge. I get that. And you know what? Maybe you're right."

"You don't have to say that on my account."

"I'm not." Natalie passed her a reassuring smile.

"What about your contract?" Helen asked.

"I'm pretty confident they'd release me entirely if I asked."

Ana set her glass on the kitchen counter as her emotions blew past her logic. "I better get home. Long day." A total lie, but she didn't want to dampen the high spirits and she wasn't very good at celebrating these days. "Congratulations," she said to Natalie before fleeing the scene.

Natalie stared at the door as it closed behind Ana.

"Give her time," Helen said. "She's happy for you underneath it all."

"Yeah," Natalie said, not at all convinced, given Ana's situation. She hadn't meant to upset her, and maybe the overt celebration in her presence had been insensitive. Underneath it all, however, was the fact that she missed Ana desperately and remembered a time when it would have been her and Ana celebrating together.

"You must be beyond excited for this," Audrey said from her spot on the couch. She lay on her back staring up at them.

"I am. In fact, I'm not sure it's fully sunk in yet." The truth was that while she was happy, it didn't feel the way she once imagined it would. But then again, since Ana's accident, everything about the way Natalie saw the world had shifted. The luster had dimmed considerably.

"As for returning to City after the gig, I completely identify with the struggle," Helen told her, topping off her Champagne. "This might be my last season."

"You're leaving?" Audrey said, sitting up abruptly. "You can't."

Helen held up a hand. "Nothing is set in stone yet. I'm just examining my options."

Natalie set down her nearly untouched glass and considered this. "I had no idea. What gives? I thought you were bound and determined for ballet superstardom."

"Oh, I am," Helen said. "I've just been thinking a lot about what you said the first day we met, about dancing for yourself. As much as I love the art form, the classical world has never been a comfortable fit for me."

"And why is that?" Audrey asked.

"Well, first of all, it's ultraconservative."

Natalie nodded. "True."

"Second of all, I'm black."

"Shut up," Natalie said, feigning mystification.

"Funny. But I am."

Audrey placed a hand over her heart. "I, for one, am glad you confided in us."

Helen kicked the couch beneath Audrey. "The truth of the matter is that I'm tired of a bunch of old white guys deciding that my body isn't right for classical ballet. And I'm not singling City out, because they've been supportive. It's the people who come with the institution: the reviewers, the patrons, and the armchair commentators. It's the same message I've heard since I was ten, that my legs are too muscular or I don't fit the typical mold. It's all a bundle of excuses. I'd rather take the power right out of their hands and be my own kind of pioneer. Dance *my* way. Maybe that's ballet, maybe it's not. But it's going to be my choice. Fuck those guys."

Natalie grinned. The longer she knew Helen, the more she adored her. "I like the way you think."

"So the point of this little pseudo confession is if you ever run into a project that sounds like it might fit, please give me a call."

"You're on. And trust me, I will be on the lookout. We would be kick-ass together on something collaborative." The two touched their glasses together in the sealing of the unnamed pact.

"Am I chopped liver over here?" Audrey balked.

"You can come, too, Audrey," Natalie told her. "Though I feel like you're on the rise with City."

"Oh, I'm not going anywhere. I just enjoy being desperately wanted."

With that Helen tossed a pillow her way, smacking her square in the face.

"Or clobbered by a pillow. Either will do," Audrey said, as the group dissolved into celebratory, Champagne-laced laughter.

CHAPTER NINETEEN

Natalie's fourth rehearsal for *Elevation* had come with a hell of a learning curve. She'd always prided herself on being a quick study when it came to picking up complicated choreography, but this show fell into another category entirely. She wondered how in the world Jenna had mastered these steps and where she found the stamina to execute them each night when so much of the show was simply *her.*

Feeling a little demoralized, she exited the elevator en route to her apartment where she dreamed of ice, her couch, a hot meal, and maybe a bath before bed. The jar of peanut butter that rolled her way and crashed against her foot was an unexpected encounter. She scooped it up curiously and raised her gaze to the hallway, taking in the chaos. Groceries, lots of them, littered the space. A series of cherry tomatoes dotted the carpet, cans of green beans, corn, and a gallon of milk. With her injured arm still in the T-brace, Ana held a ripped grocery bag in her good arm and sank to her knees to pick up the casualties.

"Here, let me help," Natalie said, joining her on the floor.

"That's okay," Ana said, her cheeks dusting red in embarrassment. "The bag broke just as I was almost home. I can do it."

"You can," Natalie told her. "But we can do it faster together." In actuality, Ana would have had a difficult time on her own, as the broken bag was now entirely ineffective and she was working one-handed. "Give me your key," she said.

Ana, still struggling to wrangle the groceries, reluctantly did so. Natalie opened the apartment, piled cans from the hallway into her arms, and brought them inside to Ana's kitchen counter. When she returned to the hallway, there were only a few scattered tomatoes that she easily tracked, rescued, and placed back in the carton Ana held open.

"This was embarrassing. I'm sorry," Ana told her, still not readily meeting Natalie's gaze. "The stupid bag, and then my arm."

"Hey, it's okay. If dropping groceries was the most embarrassing thing that's happened to you today, then you came out way ahead of me." For the first time, Ana looked at her and Natalie felt her stomach tighten when their eyes locked. "I won't keep you."

As Natalie made her way to the door, she heard Ana sigh as if surrendering to an unseen foe. "Is everything okay?"

"It will be. Difficult rehearsal today. I guess maybe I bit off more than I can chew with this show."

"I'm sorry."

"Don't be." Ana surely didn't want to hear about her rehearsal troubles, given how she felt about Natalie and her relationship to the accident. "I'll let you get back to…groceries."

"All right. Thanks again," Ana gestured loosely in the direction of the hallway, "for the assistance."

"Anytime. I'm right through that door if you need anything."

"I know."

"I'm not just saying that, Ana."

Ana's eyes found the countertop and stayed there. "I know."

"Good night…I guess."

"Yeah. Good night."

It hadn't been a horrible exchange, but being near Ana now, given everything, was harder than Natalie could have ever predicted. It was Ana, but not in the way she knew Ana. She was responsible for that, she reminded herself for the fifty thousandth time. Didn't mean Ana was any less beautiful to her, even as they stood in that kitchen, or that Natalie didn't still remember what it was like to fall asleep in Ana's arms as she drifted off alone each night. It would be a memory she carried with her always, and took out when she couldn't go on any more without it.

❖

The following week, Ana forced herself to complete the exercises her physical therapist had outlined for her. It was the first time she'd done the assigned homework, and she paid for it now. The exercises didn't come easy, but she accepted full responsibility for how far behind she was in her own recovery. However, as days passed one after another, she couldn't just sit around any longer. She'd lose her mind. Maybe it was time to start taking back control. Well, what little she could take back anyway.

"You will be instructor," her father had said to her decisively at dinner just a few evenings prior. He'd taken to flying in once a week to check in on his invalid daughter, which was fine with her. It was actually kind of nice seeing so much of him.

"I don't really see myself in that role," she answered politely, and passed him the cardboard container of Pad Thai from the delivery place down the street.

"Nonsense. You have never tried. My friend, Genevieve, is freelance choreographer. You remember, yes? She teaches classes to the young people in midtown on her days off. I'll arrange to have you sit in this week."

"That's not necessary."

He raised his gaze to her in exaggerated question and then made a show of looking around the room. "What? You have a tight schedule or something I do not know about? A very pressing agenda of things? You go to class. If you hate, you hate. We won't know the hate until you go."

She shook her head in annoyance, but recognized his valid point. Not only did she not have a tight schedule, she had no schedule. "Fine. But only because you're being difficult."

He laughed. "Yes, I am the difficult one, Kotik. Pass the jump rolls."

"Spring rolls."

"That's what I said."

Genevieve Drescher had been more than agreeable to Ana sitting in on one of her classes. In her late forties now, she'd spent her career as a successful ballet dancer with a variety of companies, having toured the country twice.

"While I love working with professionals," she told Ana as she prepared for class, "this is honestly my favorite part of the week."

"And why is that?" Ana asked, very much trying to understand the draw to teaching over dancing.

Her eyes warmed. "There's nothing like watching the spark of passion when it hits a young dancer for the first time. Many of the kids take the class because they simply enjoy it. They'll go on to other things. Sports, the mall. But in the midst of the group, there will be one or two who you know won't be able to live without it."

Ana nodded, remembering that feeling from when she was a kid. Dance had consumed her thoughts from the time she woke up until she went to sleep each night. It felt like she simply couldn't learn fast enough. And while she wasn't exactly eager to sit in on the class, she found herself looking forward to maybe catching a glimpse of that spark…

As the Wednesday-night class filed into the dance studio in a symphony of preteen chatter, Ana observed from a metal chair along the wall. She watched the young dancers unpack their dance bags, stretch, and move into a series of barre exercises. Genevieve moved among them offering adjustments, critique, and encouragement. Ana studied the faces of the young students and was immediately transported back to that time in her life—when the world seemed full of such amazing possibility. Dance had been exciting. Not that it wasn't now, but there'd been an element of wonder that had worn off along the way once ballet had turned into a mechanism of ambition and not just a study in artistry.

What she wouldn't give to be in that phase again now.

"So what do you think?" Genevieve asked her on the break.

"It takes me back in a big way."

"I thought it might."

She gestured to the students. "They're so young and impressionable. I don't know if you've noticed, but several of them hang on your every word."

Genevieve nodded knowingly. "It's inspiring, no? They're hungry."

"They are. That one," Ana said, pointing surreptitiously at the redhead she'd watched throughout most of the class, "is really quite excellent. She should stick with it."

"We're working on it. Boys and Facebook are my biggest competition. Sorry. I think it's Twitter now. Or is it Instagram?"

"I sadly wouldn't know. Even if I were the age they are now, I still probably wouldn't. But perhaps mine was not the best path."

"What do you mean? Look where it got you," Genevieve said.

Ana nodded and raised her braced arm. "Exactly. Look where

I am now. I put all of my eggs in the ballet basket. Maybe a little diversification isn't such a horrible thing in the long run. There might have been room for Balanchine *and* Facebook in my life. In fact, I bet there was. I just didn't realize it at the time."

"See? You have more wisdom to offer than perhaps you thought." Genevieve strolled away but her words lingered. She was right. The accident and its effect on Ana's career had provided her with rather startling perspective.

"Are you an instructor, too, ma'am?"

Ana glanced to her right. The talented redhead stared at her in anticipation. "No, I'm not."

"Oh. A dancer?"

"Yes. Well, kind of." She gestured to her braced arm. "I'm injured and have to take it easy for a while."

"Gotcha. I'm sorry." The girl offered a sympathetic smile, but the genuine kind. "I sprained my ankle last summer and couldn't dance for six weeks. It blew."

"When did you start dancing?" Ana asked. "You're good."

"Thank you. Uh, back when I was six. My mom enrolled my older sister and me at the YMCA. She hated it, but I counted the days until we got to go again."

Ana smiled in solidarity. "I used to do that, too."

"With Ms. Genevieve?"

"No. New York. Until I was hurt, I danced with the New York City Ballet." Whether that part of her life was over or not, she wore the accomplishment like a badge of honor.

"Are you serious? You've danced with City Ballet?"

"For close to nine years. I ended the fall season as a principal."

You couldn't wipe the grin from the girl's face if you tried. "I can't believe I'm talking to you right now."

"You are, so listen to me when I tell you that if you stick with it, you have the potential to do the exact same thing. I watched your work during class."

"I do? You're serious right now?" The girl looked over her shoulder, perhaps to see if her friends were close by to hear.

"You do. But there's a slight rigidity to your movements. You're very angular and precise, but you need to learn to soften and feel the music more. Trust your performance instincts." Ana felt a bit like she was channeling Natalie's words, but that didn't make them any less true.

"Got it. Not as rigid." There was a new energy to the girl that hadn't been there before. "Anything else? This is good."

"Practice. Not just when you're in this room. At home, you should be working on flexibility, turnout, anything that will prepare your body to do what it needs to when you walk in that door."

"I can do that."

"It won't be easy. There are nights when your entire body will ache, but trust me, it will all be worth it in the end."

"I'm not afraid of a little pain."

"Good. But don't forget to carve out some time for yourself as well."

"For me? Okay." A pause. "What do you mean?"

"I mean for friends, movies, chatting on the internet. Whatever it is you like to do to decompress, because that stuff matters, too."

"Got it. Wow. Okay. This is so cool. Will you be back next week?"

Ana considered the question and heard her father's voice echoing in her head. *What? You have a tight schedule or something?* Shaking off the impulse to come up with an excuse, she faced the girl. "I will be. Yes."

"Awesome. And thank you!"

"No problem."

Genevieve brought the class back into session and the girl headed off to her position at the barre. But she turned back once last time. "What was your name?" she asked in an exaggerated whisper.

"I'm Ana."

The redhead pointed at herself. "Roberta."

Ana smiled and mouthed the words, "Nice to meet you."

Well past dinnertime, in a rehearsal room at 42nd Street Studios, Natalie was finding herself slightly out of her comfort zone. Okay, a total lie. Way outside.

"Just remember that when you head upstage, Tonya will be waiting there for the quick change." This was approximately the seventy thousandth piece of information that Ricky, the stage manager, had provided her that day. She was a quick study, but this pace was kind of insane.

Natalie attempted to commit this to memory, but as her brain no longer worked after her eight hours of intense rehearsal, she wrote it down instead. "Wait. So this is the second quick change or the first?"

He stared at her like she was a very sweet six-year-old trying his patience, and she was starting to realize that she was perhaps no Jenna McGovern. "It's the third."

"Right, right, right," she said, and flipped through her notebook until she found the first two. "I guess it's been a long day."

"It'll be even longer tomorrow. See you at ten."

"Right. Awesome. Bye, Ricky. Thanks for today. Sorry if I—"

But he was already gone.

God, she was a failure. A failure who would never dance again after this job came to an end. Maybe it had been reckless to imagine she could handle such a monumental role. The entire show practically rested on her shoulders, and what was worse, Jenna had gone out on a limb to arrange the introduction.

She was in panic mode, and as she walked home, she wished more than anything for someone to talk it through with. She sent Helen a Mayday text and waited for the reply.

Meet at McKenna's in an hour? Helen sent back.

Perfect, she replied.

Snagging a seat on the steps in front of their building, she decided to use the time before Helen arrived to go over her notes for the day, a habit she'd picked up from Ana. Her thoughts automatically drifted back to their first joint rehearsal for *Aftermath* and the tension that had been layered between them. She smiled remembering how she'd peppered Ana with questions as she warmed up, annoying her no end. If only then she could have imagined what Ana would come to mean to her, she would have skipped the rehearsal and made out with her instead. The harsh reality of the way things had ended up rang loudly like a god-awful alarm clock to the daydream. She blinked purposefully and forced her attention to her notes, ignoring the always-present pang of regret.

She had to find a way to be better tomorrow.

❖

The afternoon had been a good one. As Ana headed home following Genevieve's dance class, her spirits were higher than they'd been in a long time, which had her moving with a spring in her step. God, it felt good to feel energized again, and all from sitting in on a class!

But it was being in the midst of ballet again that had done it. Spending time in a room full of aspiring dancers, while not exactly the professional world, was like water to her thirst. She'd missed it even more than she'd realized. Maybe there was something to this education thing.

Maybe, maybe, maybe.

The concept had her cautiously excited.

As she rounded the corner to Fourteenth Street, she paused at the sight of Natalie sitting on the steps to their building, starring straight ahead as if lost in thought. The image was strikingly similar to the one she'd walked up on the night Natalie had first confessed her feelings.

The night they'd made out in the elevator…

That seemed so very long ago now.

"Hey," Natalie said as Ana approached. Her eyes seemed sad, as if she had a lot on her mind.

"Hi," Ana said back. And then, maybe because she couldn't help herself, or perhaps it was her good mood, she paused there a moment more. "You waiting for someone?"

"No. Well, yes, Helen, but not anymore. We were going to have a chat, but she had to cancel. Something about an emergency fitting at Lincoln Center."

"Ah. Been there." Silence fell and Ana released a breath. "Well, anyway, have a good night," she said, and continued up the stairs until Natalie's voice stopped her.

"I know I'm the last person you want to talk to, but I'm drowning a little at work and was wondering if…"

She closed her eyes, made a decision, and turned back to Natalie. If they were going to continue to run into each other this way, she needed to find a way to get past the blatant pain and discomfort these encounters brought with them. Maybe facing them head-on was the way to go. "What's going on?"

Natalie raised a shoulder and let it drop as tears touched her eyes.

Whether she wanted it to or not, Ana's heart ached at the sight.

"I'm not getting it," Natalie said, her voice morose, clogged with the need to cry. "The choreography for the show. The stage manager looks at me like I am the biggest casting mistake in history, and I'm terrified he's right, that I'm going to be this…very public embarrassment."

"No. Stop that." Ana took a seat on the steps next to Natalie, invested now.

"Stop what?"

"Allowing yourself to think that way. You can't admit weakness."

"Yeah, well, what am I supposed to do when that's what I'm dealing with?" Natalie asked.

"My father used to tell me that you have to eat a hippopotamus one bite at a time."

Natalie tilted her head. "What does that mean? Is that Russian?"

"You would think, but no. It means you can't overwhelm yourself with the breadth of the situation. You focus on the bite in front of you. So what's most pressing?"

"The choreography, I guess. But stage management is throwing things at me like quick changes and spacing intricacies, and it's too much to juggle until I get the steps down."

"Then you put the brakes on the rest. You have to advocate for yourself."

Natalie nodded. She seemed calmer now. "I can do that?"

"Of course you can do that. You need to communicate with them. Trust me, they want you to get it just as badly as you do."

Natalie gave her shoulders a little roll. "Okay. Yeah. I'll talk to Ricky in the morning."

"Channel your inner rebel. We all know she's in there."

Natalie laughed wryly. "What's left of her." She seemed to shift her focus. "What about you? What's your first bite?"

She raised her brace. "Getting out of this thing."

"How long are we talking?"

"If I buckle down and get serious, maybe a couple more weeks."

"Wow. That's really great."

"I know. I just have to be more diligent." They were smiling at each other, Ana realized. How had *that* happened? And Natalie's hair was longer than she'd ever remembered seeing it, and she had that little spark in her eyes again. Ana was shocked, if not a little jarred by how they'd fallen back into a former rhythm once they got to talking about work.

But that's all it is, really, she reminded herself. Convinced herself was more like it. At least, she tried. If their easy camaraderie truly was just a *work* thing, why were alarm bells clanging loudly in her brain? "I better head upstairs. Enjoy your night."

"You too," Natalie said.

As Ana climbed the stairs, she didn't have to look back to know that Natalie was staring after her. She could feel it all over as the telltale shiver she used to relish moved through her body as a potent reminder.

Chapter Twenty

There was class today, Ana thought upon waking a week later. She wiggled her toes as the rare January sunshine streamed through her bedroom window at precisely 7:03 in the morning. Smiling against its golden glow, she pulled the covers tighter around her as she stretched. Genevieve would be teaching the Wednesday afternooners again, and Ana looked forward to contributing. Not only that, but Ana had been given the green light to begin going short segments of her day without wearing the brace. Though it was a tiny battle win, it offered her a glimpse at the light at the end of the tunnel. Her arm felt stiff, but the pain was only about a fourth of what it had been a month ago, which had to be a sign that recovery was actually taking place.

Forcing herself to fully commit to waking up, she reached for her phone and focused on the screen. Her breath caught at what she saw there. A text message from Adrienne that read, *I heard Natalie killed it last night.* And damn it, she'd included a photo of Natalie in full costume coming off the stage from her first performance in *Elevation.* Apparently a stage manager had snapped it to commemorate the moment. She tossed her phone as if she'd been burned and stared at the ceiling, willing herself to return to the stasis of just a few moments ago, before complicated reminders of Natalie once again trumped all. Not able to help herself, because she was apparently a glutton for punishment, Ana retrieved her phone and stared at the photo for just a moment longer. Natalie looked stunning. They hadn't wigged the show, so Natalie's own hair, longer than even the last time she'd seen her, fell around her shoulder in tousled waves. Her lips were bolstered with a deep rose lipstick, and her eyes were overdrawn with a silver and charcoal shadow.

However, the best part of the photo by far was the radiant smile on Natalie's lips.

She looked so alive, as if she'd just conquered Everest, and perhaps she had. "Proud of you," she said quietly to the photo, and then, annoyed with herself for the temporary betrayal, set the phone down for good.

❖

"We have to quit meeting like this," Natalie said from the stoop outside the building. It had become a new favorite spot of hers.

Ana approached and offered her a small smile. "It's true. We must."

"Where are you coming from? PT?" Natalie asked as she changed from flip-flops to sneakers for her commute to the theatre.

"Actually, no," Ana said, and took a seat next to Natalie. "Believe it or not, I've been playing the role of assistant instructor."

"To?"

"Twelve- to sixteen-year-olds." Ana must have caught the look of utter shock on Natalie's face and took a minute to fill her in on how it all came about.

"I'm impressed with your father right now. It's not easy to get you to do anything." She softened the words with a wink. "And—wait a minute, you're not wearing your brace."

"It goes back on as soon as I head upstairs, but yeah, progress."

"I'm glad to see it," Natalie said genuinely. There was something about Ana this afternoon that had Natalie a little mesmerized. Her blue eyes popped against the bright blue hoodie she wore, and the dance clothes hugged her body nicely. But that wasn't it. There was the tiniest of glows on her face, reminiscent of lighter times. Natalie felt pulled in by it. "You seem happier today."

Ana shook her head. "It's weird. I always feel lighter on class days. Something about all that artistic potential and the pursuit to get better just gets my blood flowing. It turns out it doesn't even have to be me doing the pursuing."

Natalie, now excited, turned more fully to Ana. "Are you going to stick with it, do you think? Teaching."

Ana nodded, her smile growing. "Yeah, I think I might." And then a thought seemed to occur to her. "I forgot to say congratulations on your opening."

"Not a big deal."

"It's a huge deal," Ana said. "You're on Broadway."

"Right?" She couldn't help but smile. The fact that the sentiment came from Ana was everything. "Your advice worked. I ate the hippo thing one bite at a time. And now I just get to have a ton of fun up there." In actuality, now that the show was open and Natalie could breathe, she was on cloud nine, as far as work went. Things only dimmed when she stepped off the stage...

"Well, the reviews, as far as I've heard, have all been stellar."

"You've read reviews?" Natalie filed that bit of information away for examination later.

"I heard from Adrienne."

"Ah. Well, at least I won't have to write Jenna McGovern an apology letter after all. It just goes to show you that so much of this business is about being in the right place at the right time. This whole thing only happened because we were—"

"Having dinner with famous people," Ana supplied.

"Right. That," Natalie said, meeting her eyes. "But it really all comes down to you. This was your connection."

"My father's, technically."

"Stop downplaying." Natalie shook her head and turned to Ana sincerely, slowing the pace of the conversation. "I know you may hate me, and I don't exactly blame you for that, but none of this would have happened for me without you in my life. So I want to say thank you. For everything. And now I'm going to shut up and get out of here before I get any more sappy."

"Wait." Ana stood. "I need to say something here."

"You don't," Natalie said. "It's fine."

"Just listen, please?"

Natalie finally nodded, shoving her hands into her pockets for lack of anything better to do with them. She stared up at Ana, who ran a hand through her hair, seeming to search for the appropriate words. It felt like time stood still, like the whole world stopped, as Natalie waited for what Ana had to say. It mattered that much to her.

"I don't hate you, Natalie. I was angry for a while, sure. And things aren't easy, even now, but I don't hate you. I couldn't."

Natalie nodded and swallowed back the emotion that crept in at the weighted conversation. Her chest felt tight and she sucked in a breath. They'd never talked about any of it. The accident. The breakup. Not since that day in the hospital where Ana had asked her to leave. "I miss you," Natalie managed to whisper, allowing herself to go there for the first time in so long. Hearing her words out loud, the emotion overcame her defenses and stripped her of the power of voice. "I miss you a lot."

Ana nodded, the pain Natalie felt mirrored in Ana's eyes. "You better get to the theatre."

"Ana," Natalie said, as Ana ascended the stairs and disappeared into the building.

❖

Puzzles, the little wine bar in the Village where she and Adrienne had agreed to meet, was bustling by the time their cheese plate arrived. "Thank you," Ana said to the waiter, as he topped off her glass of white. She turned to Adrienne once they were alone. "This is a cute place. Where'd you hear about it?"

"My cousin brought me here once. She lives just down the block."

"Your cousin has good taste. I'm happy we're doing this."

"Me too," Adrienne said. "It's been too long and I'm so glad to see you out and about again. The recovery must be moving along; you're not wearing your brace."

"It's a supplement at this point. I use it when my arm is tired or in pain, but on the whole, I go without it."

"That's fantastic," Adrienne said, beaming at her the way only Adrienne could. It was one of many reasons America loved her. "So we've covered the teaching thing, which I happen to agree you'd be great at. What about your love life?"

Ana selected a crostini and a dab of brie. "Nothing to report. I'm concentrating on getting my life back, remember?"

"Right. And doesn't that include Natalie?"

Ana paused at the very direct statement. Adrienne didn't mess around. "It can't include Natalie," she said simply, hoping Adrienne would leave it there.

"Why not?" Adrienne sat back in her chair and waited as if she had all the time in the world.

"It's complicated."

"Try me. I have a whole bottle of wine here."

Ana sighed. Her words came in fits and starts. She didn't want to relive this. "The night I was in the cab, I had called out of the show, for Natalie. It wasn't something I wanted to do. I did it for *her*."

"Okay. So…still not following you." Adrienne sipped her wine. "Wasn't she just trying to look out for you?"

"Yes, but—"

"But despite that, you blame her for the accident?"

Frustration bubbled. Why couldn't Ana explain this logically? It made so much sense in her head. "Not directly, no. But she *is* the reason I was in that cab."

"Because she was *looking out* for your well-being," Adrienne said, her tone level.

Ana couldn't quite pull off level. "No. Well, yes, I guess, but my feelings for her were so…strong, that I gave into her, to what she wanted me to—"

"Because that's what you do when you care about someone, when they matter to you more than anything else."

The sigh Ana released was laced up tight with strings of conflicting emotion. "Even if that's true, when I look at Natalie now, *I see the accident*. That's all. I think of the fact that I'll never dance again, and that she's still out there, doing what I want to be doing."

"So you're jealous?" Adrienne asked, as if trying to desperately to understand and failing.

Was she? That seemed…so petty, especially considering she once thought she was falling in love with Natalie. But she needed to be honest with someone. "Well…yes. And no."

Adrienne blew out a breath. "I'm going to say this, Ana, and you can do with it what you will. Are you listening?"

"Yes." And she was, because Adrienne had always been a strong source of wisdom in her life, and Ana was grateful for that. She valued Adrienne's advice, especially when she still battled feelings for Natalie that she didn't know what to do with.

Adrienne took a moment and smiled at her. "I've never seen you radiate the way you did when you were with Natalie. You blossomed and glowed and every other clichéd thing in the book that happens to someone when they find that certain person. The one." She angled her head and regarded Ana gently. "But it's gone now, that glow. You think it's because you lost ballet." She paused. "I think it's because you lost Natalie."

Ana stared at her as the truth of that statement smacked her squarely in the face. She missed dancing a great deal, yes, but she'd found a way to keep ballet in her life. There was no substitute for Natalie, and she missed her—and *them*—more than words could even express. Nothing felt the same, and it wasn't because her dancing career had come to an end. It was because she didn't have Natalie.

She just hadn't fully admitted it to herself until that very moment.

"Am I close?" Adrienne asked gently, dipping her head to meet Ana's gaze.

Ana nodded slowly as tears gathered in her eyes. She stared at the ceiling a moment until she found her voice. "So what am I supposed to do?"

"First of all, you accept the accident for what it was: a horrible twist of fate that's now a part of both of your histories. Next, you tell her how you feel about her, and you don't hold anything back."

"What if she's over it? What if she hates me for sending her away? For blaming her?"

"Then you fight harder, because nothing is more important in life than your perfect person. I can attest to that. Do you understand?"

"I do."

Adrienne reached across the table and squeezed her hand. "So what are you waiting for?"

It was the fifty-million-dollar question.

"If I'm going to do this, if I'm going to have the confidence to do this, I need to get some things in order first. I don't want to be the victim who presents herself in some pitiful plea for—"

Adrienne stopped her there. "Ana, I've never known you to be a victim, but do what you have to do. Just don't wait too long."

Ana took a deep breath, terrified, because what if she already had?

❖

The music came to a close and the young ballerina finished her variation. The class applauded politely and all eyes were on Ana, as Genevieve had been giving her the floor more and more.

"That was beautiful, Tracy. Remember to keep your movements fluid as you go. You tend to separate them and we're really working toward a continuous motion, where one movement seems to melt into the next. Make sense?"

"Got it. Continuous," Tracy said, beaming.

Ana held up her hand and Tracy high-fived her as she took her spot with the rest of the class. This would be the fourth Wednesday night class Ana had dropped in for, in addition to the Tuesday/Thursdays Genevieve had set her up with taught by another instructor. Something about working with these kids gave her a hit of confidence like nothing else. They looked up to her and desperately sought her opinion in a way no one else ever had. Not only that, she got to watch them improve, which was beyond satisfying. But more than anything else, like food to a starving person, she felt a part of it all again, and connected to ballet in a way she hadn't been in months.

They moved on to group exercises, and Ana and Genevieve circled through the room, offering insight, adjustments, and tips.

"Through the toe each time," she told one dancer. "Keep that phrase in your head: through the toe. See?" She'd worn her warm-ups to class, allowing her to demonstrate for the student who watched with rapt attention. She moved down the line of mostly girls. "Pose. Step through. Pose. Good. That was excellent, Amy, but finish each movement. Don't get ahead of yourself."

"Right. I always do that. Thank you, Ana."

The eager eyes that looked back at her had a startling effect. These kids were so appreciative and willing to take her direction. Spending time with these dancers made Ana feel needed—God, like a person again, even. She was doing something that was actually of use and she was enjoying every moment of it. It didn't come with the roar of applause like at the end of a performance, but this new form of gratification was just as potent.

As was becoming typical, Roberta stayed close during the break, and they chatted about anything and everything until her mother picked her up.

"So what are you into outside of ballet?" Ana asked, as she moved about the room helping to put it back in order.

"I've always been the quiet kid," Roberta told her.

"I'm not surprised. Quiet kids love ballet."

"Why is that?"

She began to stack the chairs with her good arm. "Because it's a powerful way of expressing yourself without using words."

Roberta considered this and grabbed a couple chairs to help the cause. "You're right. I've never thought of it that way."

"At least it was for me."

"So what made you start dancing?" Roberta asked. "If that's not too personal a question."

"Not so much a what, but a who," Ana told her.

"Okay then, who?"

"My parents were both dancers, and it was sort of expected that I'd be one, too. My earliest memories are of watching them rehearse partnering exercises."

"You're lucky. Were they any good?"

Ana considered the question. "Most people think they were some of the best."

"Ask her what her father's name is," Genevieve said as she strolled past, picking up an abandoned water bottle.

"What's his name?"

"Klaus Mikhelson."

Roberta straightened and stared at Ana sideways. "You're funny."

"Sometimes," Ana said, enjoying this more than she usually did. "But not today." She scrolled through her phone and turned it around to Roberta, who immediately raced to it and stared in awe at the photo of Ana and her father, taken the last time he'd see her dance.

Roberta pointed at the screen. "You're serious. He's your actual dad, not like a friend of the family or fatherlike."

"Right. My actual biological parent."

Roberta stared at the ground in mystification. "I should probably go put this on Twitter."

Ana raised a shoulder. "It's not that much of a secret, unfortunately."

"Still. You were already the coolest person I knew, and that just like tripled, so…"

Ana smiled as Roberta scampered off.

"They adore you, you know," Genevieve said, as they walked out together.

What a strange thing to hear, Ana thought. Since when did people adore her? "They're great. Honestly. Thank you for letting me crash your classes. It's been the best time I've had in months."

"There's something to take away from all of this," Genevieve said. "I like to think you were sent to me by the universe for a reason."

"And what's that reason?" Ana asked.

"To discover what a fantastic teacher you are." Ana allowed what might actually be the truth in that sentence to settle over her. "You have so much to give, Ana. You're knowledgeable and patient and the students think you walk on water because of your résumé. Do you know how inspiring that combination can be to a young dancer?"

"I think I'm just starting to understand it myself."

"I know you're a bit at sea lately, but I want you to take some time and think about your potential for teaching. I have a hunch you've stumbled onto something you'd be really fantastic at."

"It's a lot to take in, but I'd be lying if I said the wheels in my brain weren't already turning. Thank you for allowing me the chance to explore all of this."

"Anytime. Have a great night, Ana."

"You too."

At eight the next morning, she placed an important call.

CHAPTER TWENTY-ONE

"You couldn't have called at a more opportune time," Louise told Ana as they walked the wooden hallways of SAB. She found the place eerily the same as when she'd attended as a student. Being back here now had her reeling, like she'd boarded some sort of time machine. On the other hand, she was thrilled to be back where so many of her formative dancing years had played out. "I didn't go into much detail on the phone, but Monica Bleeker's mother had a heart attack, and she's had to return to Mississippi to take care of her."

"I'm so sorry to hear that." She remembered Ms. Bleeker well. Strict. Severe. Both words came to mind.

"We were, too. She turned in her resignation at the end of last week, leaving the B1s and B2s without an instructor for their technique class. I've been filling in, but my schedule is already dense. Official applications are pouring in, but we need an interim."

"I'm thrilled to be given the chance."

"If all goes well and it's something you're serious about, you're welcome to formally apply for the position."

Ana nodded. "I'd like to get my feet wet before making any formal decision. Make sure I'm good at this."

They paused at the door to one of the studio classrooms. "You were a fantastic student and a gifted dancer. I wouldn't be surprised if you were also a well-rounded teacher. You tend to excel at things, Ana."

"I hope you're right."

"We were all devastated to learn of your accident. It almost feels like we were meant to come together this way. As an alum, you know the school and come with an accomplished résumé."

It probably also didn't hurt that she came with the Mikhelson last name, but Ana decided not to point that part out. "So what do we do now?"

"I'll get you the curriculum and you can start when you're ready."

"How about this afternoon?"

Louise looked like she could kiss her. "Even better."

Ana placed a mental check mark next to part one of her plan.

While it had taken her until the last week in the show, Natalie mentally patted herself on the back for getting her turnaround time from the final bow to leaving the theatre down to twenty-two minutes. It really was an impressive record for her.

"Ms. Frederico, you have a visitor in the lobby," Trent, the stage door security guy, informed her. "I didn't send 'em back 'cuz they weren't on the list."

"Okay, cool," Natalie said and turned off the lights to Jenna's cozy little dressing room. She was gonna miss this place come Sunday night. With her bag across her body and her winter cap already on her head, she made her way through the house to the lobby of the St. James Theatre. "Oh my God, what are you doing here? Aren't you supposed to be in LA?"

Eddie, the best damned stage manager she'd ever had, turned at the sound of her voice and she moved to him, pulling the little nerd into a bone-crushing hug. She was that happy to see his friendly face.

"I heard you'd made it to the big broad way. Like there was a chance I'd miss it. I loved every second, by the way. You were stunning up there, Natalie. I thought you were a fantastic dancer before, but this is other level."

"Thanks, Eddie. This means a lot to me that you're here. I'm only doing a four-week run, and a lot of people I was hoping would make the show weren't able to."

"Your parents?"

"Couldn't get off work."

"I'm sorry."

"It's okay. They sent flowers, and my friends here have been really supportive. What about you? How have you been?"

"I've decided to keep stage-managing."

"No kidding." This made her immensely happy, as Eddie was one of the best.

"I've got a couple of interviews set up with some smaller companies downtown while I'm here. I don't want you to feel obligated or anything, but I was hoping we could maybe have coffee this weekend if you aren't too slammed."

"It wouldn't matter if I was. I wouldn't miss coffee with you."

"Great. I'll text you. I'm sure you're off to some crazy bash about now."

Natalie shook her head. "Nope. I'm afraid those days are behind me. There's a hot bath and a bed with my name on it, as I have two shows tomorrow."

"Times certainly have changed, haven't they?"

"In a good way."

"I'm happy to hear you say that." He hugged her again and backed up toward the door. "Look at us, in the big city."

"If you had told us a year ago, I never would have believed it."

"Tomorrow then?"

"You're on."

Eddie headed out into the blustery night, and Natalie hung in the lobby an extra minute, not exactly wanting to head home. Instead, she stole a moment to take it all in—the merchandise stand that had been broken down for the night, the cash bar that had been stripped down to nothing. She strolled into the house where the ushers were vacuuming the red carpet after the audience had dispersed and headed out into the world. A singular ghost light stood onstage. She stared at it, the image somehow magical to her, the lonely light that would keep watch until they all returned and did it all again the next day. It was the kind of sentiment she would have shared with Ana not too long ago as they lay in bed, just before sleep claimed them. This time, she'd simply hold it close for herself.

With a sentimental hand over her heart, she walked through the lobby and exited the theatre through the glass doors. She made a left in the direction of her downtown subway station, prepared to head back to her apartment, where she'd be alone and living in a maze of memories.

"Is it too late for a cup of hot cocoa and some HGTV?"

Startled by the question, Natalie spun and stared hard at the woman standing near the stage door. It couldn't be. While her eyes saw Ana standing right in front of her, she wasn't sure if her mind was playing tricks on her, or if Ana just happened to be strolling down Forty-Fourth Street at eleven at night.

"Ana?"

The figure closed the distance between them as Natalie looked on in glorious mystification. "Hi."

"Hi," Natalie said, her heart thudding away in her chest. "What are you doing out here?"

"I saw the show tonight. I knew it was you up there, but I still found myself in awe. You blew me away, and my expectations were high to begin with."

"Wait." Natalie felt the tears threaten. "You saw the show?"

Ana beamed. "I did."

"Why didn't you tell me?"

Ana shrugged. "I didn't know how. God, I'm nervous just standing here."

"Don't be nervous. It's just me."

"I know. It's always you." She paused, regarding Natalie through luminous blue eyes. "That's kind of why I'm here."

As they stood under the streetlight that shone down on Ana like a beacon, Natalie tried to make sense of that statement, her heart too afraid to hope.

"Ana, what's going on?"

Ana swallowed and stepped forward. "I owe you an apology."

"You do?"

Ana nodded and tucked a strand of hair behind her ear. "And while standing on the sidewalk late at night is probably not the ideal location, I'm afraid it's now or never." She walked the few remaining feet to Natalie and took her hands in a gesture that had Natalie struck. "What happened to me was in no way your fault. I was angry and at a loss for how to cope. I think I was searching for something to blame, someone to hold accountable." Ana held her gaze as Natalie braced herself. "It never should have been you."

"No." Natalie shook her head, wanting the blame. Almost needing it. Her heart hammered with the dread she'd felt since Ana had sent her away. "If I had stayed out of it, if I had just—"

"That's just it. I don't want you to stay out of it. I want you there with me through the good times and the tough ones. I want you to give me hell when I'm being stupid, or stubborn, which we both know I can be, and I want to do the same for you." She paused, implored. "If you'll let me."

"Ana, what are you saying?" Her insides clenched and she forgot to breathe as she waited for what seemed like an eternity for an answer.

Ana gave her hands a squeeze. "I miss you, too. I miss vegging on the couch after a long day, and I miss waking up with you sprawled across me, your hair in my eyes. My life is different now. My career has to be, my focus. But you and me? That's my real life, and the one thing that I don't ever want to change." Ana took a deep breath and smiled at her. "The thing is, Natalie Frederico, I'm lost without you. And I just want to kiss you right now and make everything that's sad go away forev—"

She didn't get to finish her sentence, because Natalie did it for her, taking Ana's face in her hands and kissing her the way she'd dreamed of kissing her for weeks now. The murmur of pleasure from Ana had her in no hurry to ever stop, lost in the warmth of the lips she'd so desperately longed for.

"This," Natalie whispered between kisses, "is everything. And I never thought I'd have that again."

Ana's eyes filled and she touched Natalie's cheek. "What now?"

"More," Natalie said, claiming Ana's mouth once again and losing herself in the all-consuming sensations that bombarded her. "And this," she whispered, kissing her some more, and then some more, and some more. She didn't want it to end, and as their lips clung and her heart soared, she felt like, maybe now, it never would.

"One thing, though," Ana managed somehow to say, between kisses.

"That sounds ominous," Natalie murmured, going in for another round, but Ana stopped her.

"It's not. Ominous, that is. But before we go any further with this…"

"Long-overdue kissing?"

She smiled. "Yes, with that. Before any of…that"—she let her gaze smolder for a moment before it slipped into something more resolute—"we need to talk."

❖

Forty-five minutes later, at Ana's insistence, they were nestled in a cozy back booth at a late-night bistro known for its fancy desserts. Not exactly where Natalie would have predicted they'd end up after their amazing reunion and off-the-charts kissing session, but she was happy to be wherever Ana was. To simply be able to look at her and know that things were going to be okay again had her on top of the world.

Ana was back.

They were back.

"I can't stop smiling," Natalie told her.

"We don't have to," was Ana's reply. "But there are things to discuss."

"Okay. I'm up for it."

"Patience, Miss Broadway."

"I also like my new nickname. When is there more kissing?"

Ana shook her head at Natalie, but she was grinning and gorgeous when she did it.

They'd ordered hot chocolates—mint for Ana and dark for Natalie. The place was dim and quiet, with a few other tables in post-show dining mode. "So what I have for you is a business pitch," Ana said and sat back, looking pleased with herself, but also the smallest bit nervous.

Natalie turned her head to the side thoughtfully. An interesting turn of events. "You have a business pitch for me?" Well, this wasn't at all what she expected.

Ana held up a hand. "Before you say anything, hear me out."

Of course Natalie would hear her out. She'd listen to Ana for hours. "I'm all ears."

"First of all, you should know that you were right way back when, in the rehearsal studio, when you thought I'd make a good teacher. I do think I'm good at it, and it looks like I'll be doing some more work along those lines."

"That's great. You should start applying—"

"I've been granted an interim teaching position at SAB, instructing a handful of technique classes for the intermediate dancers through the end of the year."

"Wow, you don't mess around. When do you start?"

"I taught my first two classes this afternoon."

Natalie's mind was blown. "How is that even possible? You never cease to amaze me, you know that?"

"I'm not done," Ana said, with a raised eyebrow and a smile.

"Oh, sorry." Natalie made a sweeping gesture that invited Ana to continue.

"After getting some experience under my belt, I hope to open up my own studio. While it sounds awesome to work at a place like SAB and teach the best of the best, I can't help but wonder about those kids who fall just shy of making the cut. What about them? What if someone invested in *those* kids? They could be just as great, given the right training, and I think maybe I could be that person."

Ana beamed as she described her new plan. She seemed open and excited for what lay ahead. Not only that, but her idea sounded like an amazing one, and once Ana set her mind to something, there wasn't anything she couldn't do. Natalie shook her head in wonder. "It's great. All of it. I couldn't be more excited for you if I tried."

Ana reached across the table and covered Natalie's hand gently with her own. "I'm not done."

She laughed. "I feel like I'm on one of those 'But, wait, there's more!' commercials, and each thing just keeps topping the previous thing in a one-upmanship of awesome."

"This is where my big business proposition comes in." Ana tucked a strand of hair behind her ear.

Natalie sipped her hot chocolate. "I'm listening."

"You're really pretty when you listen."

"Is this part of the pitch?"

"Surprisingly, no. That part was just me staring at you, making up for lost time."

Well, now Ana had gone and done it. "You realize that you're in a position to get just about anything you want from me."

"Way to show your hand."

"As if I had a choice."

"What I'm proposing," Ana said, redirecting them expertly, "is that with the school in mind, we take steps to start our own dance company."

"Wait. What?" Natalie sat a little taller, because that was the last thing she expected to come out of Ana's mouth.

"Not today, not even tomorrow," Ana said in way of caution. "I'm committed at SAB through the school year, and you spoke of wanting to audition and see what came your way."

"Except I'm not."

Ana sat back in the booth, seemingly shocked. She opened her mouth, closed it again, before settling on a sentence. "You're going back? Since when?"

"Since this girl from across the hall reminded me how much I'd learned in such a short time at City Ballet." Natalie grinned. It hadn't been an easy decision, but it was the right one. "I've decided to finish out the season there because it's the smart thing to do. I'm back in rehearsal next week. After that, I'm in."

A smile took root on Ana's lips and grew. "Now whose turn is it to be impressed?"

"What can I say? I listen when you talk. Now, tell me more about this company you're planning on."

Ana gave her head a tiny shake and refocused. "Right. Well, I'm planning on something legitimate. I know you like the whole performing in garages, starving for your art motif, but I'm looking at something a little more prestigious—and trust me, I hear how that sounds."

"I translate you, Frozen."

Ana smiled and bowed her head at the quip.

Natalie pressed on. "You want to be taken seriously. I do, too, so we're in agreement."

Ana held up a finger. "Understand, I'm asking for a partnership. Fifty-fifty when it comes to any decisions."

"I can get behind that." Natalie was getting excited now as ideas were already starting to percolate. "What do you have in mind so far?"

"I want there to be a strong classical ballet component that will tie into classwork I plan on. But in addition, I'd love to see some modern dance shows on the season as well. That's where you come in. I can't seem to get the show tonight out of my head, and if you can bring even half that caliber of performance to us for our shows, you'll put us on the map."

Natalie thought on this. "So I dance and choreo the modern stuff. And you?"

"I can teach, choreograph ballet, and run the business side of things."

"Yeah, but you'll dance, too."

For the first time that night, Ana faltered. "I can't dance anymore. You know that."

"That's bullshit. You can't dance classically for City Ballet, but you can certainly dance the choreo I lay out for you. I'll make sure of it. So your arm doesn't get all bendy anymore. Big deal. You can still handle very sophisticated material."

Ana set her mug down and contemplated what Natalie said. "You truly think that's possible?"

"I don't think. I know."

"I'm willing to try," Ana said, a smile sneaking onto her face at the concept. "We'll need investors."

Natalie widened her eyes when an idea hit. "Audrey's guy, from the building. What's his name? Tad. Tons of money. More than he knows what to do with and told us over dinner that he wants to find a way to invest in the arts." She held up both hands. "What if we were his arts?"

Ana pointed at her. "Let's pitch him."

"I'll set it up. What about your dad?"

"While I never like leveraging his name or his cash flow, an exception might be in order. I drafted a proposal offering him a fifteen percent stake in exchange for an opening round of funding with a buy-back option once he's paid back with interest. I haven't sent it yet. I wanted to check with you first."

Natalie narrowed her gaze. "You have never been sexier to me. Do you understand that?"

"Does that mean you're in?"

She didn't hesitate. "One hundred percent. I also know where we might procure a pretty awesome stage manager."

"Perfect." Ana extended her hand across the table. "Partners?"

"Partners," Natalie said, shaking on it. "Now that we've altered the course of our entire lives, let's get out of here. It's late."

"Since when do late nights get the best of a wild child like you?"

"Yeah, well, lots of changes," Natalie said, cheekily borrowing the phrase.

❖

Breathless kissing in the hallway was an activity Ana had sorely missed. As her lips clung to Natalie's, seeking, exploring, and luxuriating, it occurred to her that they were making very little progress on the way to her apartment.

"I think we need to get in there, and soon," she managed to say.

Natalie pulled back and studied Ana's face. "I agree, but didn't want to be overly presumptuous."

"Stay," Ana said. "I definitely want you to stay."

And to make her point clear, she walked Natalie to her apartment in silence, opened the door, and kissed her in a way she hoped would communicate how much she wanted her to stick around. It was only a moment before the spark flickered into a fire and spread. What started as gentle and languid was now hungry and urgent as Natalie walked her into the apartment, taking control, plunging her tongue into Ana's mouth, which was, okay, wow, more than okay with Ana.

"Your arm?" she whispered, as she kissed down Ana's neck, igniting sensations Ana didn't know existed.

"Will be just fine."

Clothes were beginning to come off. Shirts first. God, she loved the sight of Natalie in her underwear. She dipped her head and kissed the tops of her breasts, palming them through the yellow bra. "God, I've missed you," Natalie breathed. "You don't understand what you do to me."

"I want to do more." Ana licked up the column of Natalie's neck, kissing across her jaw until she found her amazing mouth and lost herself in its warmth. Before she knew what was happening, she found herself flat on her back with a gorgeous woman sliding on top of her. They were moving together and against each other at the same time as little sparks of pleasure had Ana craving, needing, searching. Natalie pushed her leg between Ana's and upward, drawing a moan of desperation. Ana had to have more. It had been so long, she couldn't wait. Natalie seemed ready to oblige, and in a matter of seconds, had Ana's jeans and bikinis off, leaving her naked and writhing beneath Natalie.

"Look at you," Natalie murmured, losing the last of her own remaining clothing before she settled back on top. Ana's hands moved to her backside, so firm yet soft at the same time. She pulled Natalie in closer, as close as she could, angling for release. Natalie began to move and Ana knew undeniably that she wouldn't last long. She was already drenched and throbbing. She slipped her hands between them and settled her palms, once again, on Natalie's amazing breasts, massaging them, taking the nipples between her thumb and forefingers and twisting ever so slightly.

"Oh God," Natalie said, and took a moment before moving against Ana faster this time, and with purpose. Just when Ana thought she would explode, Natalie withdrew contact altogether, leaving Ana blinking up at her in a silent plea.

Natalie cupped her face with one hand and crawled down her body. "I'm not going anywhere."

The explosive sensations of Natalie's open-mouthed kiss on her center had her clenching the sheets in her fists and squirming beneath the potent touch of Natalie's tongue as it snaked up and around her most sensitive spot. Once. Twice. Three times. Ana couldn't think straight. Four times. She was totally undone. Five times and she cried out as her body erupted and the orgasm shot through her hard and fast and wonderful. She rode it out as Natalie held her in place. She kissed her way slowly and gently up Ana's body until they were face-to-face.

"Can we do that again?" Natalie asked. "Please?"

"I think a little recovery time might be called for."

"One more time," Natalie said playfully, reaching between Ana's legs and beginning to play.

Ana gasped, still overly sensitive, and caught Natalie's wrist. "Recovery time is called that for a reason." But she couldn't help but laugh at Natalie's tenacity.

"You're killing my dreams."

"I know, and it's awful. You know what's not awful?"

"What?" Natalie asked, and kissed just above her collarbone.

"What you just did to me. Because that was, in fact, the opposite of awful. Mind-shattering, even."

"So, again?"

Ana laughed. "Nope. But I have an idea of a few other things we could try." Without another word, Ana maneuvered herself around her injured arm and with her good hand reached between Natalie's legs and slid purposefully into wet warmth and reveled at the feel of it, pushing in farther, then out again. God.

Natalie closed her eyes and swore quietly, instinctively pushing against Ana's hand for more. They lay facing each other on the bed, which offered Ana the delicious opportunity to watch Natalie's reaction as she touched, played, and maneuvered her way to delivering to Natalie the pleasure she'd just received herself.

"You're so ready," Ana whispered, sliding her fingers in and then out again.

Natalie covered her eyes as her hips moved faster.

"I want to see you."

Natalie moved her hand and met Ana's eyes, her lips parted, her breath coming in quick pants. Ana had never been so captivated. "What do you need?" Ana asked her, already knowing the answer. The teasing motion of her thumb had gone on long enough.

"Touch me and I'm gone." Natalie swallowed. "That's all I need."

Ana pushed into her one last time and pressed her thumb firmly to Natalie's most sensitive spot, pulling a desperate sound that turned to a tantalizing cry of release from her. She watched as Natalie tossed her head back and went still before bucking wildly against Ana's hand. Ana traced back and forth again and again. She would never tire of the sight of pleasure as it washed over Natalie, beautiful and vulnerable beneath her touch.

"Look at me," Ana said, easing herself on top.

Natalie blinked, clearing her focus, and stared up at Ana. "Hi," she said quietly. Sexy to adorable, in the course of sixty seconds. What was this girl doing to her?

"I don't ever want to be apart from you again," Ana whispered.

"Me neither," Natalie said. She reached up and touched Ana's hair. "Please don't leave me."

The request was so simple, yet so poignant, that Ana felt the large lump in her throat in response. She sat up in bed, working on how to explain what was in her heart.

Natalie followed her. "Hey, are you okay? I didn't mean to upset you."

Ana looked at Natalie and shook her head. "You didn't. When I think about the last two months, one thing is startlingly clear. Nothing I did following the accident, no progress, accomplishment, or decision would have ever felt complete unless you were right there with me. You were the only path back to myself."

Natalie's eyes glistened. "I was the path?"

Ana nodded. "The whole time. And this next part I've never said to anyone, so it's kind of a big deal."

Natalie threaded her fingers through Ana's and listened patiently.

Ana kissed the back of her hand and met her gaze. "I love you, Natalie." The unguarded smile that appeared on Natalie's face filled every crack in Ana's heart and she was whole again. "There's no doubt in my mind that we were meant to come into each other's lives and frustrate the hell out of each other so that we could fall slowly and desperately in love. Obstacles be damned."

Natalie laughed through the tears in her eyes. "I love you, too. I didn't even know it was possible to feel this way. When you ended things, you took my heart with you. I'm so glad you brought it back."

Ana kissed Natalie because there was no way not to, and when she did, her own heart sighed, mended once and for all.

They were in love.

And there was nothing better.

"Again," Natalie murmured through the kiss.

Ana smiled against her mouth. "Definitely again."

As she lay there an hour later with Natalie drifting off in her arms, Ana knew that she was right where she was supposed to be. The future loomed in front of them, scary and exciting and full of all sorts of amazing possibility. She couldn't help but wish for a glimpse of a year down the road. One thing was certain, however. When she and Natalie were together, there was nothing they couldn't do. The woman in her arms had shown her another way to live, had opened her up to the wider world, and Ana was ready to tackle it.

"I love you," she whispered, careful not to wake Natalie, but wanting to say those three words to her every day, every minute, every second of the rest of their lives, and never miss another chance. She placed a soft kiss on Natalie's head and snuggled into her. With a deep sigh, she drifted off, happy and relaxed and at long last, whole.

Epilogue

One Year Later

Natalie stood in the wings and watched as the curtain came down on First Position's opening-night performance. Her heart nearly exploded with pride at what they had accomplished in just over twelve months. The downtown theatre that the company called home was on the smallish side, with roughly four hundred seats, but to her delight, every last one of them was filled. As the applause crescendoed, Natalie took her spot onstage alongside Ana, who played Juliet in this modern retelling of the Prokofiev classic—in this version, featuring two women. Following her bow, Natalie took Helen's hand on one side and Ana's hand on the other, and the company bowed together. The audience wasn't through with them, though. Natalie couldn't remember a longer lasting ovation, and she looked out over the sea of faces, soaking it in, spotting friends and family clapping and smiling for their newest achievement.

This was a night Natalie would never forget. She stole a glance at Ana, who smiled back at her and subtly mouthed the words *I love you.* She'd never seen Ana as happy as she'd been in the weeks leading up to First Position's debut. While it seemed they worked night and day at rehearsal, interspersed with business meeting upon business meeting, the work had never been more fulfilling.

They changed quickly from costumes to party attire in the small dressing room they shared one floor above the stage. As they prepared to leave, Natalie took a moment to really drink Ana in.

"You're a knockout," she told her. Ana had selected a modest red cocktail dress with a slight dip in the front. That tiny glimpse of cleavage would be Natalie's undoing by the end of the party, a position she'd been in before.

"Are you sure?" Ana asked. "I feel a little, I don't know... *noticeable* in the red dress. Red stands out."

"I have news for you." Natalie stole a kiss. "You stand out in any room you walk into. You're statuesque and beautiful. It's your lot in life. You're also a fancy artistic director now, so it's your job to stand out and look important."

"Okay, note to self: Stand out. Look important. And what's your job?" Ana asked, amusement now sparkling in her eyes.

"To wear a slinky black dress and be your brooding sidekick."

"You don't brood."

"I know, but I can work on it." She hiked her chin toward Ana's arm. "How's the wing?"

"It aches a bit, but that's to be expected. Once the show's in me a bit more, it should stretch and accommodate better."

"Okay, but communicate with me."

Ana softened. "I love communicating with you. And doing other things with you."

"You cannot flirt with me while wearing a red dress I can't take off you. There shall be no more flirting until later tonight."

"I can't promise."

Natalie shook her head. "Ready to do this thing?"

Ana took her hand. "Never been more ready."

Having declined Klaus's offer to secure Sardi's for the opening night gathering, they had instead selected a spacious and industrial Italian restaurant not far from the downtown theatre. As they entered the room where their guests mingled, a round of applause erupted. On one hand, the celebration reminded Natalie of those days when she performed with her friends in LA, and the raucous parties that led into the morning hours. But in fact, this gathering also felt inherently different. While she loved the former Never-Never Land version of herself for what she had and had not known, she recognized all the growing up she'd done in the meantime. This party felt like a culmination of those changes.

They spent the next two hours working the room, greeting their guests, thanking their investors, and hugging friends and family.

"The show was spellbinding," Adrienne told them, as she hugged first Ana and then Natalie. "The melding of styles up there was so seamless, I found myself lost in the story."

"Thank you," Natalie said, genuinely moved that Adrienne saw value in their work. "A lot of Ana with a little bit of me tossed in."

"More than a little," Ana corrected.

Jenna sipped from a glass of bubbly. While she'd not been able to see the show due to an *Elevation* performance of her own, she'd raced over to the party right after. "And how's the teaching going? I've told several people they should look you up."

"You don't know how much I appreciate that," Ana said. "We have classes three times a week. I teach the majority, but our friend Helen has recently picked up two classes as well. The space is amazing, and we're getting it for a steal."

"We're already using the classes as a feeder school for First Position," Natalie added.

"Oh, hang on a minute," Adrienne said, and signaled to someone behind them. "I want to introduce you to my cousin, Jessica."

"That's right," Ana said. "From the advertising world. I was counting on you to make this introduction. We're in desperate need of professional assistance."

Adrienne grinned knowingly. "You're about to have your pick of agencies." Natalie turned as a striking brunette headed their way, holding hands with an equally attractive blonde. "Ana, Natalie, allow me to introduce you to Jessica Lennox and Brooklyn Campbell, both advertising extraordinaires."

"Oh, you work together?" Natalie asked, offering her hand.

"You'd think. But no," Brooklyn said. "This one works for the enemy."

"Correction," Jessica said, smiling at Brooklyn sweetly. "This one does."

Adrienne raised a hand in way of explanation. "These two are married and adorable, but own rival advertising agencies."

Jessica jumped in. "Before you feel awkward about the competition between us, we took a look at the dance company and what you might be looking for. I think Brooklyn and her partners at Savvy might be the best match."

"Which I'm thrilled about," Brooklyn said. "Because you guys are kick-ass." This girl was fun and bubbly and Natalie already liked her. "I saw the show tonight, and ideas are already floating around in my head. I'll let you enjoy the party, but maybe we can meet next week along with one of my business partners, Mallory, and discuss some options."

Ana looked just as excited by the concept as Natalie was. "That sounds perfect. I'll look forward to your call."

"And if you don't get what you need from Savvy," Jessica said, "Adrienne knows where to find me." She then sent a playful look to Brooklyn, who gasped at the quip. "We're gonna get out of your way, but thank you for having us, and have a fantastic night."

"Your show rocks," Brooklyn said over her shoulder as they walked away. "Let's be friends."

"You're on," Natalie called after them.

"They're fun."

"They are," Jenna said. "We'll all get together sometime."

Ana pointed to Jenna. "Yes. Make it happen."

"We will. It's a promise. Now go play with your other guests," Adrienne said. "We don't want to get in trouble for monopolizing the important people. Plus, we're seeing you next week, right, for dinner?"

"That's the plan. You're gonna love the new place. Tall ceilings to make me happy, and not too far from Shake Shack. Priorities," Natalie said and hooked a thumb at Ana.

Jenna laughed. "We can't wait to see it."

"Proud of you," Adrienne said, pulling Ana in to a final hug. "And FYI, I see your father sighing expectantly at the front of the room."

"Thank you, and we're on it," Ana told her.

Klaus Mikhelson was doing that pretend annoyed thing he so often did. Natalie now found it rather endearing, as she did him. His larger-than-life persona just took a little getting used to was all. Over the past year, he'd visited several times and seemed to have developed an appreciation for Natalie, despite what he sometimes seemed to project.

"This dancing you do tonight is not true ballet," he told them after their initial greeting, punctuating the statement with a long pause and a pointed Russian stare. "But I like it."

Ana smiled. "The second show of the season is entirely classical, Papa. No worries."

"What? Do I look worried? I'm not worried. That is just my Russian face."

Natalie pointed at him. "Ana makes the same one."

He laughed loudly. "I've seen it, too!"

"Thank you for being here, Papa. It means a lot to me."

"I would not miss the big opening of my fifteen percent. My fifteen percent did me proud." Ana beamed at him, and Natalie remembered how very important his opinion was to her. "I have to go now, though. I'm going to try the romance with the woman over there who sat next to me."

Natalie followed his gaze to Louise from SAB. "Oh wow, really?" she asked him.

He looked at them knowingly. "She has hot pants for me."

Ana covered her ears. "You're my father. You can't say that to me. Don't make me start reciting the alphabet."

"Go get her, Klaus. Go do the romance," Natalie said. With one quick and determined nod, he was off.

Ninety minutes later, and the little soirée had come to a quiet close. Natalie took a moment to let it all wash over her. The show was a hit, the party was a hit, and now she got to head home with the woman she loved. She thanked the universe for bringing her to this day, this spot, alongside Ana. As they headed out into the night air, hand in hand, she paused on the sidewalk. Ana had taken her hair down from the clip she'd worn it in earlier. The high heels were tucked away in her bag and the little bit of added color she'd applied to her lips had long since faded. But standing there under the night sky as she was now, she had never been more beautiful.

"What?" Ana asked, self-conscious.

"I'm memorizing you. Memorizing this."

Ana relaxed into a grin. "And why is that?"

"Because it's a moment. A real moment."

Ana was kissing her then, and Natalie melted against her, lost in the heat and softness of her touch. A shimmering perfect moment indeed.

The first in a lifetime of perfect moments to come.

About the Author

Melissa Brayden (melissabrayden.com) is a multi-award-winning author of seven novels published with Bold Strokes Books. She is hard at work on her eighth and loving the writer's life in San Antonio, Texas.

Melissa is married and working really hard at remembering to do the dishes. For personal enjoyment, she spends time with her Jack Russell terriers and checks out the NYC theater scene several times a year. She considers herself a reluctant patron of the treadmill, but enjoys hitting a tennis ball around in nice weather. Coffee is her very best friend.

Books Available From Bold Strokes Books

A Class Act by Tammy Hayes. Buttoned-up college professor Dr. Margaret Parks doesn't know what she's getting herself into when she agrees to one date with her student Rory Morgan, who is fifteen years her junior. (978-1-62639-701-9)

Bitter Root by Laydin Michaels. Small town chef Adi Bergeron is hiding something, and Griffith McNaulty is going to find out what it is even if it gets her killed. (978-1-62639-656-2)

Capturing Forever by Erin Dutton. When family pulls Jacqueline and Casey back together, will the lessons learned in eight years apart be enough to mend the mistakes of the past? (978-1-62639-631-9)

Deception by VK Powell. DEA Agent Colby Vincent and Attorney Adena Weber are embroiled in a drug investigation involving homeless veterans and an attraction that could destroy them both. (978-1-62639-596-1)

Dyre: A Knight of Spirit and Shadows by Rachel E. Bailey. With the abduction of her queen, werewolf-bodyguard Des must follow the kidnappers' trail to Europe, where her queen—and a battle unlike any Des has ever waged—awaits her. (978-1-62639-664-7)

First Position by Melissa Brayden. Love and rivalry take center stage for Anastasia Mikhelson and Natalie Frederico in one of the most prestigious ballet companies in the nation. (978-1-62639-602-9)

Best Laid Plans by Jan Gayle. Nicky and Lauren are meant for each other, but Nicky's haunting past and Lauren's societal fears threaten to derail all possibilities of a relationship. (978-1-62639-658-6)

Exchange by CF Frizzell. When Shay Maguire rode into rural Montana, she never expected to meet the woman of her dreams—or to learn Mel Baker was held hostage by legal agreement to her right-wing father. (978-1-62639-679-1)

Just Enough Light by AJ Quinn. Will a serial killer's return to Colorado destroy Kellen Ryan and Dana Kingston's chance at love, or can the search-and-rescue team save themselves? (978-1-62639-685-2)

Rise of the Rain Queen by Fiona Zedde. Nyandoro is nobody's princess. She fights, curses, fornicates, and gets into as much trouble as her brothers. But the path to a throne is not always the one we expect. (978-1-62639-592-3)

Tales from Sea Glass Inn by Karis Walsh. Over the course of a year at Cannon Beach, tourists and locals alike find solace and passion at the Sea Glass Inn. (978-1-62639-643-2)

The Color of Love by Radclyffe. Black sheep Derian Winfield needs to convince literary agent Emily May to marry her to save the Winfield Agency and solve Emily's green card problem, but Derian didn't count on falling in love. (978-1-62639-716-3)

A Reluctant Enterprise by Gun Brooke. When two women grow up learning nothing but distrust, unworthiness, and abandonment, it's no wonder they are apprehensive and fearful when an overwhelming love just won't be denied. (978-1-62639-500-8)

Above the Law by Carsen Taite. Love is the last thing on Agent Dale Nelson's mind, but reporter Lindsey Ryan's investigation could change the way she sees everything—her career, her past, and her future. (978-1-62639-558-9)

Actual Stop by Kara A. McLeod. When Special Agent Ryan O'Connor's present collides abruptly with her past, shots are fired, and the course of her life is irrevocably altered. (978-1-62639-675-3)

Embracing the Dawn by Jeannie Levig. When ex-con Jinx Tanner and business executive E. J. Bastien awaken after a one-night stand to find their lives inextricably entangled, love has its work cut out for it. (978-1-62639-576-3)

Love's Redemption by Donna K. Ford. For ex-convict Rhea Daniels and ex-priest Morgan Scott, redemption lies in the thin line between right and wrong. (978-1-62639-673-9)

The Shewstone by Jane Fletcher. The prophetic Shewstone is in Eawynn's care, but unfortunately for her, Matt is coming to steal it. (978-1-62639-554-1)